18 Reflections

and

3 Statements of Relief

18 Reflections

and

3 Statements of Relief

by
Chris Statham

Author: Chris Statham
Cover painting by King Yonas
Cover design by Steven Booth
Book & e-book design by Zvonimir Bulaja
Editing by David Kaplan
Proof reading by Wax Ligomba
Poetry by Chris Statham

Published by **www.creativityxroads.com**

First Printing, 2020

Paperback ISBN: 978-1-9161867-0-5
Ebook ISBN: 978-1-9161867-2-9

Also by Chris Statham

The Afronia Series
Crying for Afronia (Volume 1)
Escape from Afronia (Volume 2)
Dying for Afronia (Volume 3)
Afronia Rising (Volume 4)
Developing Afronia (Volume 5)
Afronian Revolution (Volume 6)

Prose, Poems and Pictures Series
7 Days in 1 Week (Volume 1)
52 Weeks in 1 Year (Volume 2)
10 Years in a Decade (Volume 3)

Other Fiction
Paperback Writer

To Mike

Book Cover Description

The painting is of me, the protagonist at the heart of the story. To the left, I'm wearing a green t-shirt and carrying a football, this represents my time as an idealist volunteer in Tanzania, before then going to university and studying marketing. The yellow background represents my youth, joy, hope and naivety.

In my mid-20s to early 30s, I went from hell-raiser to family man. This comparatively sober lifestyle is represented by my wearing of a suit and tie. The blue background signifies: peace, order and loyalty.

Just as I'm getting used to a settled life and planning my family's future, my life goes into turmoil. Finding myself backed into a corner, I put my business experience and energies into becoming a gangster. This might sound like a big leap, but trust me, once you've read my story, you'll understand. And by the way, the red background epitomises the energy, passion and danger of that time in my life.

TABLE OF CONTENTS

POEM—MY WAY

My time is near.
Soon, no more sunsets.
Regrets,
I have a few,
smiles,
even more so;
I've always done it my way.

You might not agree
with what I've done.
Rules broken,
hearts destroyed,
goals reached,
more rules broken;
always doing it my way.

I've lived a full life
and seen the world.
I've been high as a kite
and low as a whale;
always living my way.

Celebrated successes,
commiserated failures;
both too many to mention.
I've lived my life
and done it my way.

Family I was born to,
loves I've had a few.
Friends, many a comrade,
enemies, firing cross and bow.

I've lived
and I will die,
My Way.

Reflection #1— A Preamble

It's August 1996, I'm 19 and, I have just received my A-levels results. By a whisker, I have enough points to go to Lancaster University in a little over a year. But, before then, I would be a volunteer teacher in Tanzania on the dark continent and where according to the news cycle, war, corruption, famine and disease are all rife.

My story tracks the life crossroads I've passed through and which has brought me to this salty conclusion. Death is almost certain, though I know not whether it will be by water, a shot to the head or some other dastardly way. The only thing I know as I watch my assassin smoke one of Havana's finest, is that I have lived life my way.

As I'm about to meet-my-maker, I think about my many varied experiences along a most interesting life. I will relive it for my own pleasure in my last minutes on this mortal earth. I will relive it because it would seem a pity if my story were to be forgotten with my passing. I recall it for my, and hopefully your, entertainment. I will remember, so that you, my dear reader, don't make the same mistakes I've clearly made.

This is not a story of a great man who did great deeds, but rather a story of an ordinary man, who, through the fickleness, of life did some extraordinary things. This is an honest book and as such there is no place for false modesty. To conceal achievements and failures would be to produce a book that was not only dishonest but also dull. Thus, where I did something well, I will say so, for that is how I perceived it at the time. Where I did something badly, wrongly, or in many cases foolishly, I shall confess all.

The book is truthful and any such inaccuracies are unimportant and inadvertent. You may wonder how I am able to recall such details of events. Well, I have a good memory and, the many mini-stories within, are, as I hope you will agree, memorable.

I shall tell you the truth, the whole truth and nothing but the truth about those things that I believe to be important, interesting or entertaining as I watch my Cuban cigar smoking nemesis sit contentedly on a rock looking innocently out to the wide blue yonder without an apparent care on his stubbly face.

My name is Liam Stranger and I had lived my way. Please read on as I take a trip down memory lane and relive fifteen years of my life. I start with my last carefree days at university as that is where many a lasting friendship was conceived.

1. Friendships

It was five in the afternoon on the 25th of May, 2001, four years to the day since I summited Mount Meru in Tanzania, that being the penultimate activity and pinnacle of my nine-months as a volunteer teacher in Tanzania... this before becoming a debauched student.

There was just over a week remaining until the end of university life and out into the real world, where finding a job (rather than beer) would be the order of the day for me and the many hundreds-of-thousands of soon to be graduates. However, there were still ten days to go before my new reality set in, and that meant plenty more beers to be drunk, parties to attend, and women, as Lewis would say, chance.

'Toilet stop!' I shouted in the middle of a PlayStation marathon. As I stood up, I offered a silent prayer to the Sony God, Don't let the other three commit various acts of skulduggery while I'm doing the necessary. I was certain my prayer would not be answered, but having recently started my sixth beer of the afternoon I had no choice but to go; I was desperate.

'Do us a favour,' this from Jim as I was leaving my bedroom, 'be a mate and get us a beer.'

I assumed that this request was partly due to Jim actually wanting another beverage, but also so that I would be away from the game longer than necessary and thus more opportunity for my lead to be reduced. 'I'm not your slave—'

'No, you're a fecking eejit,' Lewis, who was Irish, interrupted my sarcasm.

There was nothing unusual in this sort of conversation, especially when there were PlayStation bragging rights on the line. Like the good mate that I was though, I did the honours and came back with four cold cans. It wasn't your top quality lager but the best bargain that could be found at the campus supermarket.

'You cheating fuckers,' I proclaimed as I re-entered my bedroom, inside of which was a single bed and which I'm happy to report was occasionally occupied by a female body. A cupboard, though most of my clothes would end up crumpled on the solitary chair. And a washbasin, which, when I was too tired, lazy or drunk, I used as a urinal. 'I get you a beer and you kill me; what thanks is that?' I rhetorically asked, adding, 'and you nicked my frigging chair,' this directed at Jim.

'You snooze, you lose,' this response coming from the relative comfort of my aforementioned piece of furniture, a broad grin on his cheeky, dimpled face. 'The pillow is all yours.'

As Lewis and the Welsh Wizard, Dewi, were sitting on the bed, I had little choice but the lumpy pillow on the floor which Jim had so recently vacated in favour of my clothes strewn chair.

After the five-hour PlayStation session, we went to the Pendle College bar, commonly known as The Airport Lounge due to its open plan design and large glass windows which looked out onto the rolling Lancastrian hills.

As Lewis lost the gaming competition, he bought the first round of drinks. 'Stella,' I ordered.

'Kronenberg,' Jim requested.

'Fosters,' Dewi instructed.

'You shandy drinking, Welsh poof,' Lewis, predictable in his commentary on our flatmate's choice of alcohol.

'I've got my last exam tomorrow, I'm taking it easy,' Dewi, not rising to the bait calmly asserted.

'You take it easy every night. Your countrymen would be embarrassed by your lack of drinking capabilities.'

Drinks paid and the ribbing of Dewi finished, we went upstairs where there was table football, darts, various fruit machines and three pool tables. The slabs of green baize were themselves nothing special, but a game only cost 20p and which compared very favourably to 50p in other college bars or £1 in Lancaster town. This cheapness was either very good or bad depending whether you were playing or waiting; it was common practice to create a mountain of 20p coins.

'What's it going to be, Killer Pool? The usual rules?' Jim suggested. 'One pound to enter. Breaker gets two shots unless they foul on the break. Three lives each. Foul or miss a pot, lose a life. Pot the black, gain a life. Re-rack when there is one ball left, but you can't move the white or the last remaining ball; sound good?' Everyone agreed to the parameters.

Before I broke, Gillian, (who lived opposite me) appeared at the top of the spiral staircase. She was an attractive girl with shoulder-length curly hair and an olive complexion... though her most striking feature was the size of her breasts and which in her thick Cumbrian accent she would describe as, "absolute monsters", this often followed by, "the bloody things give me bastard backache!"

'Are you joining?' I asked.

'Sure.'

With an extra pound in the pot, I broke, the white unerr-ingly finding its way into a corner pocket—I lost a life. 'Tits to that,' I cursed having been distracted by Gillian's assets.

The game carried on a pace, only interrupted by profan-ities whenever someone lost a life. 'What are you up to for summer?' I asked Gillian in-between shots.

'I have to organize accommodation before I start at the teacher training college. How about you?'

'The partying finishes next Friday and then I'll start look-ing for a job. I've been emailing CVs, left, right and centre, but so far no positive replies.' I paused, before adding, 'I will go travelling before settling down though, that's for sure.'

'You should come to Dalton for Super Sunday.'

I'd heard many stories about these bank holiday Sabbaths. 'I could well be up for it, that's if the liver is still in one piece.' The next nine days promised to be massive. Wednesday was ten-pin bowling in Morecombe followed by The Carlton, the university nightclub in the seaside town. Thursday was hockey club drinking games. Friday the campus bar crawl. Saturday was one last night at the SugerCube, the university nightclub in Lancaster town. Sunday and Monday were planned days of rest, though who knows what might happen. The final Tuesday, Wednesday and Thursday were devoted to college parties.

Gillian ended up winning the first game of killer pool and while the table was being re-racked, Dewi started up conversation, 'I need one last look through the books.'

'What exam?' I knew it would be marketing related but not which one; we were doing the same degree.

'Retail marketing. It's boring as shit, but easy.'

'Any consolation, direct marketing wasn't fascinating either.'

'What are you doing next? Back to Africa?' this referring to my nine-months in Tanzania and which had transformed me from boy to man. It had been an experience of uncertainties and relative hardships, though the highs more than made up for any lows. I had Malaria for six weeks, taught classes of 50 kids, organized the first ever school sports day, helped run the school tuck shop and funded the building of a laboratory. I'd travelled around Lake Victoria and hitchhiked down to South Africa on the back of trucks. I'd seen the wonders of the Serengeti and Ngorongoro Crater, and scuba-dived in Lake Malawi. I'd heard countless jokes over beers with locals, fellow volunteers and travellers from all over the world. It had been one hell of a wild ride. I fully expected fate would take me back to Africa one day, I just didn't know when or in what capacity.

'That's where my heart is,' I answered truthfully, 'but I have to pay off my student loan first; volunteering is not financially feasible.'

'The realities of life truly suck,' Dewi agreed. 'Once we start working, it'll be easy to get into the lifestyle of: bored in the office, wedding, mortgage and kids. Before we know it, we'll be forty, have a beer belly, a couple of sprogs and, God only knows how many other responsibilities.'

'We need a few stories for when we are sitting in a rocking-chair, slippers on, smoking a pipe and have grandkids on our laps,' I joked, though in truth I was petrified of the life Dewi had articulated.

After the Welshman left to do some last minute revision—I having chosen different modules and my exams behind me— continued playing pool, drinking beer, chatting philosophically and trying to come up with genius ideas that would make me a quick million bucks to fund my travel plans.

2. WE ARE SCREWED

Waking rather bleary eyed on Wednesday morning, I stumbled into the shared kitchen. While having my customary cup of tea—or "brew" as it was more commonly referred to in the northern climes of England—I started reading a newspaper article that had caught my eye

Middle-class young, the first generation to fare worse than their parents
The Prime Minister's, Social Mobility and Child Poverty Commission, issued a grim warning to the income earners of tomorrow, "There is a gathering perfect storm of graduate debt, lack of finance for first-time home buyers and, increasing job insecurity."

Generation Y are on track to be the first generation in more than a century that are materially less well off in adulthood than their parents. Leaked findings revealed, the existence of a national trend not experienced since the early 20th Century, where children from families with above-average incomes, as well as the most deprived, are set to have a worse standard of living than their baby-boomer parents, the generation who never had it so good and who in many cases are spending their children's inheritance on holidays and other luxuries.

The Commission warned, government initiatives have all too often been aimed at the poorest 10%. Yet the inability to get on in life is now a growing concern for middle-class children due to poor wages and housing costs. A grandmother in her 80's can expect a better standard of living than her grandchildren.

Not-withstanding my uncertain future, Wednesday was otherwise shaping up to be quite a day. First, I'd strategically arranged to meet my parents at lunchtime, this in the hope for something tastier to eat than baked beans with cheese and mustard on toast, my usual fare. They were passing by on their way back from a trip round Scotland and were going to collect the majority of my belongings, my 1.6 litre Vauxhall Astra—which I'd optimistically named the White Lightening—not large enough to accommodate my accumulated clutter.

'How was your Scottish trip?'

'Excellent,' Liz, my mum, replied while proceeding to hug and kiss me. 'The weather was great and the scenery beautiful; just what we needed. How did your final exams go, Darling?'

'As well as can be expected,' I honestly informed them having done a reasonable amount of revision. However, it was my coursework which might let me down. I didn't go to the library very often, believing, or should that be deluding myself, that university students should come up with their own theories rather than regurgitating others.

'As long as you've done your best,' Mike, my retired military father added.

Post lunch and my belongings now squeezed into my parent's car. 'Thanks for picking up my things.'

'It fitted in well with our journey. Besides, I don't think you would fit everything into your little car.'

Why my mum always referred to the White Lightening, as, your little car, I didn't honestly know. I let the comment pass not wanting my parents to stay longer than was absolutely necessary. 'I'm going to Gillian's next weekend and will be home on Monday,' I informed them.

'That sounds fun, but, more importantly, how's the job hunting going?' There was always a "but" with Dad.

'I've applied for a few jobs, but nothing very encouraging. Once I have enough money and, before I start the whole career thing, I'm going traveling—'

'I'm not sure that's a good idea,' my father annoyingly interrupted. 'There will be lots of people looking to start their careers and if you don't start soon you'll end up having difficulties getting that elusive first job; besides, we're certainly not paying for your galivanting.'

'I wasn't asking for money,' I replied sarcastically, irritated at being talked down to even though I knew what he was saying was wise advice. Notwithstanding that, I had the rest of my life for boring bullshit. Sun, sea, sand, and with any luck, sex, was a much better imminent plan. If I could find a job at a beach resort, even better.

'You don't want to be doing bar jobs for ever,' my dad responded, referring to the part-time work I had been doing throughout university holidays.

'Don't be such a snob!' I was now quite irate. 'I have lots of friends who work in the service industry.' Sensing the conversation turning into an argument, 'Thanks for lunch, it's appreciated; I'll put the kettle on,' I said, knowing my parents wouldn't leave until they had their after-lunch cup of tea.

'We'd better get going,' this from my father post cuppa. I could see him calculating if they would be back in time to watch the eight o'clock news,

'Don't get up to too much mischief,' my mother chipped in. I had heard that sentence a-thousand-times before, but little did she know how the rest of the day was planned. With a kiss on the cheek for mum and a handshake with dad, I waved to the back of their departing car. Let the games begin!

3. A Day on the Tiles

Eight minutes after my parents had once again left my life, I'd had a shit, shower, shave, put on my lucky boxer shorts, applied an excess amount of aftershave and, had run to the underground bus stop, where I jumped on the double decker just as it was pulling away. After paying my 80p fee, I went upstairs and saw the lads identically attired in their Ben Sherman shirts.

30 minutes later, we arrived in Morecombe, the once popular seaside town which had been in steady decline since the advent of package holidays and budget airlines. The wind farm out to sea was a metaphor for the need to adapt. Appropriately enough, the rainy weather extenuated this rather depressing picture. It was impossible to imagine walking along the promenade on a glorious golden English summer day licking an ice-cream… like the postcards still portrayed.

My friends and I didn't give a toss about the past, present or future of Morecombe as we made our way along the esplanade, salivating for our first beer of the day.

'Boys,' Lewis, who considered himself an alpha male, started, 'what's the competition going to be?' This in reference to the £2 we'd each put into a kitty during the bus trip. 'Who pulls the ugliest girl?'

'You're onto a winner, Dewi,' Jim pointed out.

'Any hole is a goal… and it's more than you've managed in recent times.'

'Last week,' Jim defensively answered. 'She was a nice girl.'

'You mean, nice personality,' Lewis, who thought he was a lady killer, mocked.

'When was the last time you pulled anything, Jim… other than your miniscule cock?' I joked, and so the banter continued until we reached The Super Bowl and which contained a dozen ten-pin bowling lanes, a neon lit diner, two pool tables, fruit machines galore, various shooting games, an air hockey table and most importantly a bar.

Everyone put £20 into the alcohol kitty, this enabling the ten-pin-bowling drinking game. The rules were straightforward: if you knocked five or more pins over, there was no forfeit. However, if you only managed to knock over four pins, you had four attempts to finish your drink. Three pins, three attempts. Two pins, two attempts. A pathetic one, and you had to down your drink in one. Low and behold no pins knocked over, the forfeit, finish your current drink plus a mystery concoction of the strongest, foulest spirits the others chose.

The first couple of games were the easiest as everyone was sober and trying to score well. But after three hours, four games, six pints, two shots and no one caring anymore, the average plummeted. The last game was a farce. Dewi and I were engaged on a clay pigeon shooting simulator, Jim was on the fruit machines, and Lewis was trying to see if he could hit the roof of the alley with his bowling ball—he did.

Our noise and general boisterousness finally became too much for the manager. 'That lady over there,' she pointed, 'has complained about you lot.' I saw a young boy having his birthday party. Standing behind the manager was the one and only bouncer who didn't look physically imposing but did have a certain aura that would make you think twice before throwing the first punch in his direction.

'Alright, son,' the bald headed, pit-bull faced bouncer, said to Lewis and who had assumed the role as leader in this confrontation, 'it's time you moved on.' His tone of voice brokered no argument.

'Oh, yeah, or what?' Lewis sarcastically replied in a show of bravado.

'The manager told you about the complaint,' the bouncer stated in a steady voice that conveyed one way or another we would be leaving.

'Ok… we'll be quieter. Dewi, get us another beer, mate.' It was pure bluster by Lewis and I suspect only because there were ten of us.

'Get your shoes and leave, NOW!' the bouncer raised his voice and took a step closer to Lewis who was in range of a left jab from the man's ham sized fist.

'Or what?'

'I don't like your tone, son,' this in a voice of finality. 'If you're not out of here in two minutes… I'll call the police.'

'Alright, keep your hair on,' Lewis smirked while looking at the baldy.

I was happy to move on, knowing, the longer we stayed the greater the chance that the pool table cloth would be ripped, a bowling alley ruined or someone injuring themselves. Drinks quickly consumed, Jim asked, 'Burger King or McDonald's?' The group split into two. Five minutes of walking and talking later, Lewis, as he always did on such occasions, suggested we race the final 500 metres to McDonald's. This consisted of running up and down kerbstones, over a roundabout—while trying not to trample on flowers—before hurdling the chains around the McDonald's car park. Coming into the final bend, Lewis, a natural long distance runner, had a five-metre lead over Jim, a sprinter. With fifty metres left, Jim caught up to Lewis, hurdled the first chain though his trailing leg caught the second and propelled him at a frightening speed chin first into the tarmac with a toe curling thud.

As Jim lay prostrate, I, panting heavily, surveyed the damage. Blood was flowing freely from various facial grazes and his new Calvin Klein jeans were torn. Remarkably, there seemed to be no breakages. Jim didn't seem in too much pain despite his injuries and which included a chipped tooth.

'You eejit,' Lewis, addressed Jim while patting his trouser pockets for his mobile phone to call the emergency services.

Jim gingerly stood up and did an assessment. 'It could've been worse.'

'The stupid eejit that I am,' Lewis, not listening to the blood stained Jim, continued. 'I left my fecking phone at the bowling alley. I'll pop into MacDonald's and get them to call you an ambulance.'

'Fuck it,' Jim replied, the alcohol anesthetizing his pain. 'I just need a wash up. I can't miss the last ever night at The Carlton; after a few more drinks, I won't feel a thing.'

We entered the home of Ronald McDonald and received many a look of disgust, amusement and, in some cases astonishment. Ten minutes later and gastronomically satisfied, we made our way to a pub where we'd arranged to meet the Burger King group. On the way, I needed to make a detour. Unzipping my fly, unwinding my tackle and as the beer induced pressure in my bladder started to subside, a police car came into my peripheral vision… and then slowly to a stop… ten metres from where I was now hiding behind a tree. Shit! Do I stay and hope for a slap on the wrist or do a runner? I quizzed myself.

'Been out drinking, have we?' the Police Constable rhetorically asked.

'Sorry, officer; weak bladders run in the family.'

'If you keep lying to me, son, you'll be locked up for drunk and disorderly.'

'You can phone my doctor,' I doubled-down on my lie.

'I don't for a second believe a word you said. However, I've more important things to do. I will only caution you, this time. If I get a call later and you're involved, there'll be no second chances.' I audibly sighed, relieved, literally and proverbially.

'Where the fuck have you been?' Lewis queried once I'd entered the pub. 'I thought you were having a piss... did you also have a dump?' This met by laughter from the lads and disapproving looks from customers.

'A rozzer tried to arrest me for having a wiz,' I nonchalantly started to explain. 'I blagged my way out by telling him it was a medical condition; the daft copper believed me.'

4. AND THEN A NIGHT ON THE TILES

Two hours of moving from one pub to another, it was soon time for one last night at The Carlton nightclub. Although it lacked an appealing décor, it had a very captive audience, i.e. drunk students wanting cheap drinks. I ordered half-a-dozen double Jack Daniels… for me (it was happy hour) and a Carlton Crusader which consisted of vodka, Southern Comfort and Crème de Month all mixed in a slush puppy and served in a mini plastic yard of ale. I staggered on to the dance floor and pulled a few moves, which might not have impressed any girls but did give my friends a good laugh.

Some hours later, I found myself at the bar and realised we were no longer a group of 11. Some had met girlfriends— long-term or newly made—while Jim and Lewis were searching for a chili donor kebab. As such, I made my way to the nightbus, where, on the upper deck, a pyramid of bodies was singing: how many can fit on the back seat of the bus?

One girl caught my attention, my eyes being drawn to her generous bosom, and who I later found out was called Kate, was also alone. 'Good night?' She smiled.

'Can't argue. The Carlton is always the same cheesy music and lots of drinks. Besides, who says the A-team and Jim'll Fix It are bad tunes?' These two being Carlton classics and before the Jimmy Saville paedophile expose.

'Where are your mates?' Kate enquired.

'Your guess is as good as mine; yours?'

'I came out with the lacrosse girls. Some got hammered, others hooked-up; I was the only one left at the bar… lightweights.'

Shall I cut to the chase or play it cool? I leaned towards Kate and looked into her eyes. 'What college are you in?'

'Furness.' She had picked up the sexual undertones to my reasonably innocuous question.

I HAVE A WINNER! I moved closer to Kate and placed my hands on her thighs. 'You're very beautiful.' Two seconds after my corny words, we were seeing who could get their tongue furthest into the other's mouth, this accompanied by wolf-whistling and cheering from the back seats of the bus.

I glided my hand up the smooth inner thigh of her parted legs, and on her part, Kate's hand was exploring inside my trousers. 'All in good time,' she whispered in my ear while squeezing my erection. 'But, if you want me, you're going to have to catch me,' this as she pulled her hand out of my trousers and started walking down the stairs as the bus pulled into the university underground parking bay.

By the time I got off, Kate was already out of sight. I ran up the stairs two at a time, but reaching the top, Kate was nowhere to be seen. Fuck, fuck, bollocks, wank, I swore to myself. Fucking typical, my first chance of a shag in a while and it all goes tits up. I started walking despondently in the direction of her college.

'WHERE ARE YOU GOING?!' Kate, shouted at my back. 'I'M OVER HERE!'

I turned and saw her waving; all was not lost. Kate ran in the direction of the library and I followed in hot pursuit as she went into the public toilets. By the time I reached the lavatories, she was leaning back seductively on the washbasins. 'Now, you can collect your prize,' she said with a mischievous, lust filled sneer. I grabbed her hips and forcibly pulled her towards me. I put one hand up her skirt and felt her wetness, my other hand groping her breasts all the while my erection pressed into her. She parted her legs and let out a moan, then pulled down my trouser zip and inserted her hand. We heard a noise outside. I pulled Kate into a cubicle. Quiet once again, Kate undid my belt and pushed my trousers down. 'Do you have a condom?'

'No, do you?'

'No.'

'Fuck,' we declared simultaneously, both laughing at the bad pun.

'Is there a condom machine here?'

'I didn't check. It's the first time I've been in this position in these toilets.'

'You've been in similar circumstances in other toilets?' I asked, pulling up my trousers and not caring if she had.

'Maybe, maybe not,' she coyly answered while seductively licking her lips.

To my great relief, there was a condom machine. I searched through my pockets for the required £1 coin, but my fingers only found a solitary 20p piece; I forgot I had borrowed a pound for the return bus ticket, my pockets having been totally emptied.

'Do you have a pound?' I prayed she would reply in the affirmative. 'I'm totally skint.'

'No condoms, no money… you better make it worthwhile,' Kate joked while handing me a £1 coin. Though I'd only known Kate for half-an-hour, what I saw I definitely liked: a fox, up for sex and a good sense of humour—a winning combination.

I pushed the coin into the machine and heard the reassuring thud as the packet of condoms crashed down. I returned to the cubicle and saw that Kate had hitched up her skirt and undone her blouse. 'Ribbed, strawberry flavoured, or glow in the dark?'

'Ribbed always feels good.'

Insanely smiling, I pushed my trousers down and put on the grooved condom as requested.

'Sit on the toilet and I'll straddle you,' Kate ordered and I didn't protest. Unfortunately, in my haste, I didn't put the toilet seat cover down first, but it was too late, Kate had already moved into position. Five minutes later, she got off, pulled down her skirt and did up her blouse, I, on the other hand, was less dignified, a red ring now on my bum much to her amusement.

'Yours or mine for the second round?' she wanted to know, my ego and libido suitably satisfied.

5. A GENTLEMAN DOESN'T REVEAL HIS SECRETS

After a morning shag, shower and cup of tea, Kate left at 11:00 to study for her final exam that afternoon. 'Am I going to see you again?'

'I'd like that,' and I genuinely did.

'I'd like that too,' Kate confirmed with a final kiss on the lips. Mobile numbers exchanged, she left and I went to the kitchen to get my third cuppa that morning.

'Fancy a brew?' Gillian asked in a hungover voice. 'Who was the lovely lady leaving your room?'

'Cheers, dears, a tea would go down a treat. And, that was Kate.'

'Where did you meet her? The Carlton, I presume?'

'Well, sort of,' I replied not willing to reveal all the dirty details. 'How about you?'

'Bit of a snog with a hunky footballer,' Gillian revealed. 'He was hammered and vanished into the toilets not to reappear. He must have been sick or fallen asleep?'

'A possibility,' I agreed. I'd had such an experience three weeks earlier. As best I could remember, and cobbled together with what friends had told me, I'd managed to fill up a sink with vomit before collapsing into a toilet cubicle and falling asleep only to be woken three hours later by bouncers. On that occasion, I also hadn't put the toilet seat cover down. I'd slept in blissful unconsciousness for three hours which proved a very bruising experience for the next two days.

'What are you smiling at?'

'Carlton incidents.'

'Including last night no doubt. Are you going to see her again?'

'Hopefully, but you never know how these things will work out, do you. Any plans for today?'

'No. You?'

'Watch a video or two; it's the hockey club piss-up tonight.'

'Sounds fun.' And with that Gillian and I departed to our respective rooms, got into bed and watched daytime TV.

6. GOODBYE BUT NOT FARWELL

Life carried on in much the same vain for my remaining nine days at university: PlayStation, videos, cups of tea, five-a-side football, planning for life after university and, drinking more than was healthy quantities of beer, wine, shooters and cocktails.

Waking a little after 11am and, surprisingly spritely considering the previous days' drinking sessions, I saw it was shining brightly outside; it was going to be another roasting hot day. After showering, I made a fry up with all the essentials: bacon, eggs, sausages, mushrooms, beans, tomatoes, toast and the obligatory cuppa; it was just what the doctor ordered.

'Righty-ho. So, this is it,' Lewis, saying this in his usual manner of a statement sounding like a question.

'Looks like it, big man. You heading back to Dublin?'

'Yep. You got any work sorted?'

'Don't be daft. I'm heading to Gillian's for Super Sunday first,' this while looking at my female flatmate to confirm my intentions.

'Good luck, mate. You seeing Kate again?'

I'd seen Kate a few times over the past week when we were both drunk and horny. When we didn't meet up, I tried my luck with others knowing she was doing likewise. I liked her though wasn't convinced there would be a future for us post university. 'She's good at pool, funny and, great in bed, but apart from drinking and fucking, we don't have much in common.'

'What more do you need?' Lewis questioned deadly serious.

'She's a girly girl, likes city life and, apparently doesn't do camping. She wouldn't get on in Africa and that's where my life is destined.'

'Well, good luck, man. I better be off to the train station; the ferry leaves in a few hours.'

'Keep in touch.' I gave Lewis a heartfelt hug of friendship, and who along with Jim, Dewi and Gillian had become my best mates over the past year.

Reflection #2—
Young, Dumb and Full of Cum

Farewells are sad. I knew, or at least hoped, it wasn't a final goodbye to my friends, though I wasn't so upset about no longer being a student. It had been a fun filled four years. There had been much banter, too much drinking, some success with the ladies, and a time to explore the English vocabulary in lectures; in short, I was young, dumb and full of cum.

What has that to do with the rest of my story and, how did I end up with an assassin sitting yards away from me? Well, if I tell you, it wouldn't leave much to the imagination now would it? You will just have to read on if you want to find out how I went from volunteer to student to gangster. However, what I will say is that alcohol, drugs, girls and friends all play an integral part in my story of misadventure. This is not just a boozy trip down memory lane as I remember my salad days, but to give you context as to who I am and which can help explain the decisions I subsequently made.

7. Africa My Mistress

I hoped the forthcoming weekend with Gillian would be one to remember and, that I would see Jim, Lewis and Dewi sooner rather than later. However, I also knew best intentions don't always work out, life is not always compliant. It was time I moved on and which I hoped would involve a return to Tanzania or somewhere, anywhere, before summer turned into autumn, turned into a cold, wet and grey English winter.

'That's it,' I pronounced as Gillian got into the passenger seat.

'And now it's find a job and start a family time,' she finished my sentence as we pulled out of the university car park for one last time.

With foot to the floor the White Lightening lived up to its name and we were soon turning off the M6 motorway and along the South Lake District shoreline. 'It's very beautiful,' I commented having not been that particular way before when previously mountain biking in the area. Gillian nodded her head absentmindedly to my observation.

'As you know, before Lancaster I lived in Africa as a volunteer teacher. It was the most amazing nine months of my life,' I started as a conversation opener. 'Just before flying home, which incidentally was the weekend Princess Diana died in Paris, I led a group of eleven students up Mount Meru and which is five times higher than Ben Nevis. Looking sixty kilometres to the east, I could see the majestic glow of the sun slowly rising up behind the distinctive outline of the iconic, snow-capped Mount Kilimanjaro; it was the most majestic view you could imagine. As I sat at the summit, I wrote a poem and which is engraved on my heart.

Africa, My Mistress

Africa, my first girlfriend,
my first taste of love.
The smells, colours, the people;
a frankness of reality,
a vivaciousness to life.

Poverty with happy faces,
such a contrast to my fortunate upbringing.
Where someone has little,
they often have more
than one with much.

Africa, my mistress.
Her siren calls
to rekindle our love,
to chase dreams,
to follow my destiny.

'That's profound,' Gillian commented, as I threaded along narrow hedge-rowed lanes.

'Those nine months changed me much,' I eventually said after 30 seconds of comradely silence. 'I will return, I just don't know when, where, or to do what, but one-day I will return, that I'm certain. Don't get me wrong, I've enjoyed university and made many a good friend, but in the bigger scheme of things, and being that we only have one life, I sometimes imagine what I would be doing if I'd been in Tanzania these last four years rather than drinking myself silly.'

'What ifs are the big imponderables of life. Maybe, it would've been better, maybe worse, who knows? Maybe, you would have been a big game hunter, a millionaire, dead? Life-is-life and we pass through it one day at a time.'

'I know you're right,' I replied, taking time to contemplate what Gillian had said. 'I don't think I'll ever be an office suit-and-tie man like my parents wish,' this, I said in a resigned tone, so unsure of what direction my life would next take, though half expecting I would conform to the expectations of society and end up in a white collar job for life.

To a good percentage of you who are reading, that might not sound such a bad deal, but I'm not you; the prospect of pounding a keyboard in an atmosphericless office did not bear contemplating.

'What will be, will be; don't over analyse,' Gillian wisely advised. 'If life moves you in the direction of an office job, I say, go for it; it doesn't have to be forever. When the time is right you will return to Africa; you don't need to push for it now. Who knows, by going down the office route you might meet the love of your life or win the lottery. I say, if you're given hops, make beer!'

8. DOCTOR DRINK

An hour after leaving my alma mater, Dalton came into view. It's a small village with one main street which consisted primarily of pubs. Gillian's parents lived in a bungalow near the train station and a convenient three-minute walk from the ale houses.

'What's for lunch, mum?'

'Lasagne, garlic bread and salad.'

'My favourite,' I enthused, as we were joined at the table by Gillian's father and brother.

'Out on the beers?' Gillian's, six-foot-three sibling probed.

'A few, but we're saving ourselves for Super Sunday, brat,' Gillian affectionately answered. 'Are you out with the usual losers?'

'I'm going to The Three Spoons with Gary and Tim. Samantha,' his girlfriend, and who Gillian didn't think much of, 'is staying home.'

'Maybe see you out and about… but hopefully not.' The banter between brother and sister carried on for the rest of the meal.

After lunch, we were both positively looking forward to replenishing our alcohol levels. Gillian brushed her teeth and I went for the lazier minty chewing-gum option to cover my garlic breath. We took a taxi to Barrow-on-Furness, and the first thing I saw on alighting was a stunner of a woman—five-foot-eight, long blonde hair, blue eyes and a lovely tanned complexion. Wow!

'Jo's very blonde,' Gillian bitchily said when she saw me drooling.

What's not to like? I asked myself. 'What are you talking about?' I nevertheless replied.

'Jo, the girl we just passed. You were salivating. She's easier to pull than a door.'

I pretended not to know what she was talking about... all the while practicing a chat up line. How do you know Gillian? Gillian tells me you were friends at school.

We reached The King's Arms. 'The usual?' I enquired.

'Go on then, twist my arm.'

Four minutes later, I re-appeared with a Guinness for me and a pint of Fosters for her. 'Nice pub,' I commented passing Gillian the Australian lager. 'I see it has a good selection of bar snacks.'

'Scampi fries are yummy... but don't half give you fishy breath,' she said as she opened the little lemon green packet of culinary delight.

'And fingers,' I quickly added, holding two digits up and sniffing them and which brought a chesty chuckle from Gillian, the masturbatory implication unmissable.

Six hours, seven pubs, eight pints, fish and chips, and several bags of scampi fries later, Gillian and I were still going strong. We were chatting over the usual subjects: sex, self-pleasuring, sport and our former flat-mates.

Gillian had told me about her friend Babs' anal sex exploits. On our ninth drink I met the lady in question. She was a big girl in every department. Six-foot-tall—not including high heels—long blonde hair down to the small of her back, large blue eyes, and like Gillian, extremely large breasts. Man-eater, are words you could accurately use to describe her.

'You two are getting on like a house on fire,' Gillian commented ten minutes after the entrance of the Aryan goddess.

'Sorry, babe,' Babs said to me. 'I've arranged to meet friends elsewhere; meet me at the Ambassador nightclub.'

She left much to my disappointment. 'Nice girl,' I remarked. 'Where next?'

Four pubs, two hours, some amount of beers (we'd lost count) and three alcopops later, the conversation had moved onto the pros and cons of wearing a condom when receiving / giving a blowjob, this after visiting such diverse topics as: how much better rugby union was than rugby league. Why did Walkers Crisps change salt and vinegar crisps bags from blue to green? What is the best type of peanut: salted, roasted, chili or honey roasted? And, hearing about the love life of a seventy-six year old, which lasted the length of a drink in a trendy pub. This was, Gillian and I agreed, very random but all part of a weekend we would recount for years to come, 'And when our pubes are grey,' Gillian had said to great hilarity. She then informed me, 'There's a choice of two shite clubs to go to: the Ambassador which plays 70's and 80's or dance music at The Knightsbridge.'

'You can never go wrong with cheesy music.'

'I knew you would say that and why I agreed to meet Babs there. A few more drinks first?' Gillian slurred.

'You must be able to my mind read my mind.' I was also starting to have problems articulating a cogent sentence. 'A strawpeddo?'

'A what?'

'A strawpeddo.'

'What the fuck, is a strawpeddo?'

'I've never introduced you to a strawpeddo?'

'Nope.'

'It's a legend, trust me.'

'Why, because you're a doctor?' Gillian was full of mirth-ful sarcasm.

'Yes. Doctor drink. D Squared to friends'

'What are you on about, you idiot?'

'Doctor and drink both start with D, therefore… doctor drink is D Squared.' This logic applied to many things when I was drunk. For instance, a girl who was S Cubed, would be: Sexy, Stunning and Shaggable.

'So, D-Squared, what the hell is a strawpeddo?' Gillian, presumably wondering what gibberish I would come up with next.

'Oh yeah, my foggy brain forgot to answer that one, but it's legendary and I'm a legend,' I had my hands held aloft like a boxing champ as I proclaimed this. 'You get a bottle of booze, put a straw in the top, bend it over so the gas has somewhere to vanish… and then drink it in one.'

'Doctor, indeed. Well, off you hop to the bar for drinks and accompanying straws.'

Five minutes later, I returned with four bottles of Smirnoff Ice. 'I thought it would be a good idea to double up and save the hassle of going back later; what a legend I am,' I proclaimed once more, again putting my outstretched arms—two bottles of Smirnoff Ice in each hand—in the air, this time attracting the attention of a bouncer.

'Come on then, show us how this strawpeddo is done.'

I put a straw into two bottles and bent it over the lip. 'We have to drink at the same time,' I told Gillian. We each put a bottle to our lips, and then I did a 3, 2, 1 countdown with my fingers.

'Wowzer,' Gillian said five seconds later, her bottle now emptied. 'Thanks, doctor drink,' she congratulated. 'I'm amazingly impressed that you actually know something useful.' After a short pause, we started on the second of the Smirnoff Ices, this time without accompanying straws.

Time marched rapidly on and soon it was half-past-twelve. When last orders were called we'd each ordered a double Jack Daniels and Coke. The bar staff had started removing empty glasses and after the fifth time of being told: Time to go ladies and gents, by the shaven headed gorilla in the bow tie and puffer jacket—a combination only bouncers don't get told looks ridiculous—we finally left.

Gillian and I stumbled onto the high street and where two groups of lads were shouting at each other in what looked like a preamble to a fight. 'This,' Gillian informed me, 'is the aptly named—Gaza Strip.'

Giggling and staggering to the Ambassador Nightclub, once we reached the front of the queue we were asked, 'Had much to drink?' by the doorman.

The truthful answer would have been, I'm shit-faced, down to my last twenty quid and hoping to get lucky. My actual reply: we only had a couple of glasses of wine at Pizza Express.

Bursting out laughing, we paid the fee and entered the nightclub that promised, the best night for funk and retro. The DJ was playing the gay anthem, It's Raining Men by The Weather Girls. The interior was thick with faux tiger skin sofas, the barmen wore flairs, tank tops and an obligatory gold medallion and, the bargirls long cotton dresses and flowers in their hair. I was impressed with all the effort.

The Ambassador was trying its best to live up to their promise, but of more concern there was no sign of Babs. I danced with Gillian on the small pentagonal shaped dance floor before she went to the bar to buy a round of drinks. I didn't follow her as I'd located Babs… she was snogging some-one.

With drinks in hand, Gillian saw the dejected look on my face. 'I told you she was a slapper; get this vodka down you.'

'Cheers,' I said taking the drink. 'Plenty more fish in the sea.'

'Too right. See that guy in the blue t-shirt, he chatted me up at the bar; he's pretty cute.'

The fact that Gillian's night was looking up didn't improve my demur. Why is it, that women can choose who they want, but men are overjoyed with just a smile from a woman? I asked myself for the hundredth time. I did the only thing I could reasonably think of and went back to the bar.

Two hours later, the crowds were now thinned and the lights turned on. A few couples were kissing, a small queue was waiting to get their coats, one guy was fast asleep in a corner and, a dozen drunk, desperate and horny guys were dancing around two girls. There was no sign of Gillian. I went outside and saw her looking the worse for wear and holding onto a lamppost for support. In the taxi on the way home, she admitted she'd spent half the night in the toilets being sick. We agreed not to get so drunk the following day.

9. SUPER SUNDAY

Super Sunday got off to a very slow start, neither Gillian nor I surfacing from beneath our respective duvets till past midday; it was another blistering hot day. Somehow my body had managed to heal overnight, Gillian on the other hand was at Death's door and only wanted multiple cups of sweet tea and crispy bacon and mayonnaise sandwiches. The prospect of another twelve hours drinking not appealing to her in any way. I on the other hand was eagerly looking forward to getting back on it.

'Could you get me a brew,' Gillian groggily shouted from her bed, this after hearing me plodding around downstairs.

'How many sugars?'

'You should know by now!'

I made a quick calculation. An average of two cups of tea per day, multiplied by three terms or thirty weeks, would be approximately 400 cups of tea. I certainly should know how many teaspoons of teeth destroyers she took. 'I give up, my brain's not working,' I shouted back up the stairs.

'Lots of milk and two sugars.'

I further calculated, that in the process of making Gillian cups of tea, I must have put approximately 800 teaspoons of sugar into cups of tea for her. Drinking too much alcohol seemingly does kill brain cells.

After showering, a sausage and tomato ketchup sandwich—there was no bacon left—a cup of tea and a pint of Ribena to re-hydrate, Gillian and I were ready to start another day on the sauce.

The first stop was Tim's house, where by the time Gillian and I arrived, the party was already in full swing, including a group of girls in short skirts, crop tops, plenty of cleavage, tattoos of various shapes, sizes and colours, and belly-button piercings. We were offered a choice of drinks: Fosters or Guinness, red or white wine, a variety of soft drinks; Gillian had another cup of tea, I, Irish stout.

By mid-afternoon it was pub time. 'Can you do the honours?' I asked Gillian. 'I need to go to the bogs.'

30 seconds later, 'Ah... woops... sorry,' I stammered, as I saw a surprised middle-aged woman. In my haste I had accidently gone into the ladies.

'Cheeky young man; were you trying to get a sneaky peek?' the woman cackled.

'No.' I had turned crimson.

'If you want a real woman, come find me,' she offered to my surprise; I wasn't sure if she was serious or mocking.

Done with the necessary, I returned to the bar where Gillian was chatting with Jo; she looked even sexier than yesterday.

'Why did you go into the women's toilet?' Gillian had a straight-face though I could sense her smirk.

I gave her a withering look for her purposeful attempt at embarrassing me in front of Jo. 'I was in a bit of a rush,' I stammered, my face turning red. 'I saw a green sign above the door with a little man running... easy mistake,' I explained; Jo didn't look impressed.

'But what were you doing in there... for so long?' Gillian further prodded.

'Just as I was about to let Mr. Biggy out the cage, a lady came out of one of the cubicles and told me where the gents were.' Gillian laughed. Jo stayed stonily silent. I kept blushing.

Last orders were called after what seemed like just a few minutes, but which must have been many hours. 'Do you want to go somewhere else?' Gillian queried. 'This pub is one of the few that actually stops serving at eleven, most others have a lock-in.'

'Lead the way,' I unhesitatingly replied.

On first impressions, and even after a few beers, the next bar, The Jupiter, didn't look as welcoming as where we'd just left. However, there was a band of sorts in the corner: The Dalton Motley Crew and who were dressed in leathers, had long scraggy hair and beards, sunglasses and hats, and looked somewhat like ZZ Top. They were blasting out a rather bad version of Pink Floyd's Hole in the Wall. 'The locals don't bite,' my university soul-mate, who sensed my misgivings, reassured me.

All day drinking coupled with sunshine, and things soon boiled over. Gillian's brother got into an argument and though I had no idea what was going on, I stood by his side and started looking for the nearest bottle to pick up and smash over someone's head if need be. Fortunately, the bouncers intervened and the next thing I knew, everyone but Jo had vanished. I sat down next to her and we started chatting, Jo finding it hilarious that I was wearing shorts. She started pulling my leg hair… before her hand slowly snaked up inside my shorts to discover I was going commando. Shortly after this revelation we started to kiss.

When we finally left the pub the first signs of dawn were appearing, but the kissing and fondling didn't stop—we continued at a bus stop shelter. Going back to Jo's place was apparently not possible, I didn't discover if that was because she lived with, A) her parents, B) boyfriend / husband, C) some other reason. I thought it would be cheeky to go to Gillian's parent's house, so suggested, 'Let's go behind those garages,' while pointing to the opposite side of the road. Jo acquiesced. Within seconds, my shorts were removed and Jo's skirt was hitched up and she bent at the waist.

I got the third degree from Gillian when she finally woke, but I kept tight lipped. After a bacon sandwich and two cups of tea, Gillian and I agreed, that the last couple of days were our last hoorah of being a student and, that life one way or another would change dramatically over the coming weeks, months and years.

10. WILL I END UP LIKE MY PARENTS?

'Did you have a good time, darling?' were my mother's first words as I walked through the front door.

'You know, the usual,' I replied, my mum not having a clue what the usual might entail. Indeed, I was convinced mum thought I was either a virgin or gay, as whenever she asked about girlfriends, I would reply, I'm not seeing anyone though have many friends who are girls.

'You must be tired from the long drive home?'

'I'll have a shower and then sleep for an hour,' I told her. I was indeed very tired, not so much from driving but from the previous ten days of not enough sleep and far too much alcohol; it had finally taken its toll.

'Good idea… you'll need to be fresh for tomorrow when you start looking for a job.'

I knew the job conversation would arise as soon as I arrived home, and so had been preparing my answer while driving. It went along these lines: I'll go travelling for the next twelve-months and then settle down. I don't currently have any responsibilities, so should take the opportunity to explore before it's too late. I fully expected this response to lead into an argument, so figured, it would be better to have the conversation when both parents were present rather than going through the whole rigmarole twice.

'If you have any washing, throw it down,' mum shouted from the kitchen as I was walking up the stairs. Together with Sunday roast dinners and the two family dogs, getting my washing done was one of the few things I missed when not at home.

11. That Conversation

'Supper!' mum shouted one hour after my head had touched the heavenly pillow.

Here we go, I thought, though at least I'm now refreshed and ready to face the Spanish Inquisition. 'Lovely,' I said, and not just as a strategy to get on the good side of mum, but macaroni cheese with frankfurters liberally covered in tomato ketchup, was indeed one of my favourites. 'What news from Granny and Granddad?'

'The same as always. Granny's as blind as a bat and Granddad is not in particularly good health,' mum updated me as I tucked into one of the aforementioned wieners. 'They still refuse to move into a nursing home; it's all a bit depressing.'

'You should visit them,' my father suggested. 'Who knows how much longer they'll be around.'

'I will… though I'm not sure when.'

'Why? What do you have planned?' My father immediately jumped on my pause.

I realized my statement about not having much time had led me into a cul-de-sac; I couldn't now use the subtle approach I'd been planning. My parents were a contradictory sort, at times there were old school in their opinions but on other occasions quite laidback. For instance, they hadn't battered an eyelid when I had gone hostelling around the UK for ten-days with two friends at the age of fifteen. Naturally, we got into all sorts of teenage mischief, most notably falling down a flight of pub stairs, urinating from a pub balcony and puking throughout the youth hostel after a late-night return. When I told them I smoked dope, they offered words of wisdom rather than giving me a lecture. I didn't tell them about taking ecstasy most weekends and occasionally dabbling with a line or two of cocaine.

'Well, the reason I might not be able to see Granny and Granddad, is…' I took a deep breath, hoping to get my parents moral, if not financial support, 'I'm planning on working all the hours under the sun and then go to Australia. I'll spend a month here and there, and work my way round the world. Before you say anything, I have been giving it a lot of—'

'I really don't think that's a good idea,' dad interrupted disapprovingly, his eyebrows arching upwards ridiculously, this the face he involuntarily pulled when something was not to his liking. 'For starters, where are you going to get money?'

'We're certainly not funding it,' mum, adding her two cents.

'It doesn't sound like you have this planned at all, I'm totally against it,' dad pulled the trigger on the second barrel of his verbal shotgun. 'When you went to Africa you learnt about a different side of life; it was well planned and at the right time in your life.'

'I've made up my mind,' I argued. 'Many employers like potential employees to have had different experiences.'

'You already have that. It sounds like you would be travelling and dosing, not actually achieving anything other than seeing how far your budget will last,' my father perceptively reasoned as sarcasm poured out of his every word. 'If I was interviewing you, I wouldn't offer you a job.'

'There you fucking go then,' I petulantly answered back. 'And this coming from someone who had a job for life.' To be fair though, my parents' point was exactly what the university careers advisor had told me.

'We don't need that sort of language at the table,' mum admonished.

'Sorry, but let me finish. I've made up my mind and would like you to support me… but if you don't, so be it.'

'We've supported you in everything you've done and generally agreed with your decisions,' dad replied. 'But you definitely need to think this idea over and put a proper plan together. Then, and only then, will we think about giving you our backing.'

'End of conversation,' my mother annoyingly added. I had only been home a few short hours but already felt trapped compared to the freedoms of university where I was answerable to no one.

12. JOB SEARCH

The next morning, I walked up and down the high street look-ing for vacancy signs; there were none. I registered at all the local employment agencies, happy to do anything in an effort to get some much needed money.

Returning home in the early evening, tired and frustrated, I was greeted by my parents informing me, 'We will impose a living at home charge as soon as you get a job;' my mood wasn't improved.

Although drained, I went for a run, this I found the best way to get my thoughts together and come up with a plan as there was no way I was going to stay at home longer than nec-essary. My best option, I concluded, was to move to London, my rationale being, that as there were more jobs in the capital I was more likely to find one... and if the worse came to the worst, I could always sling some dope with Jim.

13. The Big Smoke

Getting off at Liverpool Street train station the next day, the city had a very different feel to it, as although I had passed through London many times before, now it was to be my place of life for the coming weeks, months and who knows, maybe even years.

For the next two days, I literally and proverbially knocked on every conceivable door from newsagent to multinational. Three days after arriving, I got a phone call from an employment agency. 'Are you available for an interview tomorrow for a role as a Hospital Pricing Executive at a pharmaceutical company?' I immediately replied in the affirmative, even though I had no clue what the role might entail. And thus one week after arriving in the big smoke, I had a job… and it didn't involve selling narcotics of the illegal kind with Jim.

Having found gainful employment, next on my list was finding somewhere to live. Jim, who I'd been dosing on the couch at his parent's house, had come to the same conclusion. He'd found a job near where I was going to start work and so we decided to be housemates.

After a few fruitless visits to rental houses which were: too expensive, too far from the office, crappy buses routes, a shit hole—we struck gold with a four-bedroom house in Uxbridge. It was not too far from where we respectively worked, it was relatively close to a tube station if we wanted a night out in central London, and the rent was reasonable. The only problem was finding housemates for the remaining two rooms. Luckily, Lewis had also been offered a job in West London, and which left us with one room to fill.

STATEMENT OF RELIEF #1

I had managed to remove my partying body from under my parent's roof in less than 72 hours. Ok, so maybe I shouldn't be so flippant or ungrateful. I now know the difficult decisions parents have to make—which they do gladly and always in the best interest of their children—though the young rarely appreciate the sacrifices made on their behalf. So, as much as I might complain about my old folks, they did a good job to support me through childhood, teenage rebellions and the start of adulthood. I'd had the good fortune to have been a volunteer in Africa and a business graduate. I salute my parents for the start in life they gave me. I'm fully aware that any mistakes I made from here on in, notably how I find myself with the tide fast approaching and being buried up to my neck in sand was entirely of my own making.

14. Weekend Warrior

The next two years passed in a flash, and thus so does my story.

Once upon a time, the prospect of living in London had been exciting... though now it had become my home; it was not living in Africa as I had envisaged. I had started to climb the greasy pole and moved twice from one not particularly interesting office job to another. I had tried but failed to save a deposit for a studio flat and which could be a long-term investment while I went travelling for an extended period of time. In essence, I lived a studentesque lifestyle, the only tweak being that instead of going to lectures I went to work; the evenings and weekends still very much revolved around drinks, BBQs, house parties, illicit drugs, chasing girls, PlayStation tournaments, and misadventures. In short, my house-sharing years were chaotic fun.

The only slightly unusual aspect of life, considering I was in my mid-twenties and living in London, was that I joined the Territorial Army. Becoming an army reservist was primarily in the hope that in a post 9/11 world, that I would be called up to the regular army and thus the decision to move away from the UK would be taken out of my hands. During training, I slept on Scottish mountains in the middle of winter freezing my nuts off. I was put in a small room filled with CS gas to practice Nuclear, Biological and Chemical decontamination drills. I went on many assault courses, long marches and practiced battlefield first aid. I fired all kinds of weapons, but thankfully, I hadn't been shot at as was the case for some fellow reservists from my unit who had been sent to fight in the Second Iraq War. Maybe, if I too had gone to the deserts and oilfields, it would better explain how my life has unfolded? But, no, apart from the Territorial Army, the only other things I considered of interest during my London years were my frequent misadventures. Even at the time, I rationalized that I was fighting the realization that my life might end up with accepting the drudgery of a boring office job for the next 40 years. As Jim profoundly commented during one particularly long Sunday drinking session: the only thing I have in common with those fucks is the carpet we walk on. His words adroitly summed up what the housemates and many of our friends felt.

15. Jonas

Shortly after starting life in London, Jonas entered my reality. 'Either of you Wombles know of anyone?' I had asked Jim and Lewis as we needed an extra housemate.

'Nope,' Jim replied.

'Nope,' Lewis confirmed. 'Advert in the paper?'

'Sounds the best bet,' I agreed, and five days later Jonas moved in, his less than eloquent first words, being, 'You PUSS-IES! Who's up for a drink?' this more an order than question. 'Let's get on it—NOW!' This as he stood on the doorstep, in one hand a suitcase and the other a bottle of whisky.

I remember sometime later that first week, thinking, how did this overweight, shaven headed, copious drug taking lout come in the top 5% of his law class, complete The Bar in super quick time, and become one of the youngest junior partners at his law firm? The answer as I soon found out, was, that between his penchant for cocaine, speed and animal nitrate—to name but a few of his favourite class A's—and his chronic, very unsuccessful gambling addiction, he had no money and so needed a houseshare with recent graduates rather than a nice apartment closer to his work in the West End... such as his salary should have entitled.

On the Saturday afternoon that Jonas moved in, and which for Jim, Lewis and I normally meant a trip to Sains-bury's to buy as many cheap French stubby beer bottles as we could afford and then playing PlayStation, charcoaling sau-sages on the BBQ, and having a spliff... or two, before going to a pub around 8pm and finishing at a nightclub... Jonas had different plans.

Unbeknown to Jim, Lewis and I, Jonas had lived in the area for the previous six years and so had many acquaintances who he introduced us to during the afternoon, including one friend who showed his prowess at eating a pint glass. Like a circus act... he swallowed broken pieces of a pint pot!

By 10pm and all of us now steaming, it was time to go home, get changed into more suitable nightclub attire, and in Jonas' case, open a bottle of Malibu and which he consumed, by himself, during the thirty-minute taxi drive to Ealing Broadway. Approaching the main junction, he jumped out of the moving vehicle, and what can only have been divine intervention, didn't run into the oncoming traffic or trip on a curb, either one of which could have resulted in being knocked unconscious or death. Instead, he sauntered into the Roundhouse Pub. Jim, Lewis and I, waited until the taxi was STATIONARY and then proceeded into the bar we'd seen Jonas enter a minute earlier, though who within the 60 seconds it took for us to reach, had already knocked over one table and was annoying many other patrons with his boisterousness. In total agreement with Lewis and Jim, we concluded that Jonas was a lunatic; we slunk off to a different, quieter pub... and one that didn't have a maniac in it.

Several hours, many beers, and some moves on the dance floor later, I was alone. I didn't know what had happened to Lewis and Jim, but this was not unusual and I wasn't concerned. Looking for a taxi to take me home, I was greeted by the sight of Jonas standing in the middle of the road screaming, IF YOU THINK YOU'RE HARD ENOUGH, FUCKING COME ON THEN! I didn't know, and didn't want to know, who this was directed at, but in that instance, Jonas turned and waved me over. As much as I wanted to run away, I was magnetically propelled towards the slow motion disaster that was moving towards a conclusion of the bloody kind until a police car's sirens could be heard and flashing lights seen.

'The rozzers. Let's GO!' Jonas shouted, presumably know-ing somewhere in his sub-consciousness that he was the cause of the aggravation.

When I woke the next day, having fallen asleep in the taxi, I was in a flat that I couldn't recognise nor had any recollection of entering. All I knew, was that there was a porn film on the 60-inch flat screen TV, showing a guy with a huge dick fucking a little schoolgirl; I was very confused.

Running my hand over my face, I felt something sticky in my ear. On further inspection, I smelled mint. It dawned on me, that while I was comatose on some random person's sofa, my ears had been filled with something, what, I had no idea.

Jonas, sitting in an adjacent chair, apparently none the worse for wear, had a big grin on his face. 'You toothpaste twat,' were his eloquent words.

16. ONE PINT, TWO PINTS, THREE PINTS, FALL

Six-months after Jonas had joined us, to our surprise, Jim moved in with his girlfriend. In his place, Alan, known to one and all as Tony, as in, Tony Scarface Montana due to his penchant for cocaine, joined the mad-house.

August 12th was Tony's birthday. As a present we bought him a lap dance. After a night of booze at the strip club, the lap dancing stage turned into a dance floor and soon thereafter it was time to go home. Being as it was three in the morning and I had no money in my pocket, and that I had been talking to one of the dancers for the last few hours, it seemed reasonable to walk home with her rather than getting a taxi. Surprisingly, Sally—I never found out if that was her real or stage name—also thought this a good idea. As we made our way, I prattled on talking all kinds of shit… until I fell into a hedge on a deceptively even piece of pavement. 'It was a tree root… a dead rabbit that I tripped over; I'm not that drunk,' I assured her while unsuccessfully trying to push myself out of the bramble bush.

The next thing I knew, I was walking down a random road. It was raining and I had no idea where I was. My hands were bleeding from the scratches, my trousers were torn, I was shivering uncontrollably and there was now no Sally. If I'd seen a bus stop I would have taken cover and dozed till sun up; alas, there weren't any. My only option, to find an unlocked porch to doss in. Several doors, a few lights turned on and, Fuck-off you drunk, shouted at me later, a random doorway was found.

After two hours of blissful sleep, I awoke, my body sore from the concrete and being turned into a pin cushion from the bramble bush. I still had no idea where I was. I walked to the end of the road and realized, I jog down this road all the time. I was only a five-minute walk from home.

That evening and looking in the mirror, I admitted, that my drinking was getting out of hand. I would drink if there was something to celebrate, drink when I needed consolation, but most of all, drink to make something happen, as something good or bad, wonderful or foolish, was better than nothingness, boredom and frustration. It was time I spent a few days away from the lads and reflected on where my life was heading.

Brooding, I decided to have a day of contemplation and culture; I went into in central London. Having visited Tate Modern and the National Gallery, I walked around St James' Park pondering life. I considered leaving the Territorial Army and joining the regular army. I decided against that, otherwise life would surely have been very different to what it is now… that is to say, ending my days in a hole on the beach, with an assassin pointing his silenced pistol at my head

Bored, and with no particular destination in mind, I was soon walking through Soho. Thirsty, I went into a pub. With an orange juice and lemonade in hand—I had given myself a challenge to see how long I could go without alcohol—I found a seat and picked up a newspaper, the headline grabbing my attention.

Work shy, drunk, anti-social and promiscuous— Generation Y

The British public define Generation Y, as: work shy, drunk, antisocial and promiscuous. Social mobility studies have shown that this trend is being exacerbated by the growing wealth gap as compared with earlier generations who could expect job security, a pension and a house.

In the internet age, and with the dramatic social and economic changes, they have been profound changes in the expectations of the lives of those moving from youth into adulthood. There are no longer the certainties of trade unions, when men were men and worked in labour intensive industries. A sense of masculinity is being replaced by the metro-sexual ideal; moisturizer has replaced working men's clubs.

As youth enter adulthood in the early Twentieth Century, and with so little room at the top of the best careers, and the housing ladder ever harder to get on, a ground breaking study has found, there is downward mobility in which people find themselves in a lower social class than the one in which they were born. The report concluded, "The later in the century a person was born, the more likely they are to find themselves with a lower social standing than their parents."

That sums me up, I thought, as I wondered how I had changed from the idealistic young man sitting at the summit of Mount Meru to a caricature.

Three beers and a double Jack Daniels and Coke later—my abstinence lasting less than an hour—I left the pub. A random guy walked up to me. 'Do you want sex?'

'No, thanks,' I replied to the pimp.

'I have lots of good looking girls,' he persisted. 'What do you like? Young or old? Thin or fat? Thai, Polish, black? I have every type!'

'I'm fine,' this said half-heartedly, the alcohol increasing my susceptibility to suggestion.

'Just look.'

Knowing I was being a fool, I followed him. Five minutes later, I was introduced to his female associate. 'Go with

Hilda,' the pimp told me. I obliged and followed Hilda down a side-street and then up a creaking, poorly lit staircase.

'Which one?' Hilda asked, as she passed me a photo album. I chose a young looking, dark skinned African girl with braids. We agreed on £50 for half-an-hour with Winnie from Cameroon.

'Love, some men are abusive with our girls. I kindly ask you to leave a £500 deposit; you'll get this back after your time with Winnie,' Hilda reassured me.

'You're kidding?' My bank balance barely had £500 in it.

'We need to make sure you don't hurt our girls,' she insisted. I was already mentally committed, and so even though I knew that what I was doing was utterly stupid, I went to an ATM, withdrew all my earthy wealth and followed Hilda down another small alleyway. We descended into a lap dancing club where I gave the £500 to the bartender before following Hilda to another poorly lit room, and by now in a great deal of anticipation.

'Just wait while I get Winnie.'

20 minutes later, and with no sign of Hilda or Winnie, it dawned on me that I had been well and truly conned. For the next 30 minutes, I frantically ran around the streets of Soho looking for Hilda; she was not to be found. I tried to find the lap dancing club that held my deposit; it was locked. Shit, what a fucking idiot I am for falling for the oldest trick in the book, I admonished myself.

Very pissed off with my stupidity, I sat in the White Swam pub for the next six-hours, occasionally visiting the lap dancing club to see if it had opened. At 11pm, I finally saw a huge man come out the doorway. 'Is Hilda there?'

'No.'

'Winnie?

'No.'

'My £500?'

'Fuck off!'

If I'd been told to fuck off now… it would have been the bouncer, rather than me ending up in hospital… as you will find out. But on that sorry night, I finally gave up hope of ever seeing my money again; I had no choice but to put this episode down to one of life's harder lessons.

More annoyed and depressed than you can imagine, I sat at a bus shelter for half-an-hour, the drizzle freezing me to the bone as I waited for the nightbus to return me to my warm if empty bed. It arrived just as I was starting to doze. I paid for my ticket with what little change I had left in my pocket and then drunkenly fell asleep, reassured that I would be woken at the terminus by the driver before then walking home.

I was awoken not by the driver, but someone's hands going through my trouser pockets. 'What the fuck are you're doing?' I shouted at the five youths, one of who was waving my empty wallet in his hand. He walked forward and punched my unsuspecting face; he broke my nose.

'Stop those thieving motherfuckers!' I shouted through my clenched hand that was holding my bloodied beak. I ran down the bus and jumped of it just as it was pulling away. 'HEY YOU!' I shouted as I caught up with the youths, 'give my wallet back.'

'Or what? You'll call the police?' the boy nonchalantly mocked. 'Wanker.'

I punched the apparent ring leader in the face. Seconds later, I was hit on the side of the head with a bottle and knocked out.

Regaining consciousness, there was a small crowd around me who'd witnessed the whole episode. 'Stay where you are,' an old, motherly lady advised. 'I've called the ambulance and police.'

'Thanks,' I just about managed to say, as I felt great pain in side of my head and sticky warm blood that dripped down my face. After receiving stitches in hospital and making a police statement, I went home and crawled under my duvet feeling very sorry for myself.

17. HAPPY BIRTHDAY

It was 8am on Wednesday 15th November and all housemates had phoned into our respective places of work to call a sickie. 'Happy birthday, mate; now get one of these bad boys down your throat, you soft Southerner,' this from Tony as he passed me a Guinness. After my first gulp of the black stuff, Jonas dropped a Baileys shot into the pint glass, thus rendering it a Car Bomb, named so after the drink's popularity in Belfast. The Baileys and Guinness started to curdle, though with much practice I managed to finish the pint before it turned into a dark alcoholic custard.

I was hoping for a lap dance from Sally at the strip club for my birthday present, and then a private lap dance… assuming I didn't fall into a bramble bush. However, there was to be no such booty shaking, Jonas informing us, the club had been raided by the drugs squad the previous weekend. Plan B was Jonny's nightclub, a former cinema which on a Friday or Saturday night would regularly pack 800 plus, pissed and drugged up ravers, but on a cold, wet, Wednesday there was a paltry 47 hardy souls. However, what it lacked in atmosphere it more than made up in cheap drinks promotion: three bottles for a fiver; it was scarcely more expensive than supermarket booze.

By 2am, the 47 had dwindled to 12 and it was time to go home. We were accompanied by Julie and Claire; I fully expected to be shortly doing some bedroom gymnastics with the later. Opening my bedroom door, a bucket fell on my head and which knocked me unconscious, this I'm told, was greeted by great hilarity from my friends, who lifted me in my vile concoction splattered clothes and threw me onto my spaghetti filled bed; Lewis and Jonas proceeded to have a foursome with the girls.

It transpired, that during the middle of the afternoon poker session, and while I was out of the room, Jonas, Tony and Lewis discussed their options of how they would stitch me up for my birthday present.

'How about putting broken dried spaghetti in his bed,' Lewis had apparently suggested. 'However drunk he might be, seeing a quizzical look on his face will be priceless'

'Yeah, that's good, but it would be more fun if he got covered in shit when he came home, especially if he was with a bird,' Jonas, the good friend that he was had suggested.

'What, you're going to dump on his head?' Tony wanted to clarify.

'No, no, no, no, non as the French would say. When we leave, just make sure he is outside for a few minutes,' Jonas, started to explain his master plan with a devious smile on his face. 'Say, wait outside for a taxi or something. I'll pretend to be having a dump, but will actually be filling a bucket with all the worst stinking crap I can find in the kitchen and then balance it on top of his door. When he opens it, the bucket will tip over and cover him in Jonas soup, the ingredients of which are: ketchup, soy sauce, washing up liquid, coffee, coke, flour, and anything else I can find.'

'You are an evil motherfucker... but a true banter genius,' Tony said appreciatively.

18. WITH HIS BAG OF SWEETS…

I woke up one day, aged twenty-six-years, three-months and twenty-five days and knew things had to change when I looked in the mirror and saw the state I was in. Life is shit. I'm doing a wanky job, have no savings to get on the housing ladder, and even if I did, prices are stupidly expensive, I told myself. I really need to do something to change things around and get some direction (rather than booze) in my life. The mirror by-the-way, was the only thing left in my bedroom, everything else, including my bed and wardrobe, having been relocated to other parts of the house the previous evening, this while I had drunkenly fallen asleep on the sofa in the sitting-room.

Three cups of tea, an egg roll and a shower later, I started to think about Steph who I'd been introduced to the previous evening, and by of all people, Jonas. Steph was five years older than me, and much to my surprise, considering how drunk Jonas and I were, gave me her number. With there being no time like the present, I phoned her and we arranged to go on a date that evening at the Dog and Duck.

After some initial small talk, as per all first dates, Steph and I soon got into a proper conversation. 'Making an impact in people's lives is how I imagined my life would work out. I planned to save money and hopefully buy a flat, then travel the world, see different cultures and experience different foods, wine… and women, while giving a helping hand where I could; I had it all worked out. Instead, I'm living in a crazy house and doing a dead end job; my soul is being killed one day at a time. I don't see any good options for how to get away from sitting in front of a computer working on Excel for eight hours a day. Living with the lads is fun, but I need to move on. Six years has passed in a flash and I have no idea where my life is heading. That's me, Steph, sorry to have blurted it out, but my head feels like it's going to explode.'

It was at this point that the hairs on the back of my neck stood up when I saw Jonas, Tony and Lewis walk into the pub and promptly walk over to our table.

> With his bag of sweets
> and his cheeky smile,
> Liam is a paedophile.

They started to chant at the top of their lungs. 'Cheers, lads. Good one. Now fuck-off!' I, as politely as I could informed them.

'Alright, Steph,' Jonas said to his friend. 'Has he told you we filmed him sleep wanking last weekend?'

'Steph, honestly, I didn't, I don't,' I stammered, but it was too late, I'd already turned crimson. 'Jonas, why are you always such a prick?' Cornered, I made my excuses and went to the toilet. Thankfully on my return I saw that Jonas, Tony and Lewis were busy at a fruit machine. 'The thing is, Steph,' I started to say as I sat down, 'before university, I was a volunteer teacher in Tanzania. I climbed mountains and saw the most amazing sunsets and sunrises that you can imagine. I organized daily sports and was teaching classes of 50 kids, some of whom were only a few years younger than I was. I travelled all over East and Southern Africa, and saw and did amazing things with amazing people. Yet for the last six years, apart from the Territorial Army, life has revolved around how much I can drink; what's wrong with me?' I asked as I looked imploringly into her eyes.

'Wow, you've lived a really interesting life and things will come clear in time. Most of our generation are in the same situation. We have great plans, but can't move onto the second stage. You can either have a good time or save money… it's impossible to do both. Like you, I want to travel, have my own house, start a family etcetera, but at the moment it's nothing more than a dream.'

'Being pissed off with life is something we have in common,' I joked, as I wolfed down the rest of my pint, not knowing that while I had been in the toilet contemplating life, Jonas had added a triple vodka to my Guinness.

Another thirty-minutes of chatting with Steph and Lewis came over to the table. 'Let's go clubbing.'

'It's a school night,' I pointed out.

'So?'

'You guys, have fun,' Steph correctly assuming the night was going to end up messy. 'I have a presentation tomorrow.'

'Good luck,' I slurred in reply. 'Next time, I promise we will meet where these fuckers can't track us down.'

Four hours later, I was woken by the driver at the bus terminal, the others nowhere to be seen. Wankers. But at least they hadn't drawn on my face, stolen my money, or poured water on my groin… all of which was par for the course.

REFLECTION #3—
A WATERSHED

You could say, that meeting Steph was the end of the first part of my life, this story. It had been six fun-filled, relatively care-free years during my formative years during which I'd experienced many of the vices known to man… and had built quite the taste for all of them. Of greater importance, I'd bonded with a group of friends who understood and liked me for who I was, not what I was or how much I had; I never pretended to be someone I wasn't with them.

It had now been two years since I'd graduated and six years since I'd returned from Tanzania. There seemed little prospect of life turning out as I had hoped or expected. During these years, and despite the occasional holiday and some successes with the fairer sex, I had started climbing a career ladder I never wanted to be on in the first place. My unhappiness with life had started to spawn anxiety; I felt trapped and did not know which way to turn. The absence of sustained adventure on one hand and the lack of financial advancement on the other, were increasingly depressing me.

There was one significant event during these mad-house years. On a beautiful summer Saturday, 17 of us decided to get a train down to Brighton for a weekender. By afternoon we were sitting on the beach enjoying the sunshine, swimming in the sea and consuming copious amounts of alcohol as we got ready for a night of pubbing and clubbing. We had vodka, gin, tequila and any other top shelf spirit you could think of, and by nightfall on average we had each drunk a bottle of spirits.

Larry had been having his fair share, but not going at it as hard as some of us. We had a cracking night and returned to the rented house as the sun was rising. I woke up to a great commotion around 8am and saw Larry covered in puke and curled up in a ball with a fever. Something was clearly wrong. We called an ambulance. He was carried out of the house on a gurney and rushed to hospital. On the way he had his stomach pumped, but was pronounced dead on arrival. We later found out that his drinking brought on a blood clot which led to a heart attack.

It was a real shock, not least as I knew what happened to Larry could just as easily be my fate. Life seemed to be slowly slipping by and for the first time I gave my future some considerable thought as I moved into the latter half of my third decade on this mortal coil. So, like Scorpion, the German Rock Group who had the hit single, Wind of Change on their 1990 album Crazy World, I too felt that the future was in the air and, I could also feel it everywhere… but I didn't know which way I was going to be blown.

19. Destiny

Two years on from my date with Steph at the Dog and Duck, and I'd been sharing a flat with her for eighteen months. Wild nights had in the most part been replaced by movie nights, and as Jonas liked to remind me, I was now pussy whipped. Time had passed quickly, and to my parents things probably looked much more positive, rosy even. I had settled down with a girl and moved on from my bachelor days. I expect they said to each other: a long term girlfriend, steady job and house, who knows what next, grandchildren?

I had left the corporate world and was working with Uncle Brian who had a small company, Absolute Hygiene and which sold industrial cleaning products. It wasn't the most exhilarating of jobs, however, it afforded me the opportunity to travel the UK making sales calls, this preferable to sitting in an office.

The quiet life had resulted in me saving enough for a deposit on a co-owned cottage (with Steph) in the Essex countryside. Our new dwelling had a unique layout, this from having been built in the 19th century as stables.

It was an exciting time. Steph and I spent most of our spare time and money fixing-up the house, hoping that we could rent the cottage to cover the mortgage while we went travelling, it being our permanent base and long-term investment.

During the early days of home ownership, and having a much needed cold beer while taking a break from tiling, I opened a cabinet drawer, the previous owner selling the house with its contents; I picked out a random bat eared magazine.

Micro Finance Malawi: facilitating independence not dependence

Micro Finance Malawi, a London-based charity provides micro loans to women in landlocked Malawi.

Malawi, bordered by Mozambique, Tanzania and Zambia, gained independence in 1964. The first multi-party elections were held in 1994, this after 30 years of Hastings Banda's autocratic rule. With a population of over 16 million, 85% of whom are subsistence farmers who live on an average of 45p a day, it is no wonder Malawi is the ninth poorest country in the world. The economy is heavily reliant on donor aid, famine is frequent, there is an estimated HIV/Aids infection rate of 10%, and a child mortality rate of 1 in 10; average life expectancy is 46 years.

The premise of microfinance is simple: it's better to encourage independence than dependence. MFM does this by providing small loans, basic business training and, on-going guidance to groups of women. The ladies develop sustainable livelihoods, work their way out of poverty, and are able to feed, clothe and educate their families which are often as large as 12 or 14 people, some of the children orphaned by AIDs.

The loans, often as little as £15, are big enough to enable recipients to set up a small business, such as farming, fishing or market trading. The difference these small sums can make is staggering. Typically, after the first loan, the women use their profits to buy food and clothing. After a second loan, they can send their children to secondary school. After a third loan, they invest in home improvement, and after a fourth loan they are running businesses that employ others.

MFM only lends to women as they are proven to be more reliable than men at repaying. Through a combination of assessment of the individual and ongoing support, we achieve over 96% repayment, the money then re-circulated to other clients.

For the next three weeks I read the article several times, though I couldn't put my finger on what exactly was pulling at my heart strings. I'd passed through Malawi on my way down to South Africa when I was a volunteer in Tanzania, the trip including a week at the beautiful Nkhata Bay where I did a scuba diving course and which gave me a new, though utterly unfulfilled passion. Nevertheless, I felt the article was linked to my and Steph's future. I thought, maybe our destiny lay in Malawi.

I did some background reading on both Malawi and Microfinance, and then spoke to Dewi who was coincidently working at a Micro Finance Institution. 'It's been a long time.'

'I've been working in Zambia for the last three years; it's the best decision of my life. What are you up to these days?'

I updated him. 'What's microfinance all about? Give me the basics.'

'It's financial services for micro-businesses, such as farmers and hawkers who can't access financial services from a commercial bank. The clients are often organized in groups of twenty and have joint liability to repay their loans.'

'I've read that microfinance is seen as the new way to help the poor out of poverty; is that really the case?'

'Certainly, it's a way to support micro-entrepreneurs who are often the sole bread-winners for their families. If you're really serious about getting into microfinance, give me a phone call anytime.' After the call, I had much to ponder.

20. THE MAN IN BLACK

Shortly after talking to Dewi, and totally unrelated, Uncle Brian had organized for me to have a chat with Martin, a fifty-something, grey bearded, thick dark-rimmed glasses wearing, black polo neck sporting motivational guru, who Brian hoped would help to increase my sales figures and which of late had been declining—like my motivation—at an alarming rate.

'What do you want to achieve?' was Martin's first question after pleasantries had been exchanged.

'Business or life?' I answered, as I poured two cups of tea.

'Both.'

'Well, I need enough money to keep food on the table and pay the mortgage. As for life, I want to do something that will make a difference.'

'A difference, in what?' he probed as he took a sip of tea and nibbled on a chocolate digestive biscuit.

'A difference for the people I work with, but also to me.'

'What do you mean?'

'Something where I'm personally making a difference.'

'How will you reach that goal? What motivates you?'

'I don't know if Brian told you, but eight years ago, I was a volunteer teacher at a rural secondary school in Tanzania; there, I made a difference. Nothing, absolutely nothing since has come close to that sense of fulfilment. I like to travel and experience new cultures. I'm a believer that everyone has a story to tell and, that you can always learn something from every experience, good or bad.'

'It sounds like you were super motivated; what happened? What can make you motivated so that you increase your sales once more?'

'I ask myself this question, and all I come up with is life. I'm a poster child for Generation Y. I'm university educated and travelled more than my parents. I have finally managed to get on the housing ladder and which I co-own with my girl-friend; I couldn't get enough savings for a deposit on my own. The stories you read in the newspapers, about binge drink-ing… that's me and my friends on weekends. Maybe, I peeked early and my expectations are now too high?'

'Life doesn't give, you have to be proactive and make things happen. No one will do it for you and it certainly won't happen just by wishing. There is no right way in life as this little story illustrates. A husband and wife were walking along a dusty road with their donkey. A passerby asked, you have a donkey, why are you walking? The man gets on the don-key and they continue. A little while later, another passerby says, you're so mean, how can a man be on a donkey while the wife walks? The husband got off the donkey and lets his wife ride. Another person passes and looks disdainfully at the man. What sort of a man are you? Why are you dusty and sweaty from walking when there is a donkey to ride? The husband and wife looked at each and decide to both walk.'

21. SOUL—WHERE ART THOU

Over the next few weeks, and with Martin and Dewi's words fresh in my mind, I did much soul searching. I finally concluded, that with my business background, changing career into microfinance would be the most logical path while also giving me the wanderlust I was craving. Thus, four months after moving into the cottage, it was time to talk with Steph about our future. 'Now that we have this cottage,' I started while rapidly making my way through my third glass of red wine, 'we can do what we want. There is nothing stopping us to travel the world. Now that we have the cottage,' I repeated, 'there is nothing stopping us leaving; the rent would cover our mortgage.'

'Sure, but we've already travelled around a bit, especially you. Now is the time to start a family, don't you agree?' Children had not previously come up as a serious point of conversation. Steph wanting to start a family in the near future was news to me, as apparently my desire to live overseas was to her. 'That's why we got the cottage in the first place... isn't it... to settle down?'

'I suppose... but there's nothing stopping us settling down outside of the UK and starting a family elsewhere, is there? If we don't go now, we'll never have the chance.'

'I'll miss our friends and family.'

'So will I... but family and good friends will always be here and we'll make new friends wherever we go; in life you have to go with your convictions.'

'It sounds like you've already made up your mind.'

'I've made no secret, ever since we first met, how I saw my or our future. It was just a matter of being the right time before making changes. We are the lucky few who are in a position financially, socially and culturally, to take a chance and let the chips fall as they do. We'll have the support of our family and friends, and if things don't go according to plan, they'll help us pick up the pieces.'

'It sounds like you've been practicing this speech?' She was correct, I had. 'What if I say, no? What if I want to stay? I like what I do, I like my friends, and I like to be near my family. I don't want to leave. Now we have the cottage, we can start a family,' she reiterated.

'In that case... we both have decisions to make,' I replied without hesitation.

'It sounds like you already have,' she said full of sarcasm as she stormed out of the room. 'You can make your mind up on the couch,' she added, as she poked her head round the door before slamming it shut, the force of which knocked over the wine glass which I had perched on the arm of the sofa, the red wine ruining my jeans.

22. KING MIDAS

Sleeping on the couch, I played the conversation with Steph over-and-over as I tried to work out all the ramifications of the biggest decision of my life. As the Clash sang, Should I stay or should I go? If I go, there will be trouble, and if I stay it will be double. On the one hand, I had a girlfriend and potential wife and mother who I liked, respected and for the most part had fun with. We'd just bought the cottage, work with Brian was ok, and despite the drop in monthly sales, I still made enough. All-in-all, I led a reasonably good life. On the other hand, if I stayed I would be giving up on my dreams. Steph, had made her position abundantly clear—her way or the highway; I couldn't see any compromise.

Not being able to answer the question, and despite it being 10pm, I decided to go for a pint at my local pub. Looking back now, it must have been fate that as I walked through the front door of The Castle, one of my all-time favourites, Lynyrd Skynyrd's Free Bird, was being played on the jukebox. I went to the bar and ordered a pint of London Pride bitter and listened intently to the lyrics. Am I a bird who doesn't want his wings clipped? I desperately wanted to know as a tear came to my eye then rolled down my cheek, my mind almost made up; the ramifications of the decision utterly unknown.

Halfway through my pint, I saw a man in his 70's sitting in the corner of the bar mentally playing an air guitar to the fantastic riffs. 'What a song,' I introduced myself.

'Indeed,' the man agreed. 'I remember when I first heard it on Skynyrd's debut album—I just wish I'd followed their advice.'

'What do you mean?' I was very interested in the answer and hoped for some insights into life.

'I was seventeen in 1973, free, young and an idealist. I was about to move to India to live in a commune, when my grandfather died. He left me a significant inheritance and which I used to start a construction business. That's what I've been doing for the last 40 years. I'm as rich as King Midas but divorced three times. My children have disowned me and I have no spirituality. I never made it to India,' the gentleman reflected with a sad and distant look on his face which bore the scars of loneliness.

'Should I follow my head or my—'

'There's no choice,' he interrupted. 'Do what your heart tells you; don't be a caged bird.'

REFLECTION #4— FREE BIRD

At the time, this really was the hardest decision I'd had to make, though once made a huge weight was lifted. I no longer felt like Sisyphus who'd been condemned by the Greek gods to roll a boulder up a hill for eternity. I'd tried to impose order on my existence, but had too many unanswerable questions; my only logical alternative, rebel and rejoice in the unknown.

Decision made, my heart had been freed and I didn't give a damn about the consequences. I realized, if I didn't try to reach for the stars, I would always wonder, what if? I think, ultimately, that was the difference between Steph and me, the willingness to risk failure for far greater reward. With her being a few years older than me, and broody, it was understandable why she wanted to settle down, but it just wasn't the right time for me. I would forever resent her for clipping my wings if I stayed… and more pertinently, I now realise I didn't love her enough to sacrifice my dreams for hers.

23. No Turning Back

I informed Steph of my decision, her response; a slap across my face. Whatever love and friendship had existed evaporated like a fart in the wind. I'd made my proverbial bed on which I now had to lie… that bed being in the spare-room and where in no uncertain terms Steph had told me to relocate.

Once all my worldly goods had been moved upstairs, I drove to meet Uncle Brian and told him that as well as leaving Steph, the cottage and the UK, I would also be leaving Absolute Hygiene. We agreed on a three months' notice period. This would give him time to find my replacement and allow me to keep earning to pay my half of the mortgage while at the same time trying to work out the details of my future.

I anticipated it was going to be a rocky but very interesting time ahead, but I also knew that if I couldn't find a volunteer opportunity within three months, then I was up shit creek without a paddle, not least, out of financial necessity. I also had no choice but to live in the cottage with an angry, moody Steph; I could ill afford paying rent on top of the mortgage and she had no intention to, 1) move out, 2) sell her half of the cottage to me, or 3) together, both sell the cottage. This was the grim reality of my pronouncement.

Declaration made, and as the clock on my three-month timer started to tick, I made my way to the community library to jot down details of volunteer organizations who I could contact. I quickly found out that most charities were concerned with the environment, teaching or working with kids, none of which floated my boat or would make use of my business experience. Voluntary Services Overseas (VSO) which hired business professionals looked to be my best bet. I also sent an email to Micro Finance Malawi telling them how their article had inspired me… though for obvious reasons, not the heart-ache it had caused Steph or the ball ache she now gave me.

The first month flew by, but little headway was made. The second month passed with few encouraging responses from organizations I had applied to, but I was increasingly putting all my eggs into the VSO basket.

Getting home after a day of poor Absolute Hygiene sales, and which included a parking fine, I found an envelope from VSO. I opened it with great anticipation and trepidation, wondering where in the world I might next find myself and hoping my choice two months earlier had been worth it. In summary, I was told, I didn't have sufficient sales experience to write grant proposals. Really? I'd been working for a small business where sales are the lifeblood. Besides, I couldn't have been that bad at Absolute Hygiene otherwise I wouldn't have been able to financially survive on a commission based salary.

The disappointing news (this a gross understatement) was the cherry on the cake of a crappy day, in fact, a wanky couple of depressing months. Thus, I foolishly decided, it would be a good idea to go for a night-time walk and drown my sorrows along the way. I took two cans of Heineken from the fridge, an oblig-atory hip flask of whisky, and every forty-five minutes or so on my Odyssey, I would be at either an off license or a pub to refill.

I walked for six hours and drank 10 pints; I've no idea how much whisky? I reckon I covered about twenty-miles, and by midnight my knees were starting to seriously hurt. On my trek, I contemplated that it might have been wiser to have done my research or organized an opportunity first before dropping the bombshell to Steph. I also vaguely recollect going to a Chinese takeaway and ordering a bag of prawn crackers… to keep me sober. As it was a warm and dry night, and I had no idea where

I was, I slept on the grass verge of the road. The next morning, I hobbled home feeling even more sorry, this from the hangover, my sore feet and legs, and being up shit creek. I only had two more weeks of working with Uncle Brian and then I was unemployed.

After a third fruitless month, I transitioned from being gainfully employed and a tax paying member of society to one relying on state benefits. Life on the home front with Steph was going from miserable to worse. Seeing me floundering, Steph left a red lipstick kissed envelope on my pillow, inside of which was a poem.

Wishes

You can wish upon a star,
but be careful for what you wish for
as you might just get it!

A toy gun… and you can be killed.
A pet dog… who can bite you.
A car… for you to crash,
dreams, smashed.

Sometimes, the grass is greener on the other side,
but that might be a small patch in a dessert of dust.
You can never know where you wish will lead—
to the Promised Land or to hell and back?

We all wish, but we can't foresee the outcome.
Hindsight is a wonderful thing, or so we say.
If you had hindsight
would you still have made your wishes,
or is it better the devil you know?

The future is unknown,
so be careful with what you wish for
as you might just get it.

24. The Internet

Two months unemployed and no promising opportunities on the horizon, I desperately needed a morale boost. So, to kill two birds with one stone, I became a health tourist, or more specifically, I used my credit card for a spot of dentistry tourism.

To cut a long story short, I was told I needed four root canal treatments—ouch, both for my mouth and pocket. With the aid of Google, I found that for the same cost of having pain in Essex, I could pay for flights, accommodation, all dentistry work done, and still have some change left over for a few beers and a bit of sightseeing in Prague—awesome!

Other than the aforementioned sightseeing, dentistry work and drinks, I also went to a nudist park and skinny dipped in the Vltava, and then onto the most extraordinary place I've ever visited. Part brothel, part internet porn, it was an excellent if somewhat seedy business model whereby punters get to have discounted sex with hookers while being live streamed onto the internet for paying voyeurs.

25. O'SULLIVAN'S

The other thing of note in my topsy-turvy world, this happening shortly after returning from Prague, I slept with Steph for the first time since we split up. Let me explain. After a cold, wet, miserable Wednesday, I got home and slowly got drunk and high. Steph, smelling the weed, came upstairs to shout at me, but after five minutes of venting her fury, she joined me in smoking and drinking, and then both of us high, tipsy and after sharing some good memories... we shagged.

There were to be a few repeat shags over the next few days, this in between the screaming matches. Split personality would be a very appropriate description of this incarnation of our relationship. Then she went cold turkey on me. I think she might have had a new boyfriend. I wonder how she explained our strange set-up? I never did find out.

Another evening, this as I was spilling my guts to Michael, the manager of The Castle, he offered me a job. By the end of my first week, I had worked ninety hours and finally had some much needed cash-in-hand... this on top of my unemployment benefits.

Working again, life quickly turned into a trance revolving between sleeping, sending applications to charities and standing on my feet serving pints. Having worked in white collar jobs since leaving university, I quickly realised that I needed to invest in some thick soled shoes, rather than thin, leather business shoes; standing all day becomes incredibly painful; I had forgotten this from my beer serving days during university holidays.

Turning my sexual frustration of sleeping alone and cold upstairs, while Steph slept downstairs, I decided to try my luck at internet dating. After a few nights of signing up to various websites and using a scatter gun approach to sending out invites for a date, I eventually got lucky.

Agreeing to meet at O'Sullivan's pub, I didn't immediately recognise Shelly; she was five years older and thirty pounds heavier than her photo. Not to mind, with the wonders of six pints I had donned my beer googles and our mouth and hands were exploring each other. What Shelly didn't have in looks, she certainly had in blowjob skills, this I found out in O'Sullivan's toilets, during which pleasurable time, I remember thinking, I might not know how the whole Africa thing is going to work out, but I'm certainly getting some exciting new experiences since splitting with Steph. I met Shelly once more, this time graduating from a blowjob to anal in a cheap bed and breakfast.

26. WHERE?

After six months of my life changing decision, I finally got some good news, I was going to Malawi as a volunteer consultant for five months with Micro Finance Malawi. However, that was not to be for another three long months of living with Steph; what purgatory.

With a new beginning finally in sight, I went back to the library to do some research. I photocopied a local business directory, with the idea that if I was going to work in microfinance then it would be good to raise some loan capital before leaving. As such, I wrote a letter to some companies.

Dear Sir / Madam

I'm going to Malawi for five months as a volunteer consultant for Micro Finance Malawi. Other than the technical support I will give as a self-funded consultant, I'm also raising funds to be disbursed as loans. The greater the amount I raise in England the more I will be able to help the greatly under-funded communities.

Yours sincerely

As I mentally prepared for the unknown, I started to organise my health requirements. I received: Tetanus, Typhoid, Yellow Fever, Hepatitis A, Hepatitis B and Rabies injections; my arm and ass were very sore for some days. It could have been worse though, but I was already covered for Polio, Meningitis, TB and Flu.

I also went shopping for an impossibly long list that MFM suggested I take with me. At the age of nearly 28, I was humiliatingly forced to plead bankruptcy to the Bank of Mum and Dad. They couldn't comprehend my decision to leave Steph, the cottage and a job for a life of uncertainty and relative poverty.

Two weeks after sending out the fifty or so letters, I received a cheque and cover note.

> The Board was impressed by the sentiment of your communication and reviewed your request together with various other approaches received. As such, we would like to support your unselfish efforts in helping others and agreed to donate £350.

There was no turning back now.

27. TICK-TOCK

As the clock ticked down to lift off, and in-between working all my waking hours at The Castle, I managed to fit in a few pints with Jonas, and who egged me on to call a local radio station and tell them my story. To my utter astonishment, a kindly listener phoned up and offered to do a fundraising concert in Jameson's Ale Bar. To raise extra money, I thought it would be a good idea to hold a raffle and so went round shops in the nearby village for prizes; people were very supportive.

On the night of the concert, unbeknown to either Paddy (the band leader) or I, there was another group playing at the Long Room; few people attended our shindig. However, the incredible part of this story was not the concert, but Paddy, who aged seventeen was involved in a car crash which left him quadriplegic. Instead of moaning and self-pity, he got on with life and ten years later now manages his band, is the lead singer and, a successful poet and theatre director. What an absolute inspiration; I felt truly fortunate to have met Paddy, his troubles putting mine into perspective.

The story doesn't finish there though. As not many people came to the concert, Paddy and I decided not to hold the raffle but donate the prizes to a kid's hospice. Two nights later, I was on one of my usual nights out on my own, and who did I meet, Gemma, one of the nurses at the hospice. After several hours talking and telling her my life story, including how I happened to be at the hospice, it was time to go home. I explained my sorry situation with Steph and she offered me her couch; what a great girl.

Soon I was counting down days, rather than months and weeks before flying to Malawi. One night, I decided to play poker in the nearby town, but not only did I lose £50, which I could ill afford, but I chose the coldest night of the year to sleep in my car. The cottage was fifteen miles from town, and so if I wanted a drink, play poker and go clubbing, I would be in no state to drive home, thus, it was wiser to sleep in my car, and which would have been a good idea… if it wasn't so frigging cold!

In an effort to raise some extra pocket money, I did two additional jobs. First, tele-selling cigarette lighters. I don't know which bright spark—pun fully intended—thought selling cigarette lighters over a phone was a genius idea, but predictably sales were minimal. Having proved my ineptitude at selling lighters, I did two days of the most mind-numbingly boring job. Through the years, I have worked at the Post Office, pubs and restaurants, car cleaning, processed credit card application forms, and telesales to Australia for Yellow Pages (and selling cigarette lighters) however, being on an assembly line and putting plastic boxes in a crate three boxes deep, by three boxes wide and nine boxes high, takes the gold medal for worse job ever. I was nothing more than a human robot. Experiencing the reality of many people's everyday lives, and being grateful for the opportunities life had given me, was yet one more lesson in the difficult ten-months since I'd become a free bird.

On my last weekend, I said my farewell to Steph and then took my few personal belongings from the cottage back to my parent's home where I stored it in the loft; I didn't trust Steph not to sell what she could. I went for a last pint with dad at his golf club, but was refused entry for wearing jeans; I hate that petty bullshit. I bought a few more bits and bobs from the MFM list, including a long wave radio, remembering that the trusty BBC World Service had kept me entertained in Tanzania nine long years earlier. I sold my 2.0 litre Renault Laguna with electric wing mirrors, sunroof and a low mileage… for a miserly £60. The relatively new tyres cost more, but only the breaker's yard would buy it; I handed over the keys with a heavy heart.

My last Saturday night was one to remember. After a few glasses of the old vino, a couple of shagging rounds and then showering, Gemma suggested I wore her makeup; I assented. Low and behold, after five minutes of expert female attention, I was duly dolled up with lipstick, makeup, eyeliner and painted fingernails. I was vamped and ready to hit the town. Unsurprisingly, we got many inquisitive and surprised looks; it was a very fun night. I would miss Gemma, but I couldn't change my mind, I'd emotionally invested too much to turn back, and besides, Gemma was also of a mind to change her life from being a secretary. Shortly after I left for Malawi, she became an English teacher in Thailand and has been doing that for the last five years while travelling the world. In my own little way, I think I inspired her.

On the last Sunday, my parents organized a family sending-off party. It was quite nice to see aunts, uncles and cousins who I hadn't seen for well over a year. Predictably, they asked the same questions I'd been hearing for the previous months: why Malawi and what is microfinance? I kept giving the same answers: it's my destiny, Malawi is south of Tanzania and, microfinance is giving small loans to micro-entrepreneurs. The truth is, I knew very little else about my future.

28. D-DAY

Soon it was D-Day, and butterflies were flying round my stomach. I knew the next five months would be a watershed in my life, just as much as when I had lived in Tanzania for nine-months before university. I was leaving everything I know behind: friends, family, career, cottage, the bitch Steph and, nice girlfriend Gemma.

Boarding the plane at Heathrow, I was a mix of emotions. I was sad to be leaving Gemma, but happy that my ten months of self-imposed hell was finally coming to an end.

STATEMENT OF RELIEF #2

I made a list of some of the things I wouldn't miss:

1. A football obsessed media
2. Chavs
3. Beer being so bloody expensive
4. Boy racers and their pimped cars
5. Image, image, image
6. Everybody trying to conform to the acceptable norms of society
7. Reality TV shows
8. Annoying ringtones
9. Constantly being asked, why Malawi? Why microfinance?
10. Not having to be a human robot or tele-selling cigarette lighters.

Reflection #5—
New Beginnings

Being less flippant, I would just like to say, especially to those who work on an assembly line or sell cigarette lighters over a phone, I'm sure that isn't your dream job. I admire your resilience and lion heartedness in doing what you have to do for your family; I now more than ever fully appreciate what that means.

Back to my story. I knew I was a very different person to when I last set foot on African soil ten years earlier. I was no longer a callow youth with excitement and naivety in my heart, but had gone through all kinds of emotional ups and downs, especially so in the last year. I appreciated that I looked back at my pre-university days through rose tinted glasses, and that I might well end up regretting my life-altering decision but, I was prepared for any eventuality... though let me quickly add, here and now, in no way, shape or form did I expect to be in my current sandy predicament!

29. WELCOME BACK

Within 48 hours of landing in Malawi, I was starting to question the wisdom of my life defining decision. The plane was one hour late. After getting a taxi into Lilongwe (the capital) from the airport, I found a small coach. I sat being roasted inside while watching those I had assumed were fellow travellers get off. I eventually worked out, the decoys were sitting inside to attract fare paying passengers.

The 30 seat coach left after two increasingly sweaty hours with 43 people on board. The road was not good. My memory had erased the need to dodge livestock who apparently had the right of way and swerving round potholes the size of bomb craters. This was not to mention avoiding traffic in the opposite direction, who were likewise doing a slalom, even round blind bends.

The further from Lilongwe we went, the windier the weather became, so much so that some of the plastic windowpanes were blown out as it started to rain. The cramped damp torture, which was supposed to last for three hours actually took five due to a breakdown and innumerable delays. This was not how I imagined my glorious return to Africa. Approaching my 29th birthday, it was clear the last ten years had made me soft and I was now the proverbial fish out of water.

30. KASUNGU

Kasungu, in the central region of Malawi, was my home for the next five months. It's like a mid-west American town a hundred years ago, with farmers, dust, rough pubs, hookers, corrupt police and stories of good old fashioned robbery. On the plus side, Kasungu had a lovely climate with low-humidity, and beautiful, if dusty scenery. I lived in a house which had: three mango and two avocado trees, a guard who slept most of the time, the landlord's twelve goats and three cows whose daily stirring acted as my 5am alarm clock. I had a long shot toilet, which consisted of two breeze blocks in a V shape and which were consistently covered in flies. Inside the house, I had two bedrooms but no bed. I slept on four sofa cushions on the floor, and used a towel and jumper as a makeshift pillow; surprisingly I actually slept quite well. I bought a bed and mattress at the market for £14, which I later found out was double the going price. Electricity was erratic at best and more often missing in action for days at a time. I had a kerosene stove to cook on... though the pans had holes in them.

I soon got into a routine at work. I sat busily at my desk tapping away at my laptop. My role was to, 1) build commercial and operational capacity of MFM and, 2) write a business plan. With this in mind, I had a long conversation with staff about what they thought was better: a loan or a cash gift? Unanimously, they said, gifts don't motivate the recipient into making the most of the opportunity, whereas a loan has consequences and so is used more efficiently.

I started visiting the women only groups. I would ride pillion behind the loan officer, this something I'd never done before. I was a little worried as we flew along at 60 mph on (thankfully) empty roads, half that speed on dusty tracks. I saw the impact MFM had on the micro-entrepreneurs. The variety of businesses and complexity of their logistics was impressive. Some women got orders for dresses and which they bought in Tanzania (where they were cheaper) imported and then sold them at a healthy profit margin. Other ladies sold veggies by the roadside, hawked second-hand clothes, made a moonshine equivalent or, ran tea shops, the availability of fresh bread surprisingly hard to find. Everyone had an entrepreneurial mind-set, but this out of necessity rather than a lifestyle choice as in the UK. It was clear how these women's lives had positively changed thanks to the support of MFM. In one village, we talked to a village-headwoman who showed us her old mud brick and thatch dwelling and then compared it to her new cement and corrugated iron sheets house. Other women who cared for orphans were now able to feed, clothe and educate their nieces, nephews and grandchildren; it was very encouraging.

After work, I would walk home at around 5:30, do exercise and then decide what to eat. Cooking was not the same, not just the ingredients but also the lack of kitchen equipment. There was no oven, steamer or Lean Mean George Foreman grilling machine and which over the previous years I had come to rely on. My meals usually consisted of two out of: tomato, onion and potato, with a variety of: rice, pasta, egg and avocado, and then generously covered in the local chili sauce. As there was no TV, DVD or PlayStation, I read a lot and was generally in bed by 9pm.

Some evenings I went to A&J's restaurant, which undoubtedly had the best food in Kasungu. I got more than I bargained for on my first outing there, when Alex, an East Londoner, who married Julie, a Malawian, told me a story; I paraphrase:

'So, mate, you won't believe what happened just before Christmas… we were approached to see if we wanted to buy a penis and scrotum. You know, apparently it helps down below. Low and behold, mate, two days later, there was a penis and scrotum in some Tupperware. I chatted to the selling pair while Julie called the police, and who of course were in town getting pissed up. Julie eventually tracked them down to the Groove2000; you been there yet? She got a taxi and brought the pissed policemen here. Mate, in the ensuing scuffle, the penis got thrown under a car. The scumbags were arrested, though a policeman left an AK47 at the bar when they left, as you fucking do; stupid pissed fuckers. To top it all, the following day, a dead man was found minus penis and scrotum. You'll never guess the next bit… it turned out to be the uncle of the two guys who were arrested; welcome to Kasungu, my friend.'

'You're pulling my leg.'

'Wish I were, mate; this place is nuts. Don't walk here after dark. Pay up the money and grab a taxi.'

'I always walk after a few drinks; it freshens me up.'

'Not here, not if you want to stay in one piece. It's just not worth the risk, take a taxi.'

'I've lived here most of my life, but I wouldn't walk 30-seconds in the dark,' Julie confirmed.

On another evening, some volunteers who lived in Kasungu organized a dinner. There was Ken, a Malawian who was married to Avisha, an Indian/Canadian—they were Christian missionaries. Stephanie, another Canadian worked at the District Education Ministry. Courtney, an American, was the District Council facilitator for HIV/AIDS. Eleanor, an Italian, worked for the World Food Programme. Patricia, who was Spanish, worked for a NGO and came with a colleague, Freddie, who was Italian. It's was great to socialize with like-minded people, all of us in our mid-20's to early-30's, motivated and passionate about our jobs. It was easy to talk about anything, from work to politics, economics and where we have travelled. In large part, this camaraderie with like-minded souls was one of my main hopes when making the decision to leave Steph and the cottage in what now seemed a lifetime ago.

One weekend, having gone pillion, I decided to learn how to ride a motorbike; it was easier than I anticipated. Another Saturday, I met Lincoln and Mavuto at A&J's. They were two local businessmen who were good company, if normally wasted. They introduced me to Jacaranda's, a local nightclub which had a reputation for aggressive young men and prostitutes; I was not put off. The music was an eclectic mix of African pop, reggae and European dance. I couldn't help but have a shuffle on the dance floor and, unlike in the UK where my moves were a source of mirth, in Kasungu they seemed to be appreciated. Leaving Jacaranda's in the early hours, a passing police patrol threatened to arrest me for being a vagabond. At the time I was a bit flustered, not realizing they wanted a small bribe to buy a drink; I hadn't yet got to understand the ways of the police… like I do now.

31. A Wonderful Weekend

As I was settling into Kasungu life, I also wanted to have some time to myself so went to Lake Malawi. On the Friday of a bank holiday weekend, I drove to Vwaza National Park. A minute from the entrance, I saw a herd of elephants strolling through the staff accommodation area. It was amazing to see these enormous, graceful animals in all their glory at such close quarters. I drove around for the next few hours and saw baboons, gazelles, vervet monkeys and various other animals, including a couple of young aggressive elephants who trumpeted at me before thankfully plodding off. It was a lovely afternoon. I enjoyed driving the 4x4 across streams and up and down rocky tracks. It was my first time to camp in a national park, and I was a little worried when I heard the hippos crashing around in the dark. It was a wonderful 24 hours, and all for £20.

On Saturday, I drove to Mayorka Village Resort in Nkhata Bay. It's built on the side of a hill overlooking the crystal clear waters of Lake Malawi and has interconnecting winding paths linking the chalets to the main relaxation area. After setting up my tent, I went snorkelling and sunbathed on a floating platform 100 metres from the shore. In the afternoon, I went for a walk up and down hills, across beaches and through tiny hamlets; it was so beautiful. In the evening I had a delicious buffet and chatted to travellers, volunteers, development workers and locals over a few beers.

As much as I liked Mayorka the next day I went to the equally picturesque Kandi Beach and where I met Elizabeth, a self-funded volunteer who had a similar story to mine, that is to say, she'd been to Africa before, had worked for multi-nationals but got bored of the 9-5 life, then worked for a small business, before coming back to Africa as a volunteer. Several drinks and some skinny dipping later, and with such a common background, we were having sex on the beach... and not of the cocktail kind.

32. Something New Everyday

Back in Kasungu, my one and only water-pipe had become blocked; I now had to walk 200 metres to pump water into my bucket. Also, the electricity had stopped, so I had to rely on my not particularly good kerosene hurricane lamp. It emitted enough light to do things round the house, but not enough to read by unless you very close, in which case, as happened, you can burn yourself.

Life was never dull. There was great excitement one Tuesday afternoon when a rogue hippo had been shot and transported to the District Assembly offices. When I went to investigate, I saw it had been decapitated and the stomach split open, the entrails loosely hanging out and onlookers given chunks of meat to take home. I had hippo steak that evening; it was very tasty. Apparently, a massive python was subjected to the same treatment a couple of weeks earlier.

One day at A&J's, I got chatting to an English couple who taught at Kamuzu Academy, the self-proclaimed, Eaton of Africa. Apparently, when it was built during the late 70's, it took up to 25% of the nation's education budget, the justification being that future Malawian leaders would graduate from there; statistically, this has proved to be the case.

33. ROAD TRAFFIC POLICE

Sometimes I had to make a trip to Blantyre, the commercial capital in the south, this as I followed up on potential opportunities for life after MFM. On one occasion, I intended a quiet night at Dougal's Backpackers Hostel, but was seduced by the pool table and beer. After a couple of games of pool and watching some tricks by a South African member of the Magic Circle, I ended following a birthday crowd around Blantyre's night spots, my curiosity getting the better of me, the night finishing in a random house and joints being passed round.

On a return journey to Lilongwe, I got caught by the police for speeding when overtaking a slow minibus. The road was apparently 50 kilometres per hour… as there was no sign saying it wasn't. I had at the time what seemed a very strange conversation with the police officer, though now know this is the norm. I was ordered to fill out a blank sheet of paper and make a statement professing my guilt. Though I knew corruption was rife, especially in the Traffic Police, and I didn't want the hassle of going to a magistrate's court the next day, I was still wary of being arrested for bribery. The conversation went like this:

'What can I do to help you?' The police officer asked.

'I'm a visitor and don't know the procedures; how can I make this quicker?' I picked my words very carefully. In the end, I signed the form… which I made… with the pen and ruler the police officer gave me.

I went to court the next day to pay my fine, but arriving at the police station, I met the same Traffic Police Officer who unexpectedly handed my driving license back; I was confused by this turn of events; I was naïve to the games the police played.

34. Not the Big Smoke

It was soon my last day with MFM, and without a doubt, those five months were the hardest, most intellectually challenging and rewarding that I'd ever had. I had done a wide range of roles, including developing a business training course and which proved very useful as you will find out.

On my last night in Kasungu, I went to A&J's to meet colleagues for my going away / thank you party. Two hours of chatting to the MFM watchman, I had my doubts whether anyone was turning up. Just as my patience was about to snap, the MFM staff came en-masse. As no one seemed to do any organizing I ordered drinks and nibbles. Half-an-hour later, I learned I was expected to foot the bill rather than everybody making a small contribution or funds coming from the office petty cash. This left a somewhat bitter taste after a wonderful five months. And so I went to my now regular bottlestores and nightclubs for one last night of drinking, playing pool and dancing with friends, before moving to Lilongwe to see if I could find some much needed paid consultancy work.

My first weekend in Lilongwe and I was in a bar watching the Wimbledon men's final. Once it had finished, and as it was dark outside, I decided to hail a taxi back to the campsite where I was staying. The first taxi that stopped demanded double the normal fare; I kept waiting. After five minutes, a pick-up with four drunken policemen pulled up. Seeing an opportunity for some easy beer money, they gave me a lift, but only after I'd haggled them down to the normal taxi price. As we passed the police headquarters, we drove in. We were followed by another police pick-up which was overflowing with policemen holding Uzis and other assorted weaponry; they also had two prisoners. After a few well aimed kicks, the first prisoner was lugged off to the cells while the other robber, who I thought was drunk, was thrown to the ground handcuffed. When a torch was shone on him, I could see that there was a hole the size of half a tennis ball where his ankle should have been. The police found the whole scene particularly amusing, even though if the prisoner did not die from blood loss he would certainly be crippled for life.

Back at the campsite and recounting my evening, a volunteer teacher told me his police story. 'A couple of weeks ago, my friend was robbed in the middle of the day. Her rucksack was pulled from her back. The police promptly found the thief and shot him dead on the spot. Unsurprisingly, after not just being mugged but as an unwitting accomplice to little more than murder, my friend left three days later.'

Later that evening, the conversation once again turned to the police. A Malawian told a story. 'One evening, as I was walking from one bar to another, I was arrested for being a vagabond. I was locked up for four days during which time all my possessions were stolen by the police.' It was a revealing evening… and I was starting to understand how the police were a law unto themselves.

35. COLD CALLING

Once settled in Lilongwe, I knew the next weeks and months were going to be very hard as I tried to forge a new career, in a new country, with relatively little consulting experience, and fast dwindling financial resources. Having burnt my bridges in the UK, I was committed to making it work in Malawi, or at least trying; I was prepared to do whatever was required.

The first few weeks I followed up on the leads I'd been cultivating over the previous months at MFM; it was just like being back at Absolute Hygiene and cold calling. I used the business training course I'd designed for MFM to get my foot into the door of potential customer organizations, but it didn't lead to any contracts.

I still had time for a few drinks. Notably, one night I went to an area where there were 15 bottlestores next to each other and the accompanying countless prostitutes. It was aptly named, Devil Street. On a Friday, I crashed at a friend's villa with a good looking Malawian girl I picked up at a bar; she was not a hooker. On the Saturday night we were spoilt for choice with multiple BBQs to attend; it was fun times. Another Friday night, I went to the usual nightspots and met a guy called Nando who'd been cycling round Africa for the previous two-and-a-half years. We went to Harry's Bar where I saw a Malawian wearing an England rugby shirt and which I quite literally bought off his back.

36. WOULD YOU BELIEVE ME?

The weeks soon turned into months and still I couldn't find any paid work despite my best efforts. It was no fun financially, emotionally or mentally constantly being told, next week, next week. My savings were depleted, so much so that I was not able to even afford to live in a house-share. My temporary tent arrangement had become permanent. For meals, I ate at a small restaurant near the Post Office. The menu was limited to rice, meat and beans, but it was reasonably tasty, came in big quantities and was cheap, the holy trinity of budget nourishment. My Visa card and MasterCard had become my option of last resort. This was the financial reality of not having an income for eighteen months while still paying a mortgage. I did have an amusing conversation one evening while getting into my tent as two backpackers were putting up theirs. They asked: what are you doing in Malawi? When I replied, that I lived in Lilongwe as a business consultant, they cracked up laughing. If I was in their position, I doubt I would have believed me either.

37. Loveness

Four long and increasingly depressing months after finishing at MFM, and during which time I had often questioned the wisdom of splitting with Steph and leaving the straightforward life behind, I was getting ever more desperate for some good news.

On a more positive note, I had started dating Loveness. One night after yet another hot, tiring, sweaty and fruitless day of knocking on doors, I was hoping for a night of passion but instead we had an argument. Old school style, I wrote her a letter, a copy of which I kept for posterity's sake.

Dear Loveness,

It's an hour since I left, and who knows what you were thinking about me or the situation we find ourselves in. You know I like you, and I know that you are leaving soon due to your complicated situation with your ex-husband. I too have a complicated life, my work, or current lack of it, leaving me physically, emotionally, financially and mentally exhausted. Getting to the point, I don't want or have the strength for a stressful personal life as well.

I've only met three girls who had a spark, something more than being friends and sleeping together, an x factor if you like. Someone who knows where they are going in life, has the motivation to do whatever needs to get there, and will take calculated risks when needed; you and I both have that.

Living life means different things to different people, and maybe that is why opposites attract... but not for me.

It's a shame you're leaving Malawi soon, though I know it's 99% the right decision for you and I wish you all the best. Ironically, before leaving the UK, I was on the other side of the coin and going out with a girl who knew I was leaving.

It's a tricky one, that's for sure, and even if there is only a short amount of time you are still here, I would rather be together than the alternative, deleting your numbers from my phone... for the third time. I'm not sure I can live in limbo till you leave.

After the writing of the letter, I decided that I would give it one more week in a final effort to get Malawi based contracts, but if I still had no success I would consider all available options, and which at the time consisted of:

1. Stay in Malawi and hope my luck changed. I was wary to leave Malawi as I knew I would have to start all over again wherever in the world I ended up. It would be very hard to establish myself and get that crucial first contract.
2. Go to the UK and hope to find work quickly, then leave for somewhere else as soon as possible;
3. Move to Columbia and live with Tony. It sounded as if he was having the time of his life with the senoritas.

38. Persistence

Just as I was giving up hope, I got a call from a private hospital to help them with their business plan. It was only five days of paid work, spread over two weeks, but FINALLY I'd earned £400. Not a lot, but enough to kept me financially going for little while longer.

Shortly afterwards, I got a call from the National Small Holders Farmers Association, who invited me to edit their Farming as a Business training manual and, conduct a three-day workshop. And then out of the blue, a Jordanian consultancy firm who had won a United Nations contract to do an evaluation on youth sexual health in Tunisia, Russia and Bulgaria, enquired if I was available to be part of their team; I immediately said, yes.

Reflection #6— Redemption

How I got chosen for the United Nations contract, to this day I have no idea, but it was just the lift that I needed after many months of trying but not being very successful. This rather exciting contract was exactly the type of work life that I'd sacrificed so much for. It was the lucky break I'd been so desperately praying for.

It was a very interesting, informative and intense couple of weeks, with long hours of meetings and report writing on subjects I knew little to nothing about. The meetings were with government ministry directors, country managers for charities, United Nations staff—all very high level. I only just about managed to keep my intellectual head above water. The money was much needed and the professional experience helped to beef up my resume.

39. Tunis

Flying into Tunis for the four-day evaluation, I was surprised to see how green everything was. I later found out that Tunisia is known as The Green, as compared to Algeria, The White.

I worked with an Aussie, Harold, who has a PhD in public health. He was a very friendly guy with a very complicated personal life. Harold was gay—I expect he still is. A lesbian friend wanted a second child with her girlfriend, and Harold did the honours as the sperm donor. The girlfriends subsequently split and are now in a four-way custody battle between themselves, Harold and the other sperm donor.

I learnt a lot from Harold, and not just the intricacies of homosexual life, but also what's fact and myth in regards HIV/AIDS:

1. The reason why there's such a high prevalence in Sub-Saharan Africa, is that HIV has existed since the 1930's. It was first discovered in the 60's in the Congo, and research only started in earnest when it hit the San Francisco gay scene in the 80's.
2. A large amount of infections are vertical, that is to say, mother to child.
3. If you get full treatment, it's apparently little worse than diabetes.
4. The virus, although extremely complex, is very weak and can only survive outside the body for two minutes.
5. Due to its weakness, there is only about 1 in a 100 chance of contracting it. This happens though the exchange of bodily fluids.

6. There is never likely to be a cure, as it attacks and mutates to each individual's immune system. However, advances in gene therapy are the most likely source for a personalized cure. This was the thinking ten or so years ago, though with advances in medicine and using cancer technology, the conversation has thankfully moved on.

Well, there you go, you've learned something new today!

40. Moscow

Arriving in Moscow, I waited for my new consultant partner. Ben, from Canada, was a friendly guy and, like me, didn't have a public health background. Unlike me, he was black and there are very few people of colour in Russia, though much racism.

As much as meetings, transport and everything else in Tunisia had been well organised, Russia wasn't. There was little time for sightseeing, though I did make it to Red Square and The Kremlin; it would have been a missed opportunity if I hadn't. Apart from being very expensive, Moscow is massive. The main streets seem to be 10 car lanes wide, and all are blocked at rush hour. The underground, as well as being very ornate, is also massive; it needs to be with 9 million people using it every day, four times as many as the London Underground.

41. SOFIA

I arrived at Sofia, Bulgaria, for the last part of the evaluation at 6pm on a Saturday night. I took the first taxi available from the airport. This was a mistake as I got scammed and paid five times the normal fare.

I was glad to have a weekend to relax and not writing reports or being on planes. As such, I stayed at a hostel knowing I was bound to find people to have a few drinks with. I was correct—I had a few beers with some Kiwis. Together, we explored the nightlife. The two work days were well organized as we (Paul, another Aussie Ph.D. in public health) raced from one meeting to another.

42. Amy

While in Sofia, I got an email from a Micro Finance Institution in Blantyre. They offered me a three-month contract. It seemed my destiny lay in Malawi.

After spending two weeks in UK, during which time I visited Jonas, Gillian, Lewis and Jim, as well as Steph—who still refused to sell the cottage—I returned to Malawi. Before getting stuck into the Blantyre contract, I spent my first weekend in Kasungu and caught up with friends.

'What are you up to tonight?' Alex asked. 'Jacaranda's?'

'Why not?'

'Julie mentioned there was a band playing at Kasungu Inn.'

'That cultural entertainment centre.' I was being sarcastic.

'It the best that's here.'

'I'll see how I do on the pool tables. If I win a few games, I'll go,' I replied. As fate would have it, I did do quite well, and so £15 to the good, and which would cover the cost of beers for the night, I made my way to Kasungu Inn

'I've not seen you here lately, what have you been up to?' This asked by Chifundo.

'Ducking and diving. Trying to win contracts. Use my charm on the girls. You?'

'The only charming most of these girls care about, are these.' Chifundo, held up a 500 Kwacha note. 'What do you fancy drinking? My shout.'

'A Carlsberg Special. Where are the boys?' this in reference to our group of drinking friends.

'At the BBQ stand. Give me a hand taking the beers over.'
And with that, Chifundo and I made our way to where Lincoln, Mavuto, Nadil and Brian were.

'Who's the hottie over there?' I asked.

'Where?' Nadil said looking around. 'Whoever she is, she's mine.'

'The one with the long legs and tight ass,' I clarified.

'That's Amy. Her parents will probably be around somewhere. She's a good girl, if you know what I mean. She doesn't normally come here. You know the way it is, a girl alone in a bar normally means she's a whore; Amy isn't.'

'It's self-defeating,' I started to reply to a conversation I'd had many times. 'If nice girls can't party because they'll be labelled a prostitute, then the only girls out drinking will be those looking for money. Well, I'm going to try my chances with her; I've nothing to lose,' I informed my friends and made my way over to where she was standing. When I reached Amy I saw she was talking to an older man, someone who I recognized but whose name I couldn't recall; I hoped he wasn't her boyfriend.

'Hi, how are you doing?' the man spoke as I was thinking of my opening line. 'I heard, you'd left Malawi? By the way, this is my daughter Amy.'

'Hi, how are you?' I offered my hand and which she accepted with a beaming smile.

'How do you know my dad, Wilbert?' That bit of information solved my mystery.

'We've had a few beers together. Do you dance?'

'Sure.'

The music was good and I was drunk, the combinations making me think I was once again the king of the dance floor. After half-an-hour, Wilbert and family were ready to depart, this much to my disappointment. However, Amy didn't leave before I convinced her to exchange mobile numbers and promise to continue our chat the following day.

Much to my delight, we did meet up. We went for a walk and then climbed the steep Kasungu Hill. At the top we sat, looked at the splendid view and chatted. 'I have very little, Amy,' I told her. 'I gave everything up in the UK, including a cottage I bought with my ex-girlfriend, and which by the way I'm still paying half of the mortgage. I'm 30 and professionally starting from ground zero. My bank account is nearly empty and I've lived in a tent for six months as that was the only accommodation I can afford.'

'I have a past as well, everyone does. It's what happens going forward that matters,' Amy said, as I put my hand on her thigh... and then round her waist... and then my lips to hers. Several hours of kissing and caressing later, it was time to go back down the hill; I had to start the journey to Blantyre and my new contract. It had been a very pleasant 48 hours and a friendship of kindred hearts had quickly developed; I was very glad destiny had returned me to Malawi.

REFLECTION #7—
LOVE, LOVE, LOVE

On the bus to Blantyre, I suddenly realised I was truly in love for the first time in my life. I knew Amy would make me a better person simply by loving me. She showed me that you don't have to let your experiences change you and that just because things in the past have not worked out in love or life that has nothing to do with what'll happen in the future. She told me, just be you. Use every experience as motivation. Use your challenges to help others through theirs. She seemed to understand me so well.

43. A Bus Safari

My new found love was given extra clarity, when just after 9pm it began raining and I had started to dose. As my bus tried to overtake a lorry, the driver (not seeing us) swerved to miss a pothole and smacked into the side of our coach and pushed us onto the grass verge. Fortunately, after bumping around, we made it back onto the road. I was sitting in the middle of the front row with nothing between me and the windscreen; seatbelts were non-existent. I would have been killed if we had crashed, I have no doubt about it.

My contract in Blantyre started well, and most weekends I arranged to meet Amy either in Kasungu, Lilongwe or she would come to Blantyre. Entering my third month of work, I took a week's break to help Amy who had organized a field trip in Kasungu National Park. For the majority of students and even some of the teachers, this was the first time they would see Malawi's natural wild life. Amy had pre-arranged permits into the park and to use the hostels for accommodation, all that was missing was the hire of a coach for three days; I was more than happy to pay for it from my unexpected United Nations contract windfall.

When the day came, it was up at 4am and at school by 5. Predictably, we had to wait two hours for the coach to arrive. Once aboard, and after a detour to the market to buy groceries for the staff and students to cook at the hostels, we were finally under way. We arrived at the National Park by midday and we were greeted by the sight of gazelle grazing but who scattered at the sight and sound of the ancient coach approaching; the elephants, giraffes and warthogs were not so perturbed.

In the evening, with the students in the hostels, Amy and I went to the tented camp. There was meant to be electricity, but wasn't; the generator also not working. There was supposed to be hot water, but that wasn't working either. However, there was a comfortable bed and no mosquitoes; most importantly, we had each other. 'This is one of the most uplifting things I've ever done. I don't know how else to describe seeing so many smiles,' I said as Amy lay in my arms.

'It's great that you could come. Thanks for covering the cost of the coach otherwise we wouldn't have managed.'

'Over this last year, I've found my soul again,' I contemplated aloud.

'I know exactly what you mean. It sounds like you had hard choices to make with powerful consequences, but you made the correct decisions for the right reasons and now reaping the benefits.'

'Meeting you for one.' I kissed her on the cheek. 'I honestly think coming to Malawi was the best thing I could've done. It wasn't an easy decision to leave Steph. It was a real challenge living under the same roof in different beds for so long. I don't know if I told you, but I got an email some time back from her agreeing to sell the cottage. She organized a lawyer, but to our horror, the previous owner had made structural changes without the proper papers; no one will buy the cottage. And then last week, I got an email from the bank asking why only half the mortgage was being paid. This was news to me as I've always paid my share. It sounds like Steph has stopped paying her part after the problem with selling the cottage. Maybe, she was the wiser of the two of us. I can't really blame her for walking away, after all, the cottage is now in negative equity and can't be sold. I can't afford the mortgage. This weight around my neck from my past life is very heavy; I hope it doesn't pull me down.'

'It will sort itself out; don't stress too much.'

'The last few years have not been easy. First I was unemployed, then volunteering, and now for the last nine months only getting lowly paid contracts, apart from the short United Nations one. I think I have no option but to hand the keys to the bank and put the financial and emotional disaster of the cottage and Steph down to experience.'

'Life has its reasons. What doesn't keep you down will only make you stronger.'

'My reward, meeting you,' I gushingly replied as I kissed Amy and thought how she was everything Steph wasn't.

44. ONE LAST WEEKEND

Two months later and it was my last planned weekend in Malawi. After finishing the Blantyre work, there was once again no sign of a new contract on the horizon, no matter how many proposals and CVs I had sent out. I really wanted to spend more time in Malawi with Amy, but I had to accept my financial limitations, and if that meant going back to the UK for some time, then so be it. But first, I was to have one last weekend with Amy in Kasungu so that we could plan our future. 'I hope I'll be back in Malawi soon, or you could come to the UK,' this being in the days before Brexit and harsher immigration rules.

'We could start somewhere else, like we talked about. How about in Columbia with your friend Tony?' she suggested.

'Something will work out.'

'What will you miss about me?' she asked, both of us not wanting to dwell on our uncertain future.

'Your laugh, your smile, your positive attitude… your ass.' The last comment got me a punch on the arm.

'And Malawi?'

'There are many things I'll miss. Some good, some bad, some funny, some sad, but all typically Malawian:

1. Bad wigs… whether on pretty young girls or grannies
2. Needing to push a taxi backwards to start it
3. All sorts of things on someone's head, especially suit-cases and water buckets
4. Misunderstandings between Malawians, Asians and Whites

5. Bottlestore culture
6. Eating birds, mice and smelly little dried fish
7. Becoming addicted to Nali and Malawi Gin
8. Being called Jesus, due to being white and having longish hair and a beard
9. Music blasting out of bars, with bad speakers all day and night
10. Everyone wearing spotless, well ironed and starched shirts... apart from me
11. The hypocrisy between church and actual living. It's taboo for boyfriend and girlfriend to live together, but seemingly nothing wrong with husbands having mistress or using prostitutes
12. Always being asked, what church I go to, then explaining I'm an Atheist
13. People pissing wherever they like
14. Eating all food with hands, but liking the idea of bowl of water being brought round the table before and after a meal
15. Constantly being referred to as Mzungu (which dear reader, means, a white)
16. If shops don't have the correct change, inevitably it is the customer that loses out
17. The daily witchcraft stories in the newspapers
18. The incorrect use of English sayings and slang.'

'Wow, what a list,' Amy laughed. 'Has Malawi changed you as a person?'

'How have I changed during my time in Malawi?' I repeated, while thinking hard before giving an answer. 'My views, aspirations, feelings, persuasions, and indeed my whole personality has been influenced by the past 24-months, plus the twelve months prior with all the Steph hurdles. I'm definitely now happier with the person I've become, if that doesn't sound conceited. I know who I am and what I want, and will do absolutely whatever I need to get it. I don't know what will happen next, though I hope it will be with you, somehow, somewhere, doing something. I think I'm at the beginning of another major crossroads in my life, but I'm comfortable and confident to move onto the next stage; I hope it will be with you.'

'Any final thoughts?'

'That one, I have a definite answer. I would suggest to anybody who has the opportunity, a willingness, and a deep desire to make a radical change in their life, to go for it and sod the repercussions. If you're not happy you can't make people around you happy. It doesn't have to mean working in Malawi or microfinance but, something you have a passion for. Through new experiences and meeting different people, you can learn so much, not least what sort of person you are. If you haven't got much time or are not willing to create a Tsunami in your life, then go travelling. Don't just do the touristy things or stick to the cities, but go off the beaten track. Visit a friend teaching in a village school, it will be a lot more interesting and will dispel misconceptions. Stereotypes are largely extenuated on package tours. For example, people who have visited a Masai village, often claim to have seen, "the real Africa", when they have only seen one small, unrepresentative part.'

45. Quick Thinking

That evening, Wilbert and I went into town for a quick drink... but which turned into a five-hour session. As we returned home around midnight, we heard a commotion coming from within the house. I didn't think much of it as it was not uncommon for there to be an impromptu party. As we opened the front gate, we saw Wilson, the guard, badly bleeding. 'There are burglars, five of them,' he informed us as he wiped blood from the multiple cuts on his arms and torso.

'Fucking hell,' Wilbert whispered. 'Wilson, go to Brown,' their neighbour, 'and tell him to go to the police.' Wilbert knew by experience that just calling the police would be a waste of time.

'We have to do something,' I said in state of shock. 'Do you have weapons?'

'Follow me.' Wilbert ran to the garage and after some rummaging around found two machetes and handed one to me.

We entered the house through the kitchen, and keeping as quiet as possible crept silently along the corridor. 'If you rape me,' I heard Amy say in a terrified voice, 'you'll die soon enough... I have AIDS.' I was momentarily stunned and considered all the times we had sex over the previous months, sometimes without protection.

'We all are,' Mary, Wilbert's wife confirmed, while Wilbert and I sneaked closer.

'You lying sluts,' one of the attackers shouted. 'If you are positive, then we'll give a quick death so you can't pass your bitch disease on.'

Hearing that, Wilbert and I rushed into the living-room, and flayed wildly with our machetes. Taken by surprise, three of the burglars rushed out of the house taking what they could. 30 gory seconds later, the two remaining attackers were pinned to the ground and being viciously beaten by the women.

'ENOUGH,' I shouted, automatically trying to take control of the situation. 'Amy,' she didn't look hurt, 'check on Wilson and make sure Brown has gone to the police. An ambulance needs to get here as soon as possible.' Amy departed, but not before giving me some bath towels and holding them to my arm and forehead which had deep cuts and was bleeding profusely. With the adrenalin flowing through my veins, I hadn't noticed my injuries.

Twenty minutes later, the police and ambulance arrived. The two burglars were taken to the police station and I to hospital for stitches and a blood transfusion. 'My God, what a night,' I said relieved. 'I'm just glad we came back when we did and not a minute later.'

'And you were quick thinking to say we had HIV,' Mary congratulated Amy.

46. Life Changing

Much to my surprise, one month later I returned to Malawi as another small contract had come up. This allowed more time for my love for Amy to bloom, her infectious enthusiasm lighting up my life. We went on romantic weekends away, had fun with friends, and both did what we could to earn money hoping that soon we would be able to travel together. The sex was as good as ever.

Everything seemed to be going in the right direction and the tough decision I made several years earlier now seemed to have defiantly been worthwhile. There was one cloud on the horizon, but whether it was a blessing or not, at that stage I couldn't tell.

Hi Jonas,

This is probably the most life changing email that I will ever write… can you guess what it might be about???? Amy's pregnant. We found out last week and it blew me away. I've been finding it hard to concentrate over the last couple of weeks, wondering what we should do. I know there are only two options, abortion or keep it. I have no ethical or moral quibbles about abortion, and it is something that we talked about. The idea of being a parent is worrying if I can't financially support Amy and the baby. Being an independent business consultant doesn't give me job security.

I love Amy even though it's been a relatively short amount of time we've been together. But for the first time in my life, I'm thinking of someone other than myself; this was never the case with Steph.

Marriage is another question. I know a baby does not necessarily mean wedding bells, but I was thinking about popping the question anyhow.

I really need your advice on this one. You meet lots of interesting people and no doubt you have come across situations like mine before. You are a good source of wisdom and I truly need some now; your views, I truly respect.

It was true, I really did love Amy, and still do for that matter. Having such a weighty decision to make, while realizing that I wanted to spend the rest of my life with Amy, I knew I must be in love.

47. Sage Advice

Jonas, the good mate that he was, replied within 24 hours.

I'm sorry to hear of your difficult situation, but whether it is bad news or good, it's not for me to say. I'm truly honoured that you feel you can share this and that you've come to me for advice. No one has done this with me before concerning such news. I'll try to assess the situation as best I can and hope it'll be some help.

Do you know the due date? Have you said anything to your parents or brother yet? I wouldn't mention anything to them yet about the pregnancy or talk about abortion until you and Amy decide the best way forward. It will only make the situation far more difficult than it already is. On the work front, if you have the baby, you must have a guaranteed income rather than self-employment; having a family doesn't facilitate individual lifestyle choices.

I'm sure you've spent hours talking to Amy, however, take yourself out of the equation for a minute and put Amy on the spot about what exactly she wants... baby or no baby? Malawi or somewhere else? If somewhere else, where?

Don't start worrying about marriage or the child's upbringing yet. There will be plenty of time to address those issues in the future. The most important questions are, does Amy want to have your baby and, do you want to become a father? One cannot happen without the other.

I don't know if any of this is of much help, but I'm sure these are the right questions to be asking at this stage. Best of luck, mate, and contact me anytime about anything.

48. PARENTS… AGAIN

With Jonas' words in-mind, and having talked everything through with Amy, and knowing I still needed to sort out the ongoing financial mess that was the cottage, I decided to go to the UK for a week; it made for an interesting Sunday lunch.

'It seems to me that you are in a very sticky situation.' This was an unfortunate pun from my father. 'I won't say, bad luck or, it could have happened to anyone, because it couldn't have happened to me. There was no way that I could have been in the situation that you are now in. This is not because I was particularly skilful in the use of contraceptives, but living in a different age, we didn't cohabit before marriage and thus didn't have sex before our wedding day. You live your life by different standards and which is your right, but it is risky and you have been caught out.'

'If it had been Steph who was pregnant,' I started to reply, now that my father had come to his sanctimonious end, 'then I would've been afraid as I wasn't happy with my life with her, but I am happy and confident for a future with Amy. In an ideal world, Amy wouldn't be pregnant and my decision about marriage would have been delayed, though it is something I had already thought about.'

'On the one hand you have a moral obligation to marry her and provide your child with a recognized father,' my dad carried on, 'and not be born a bastard, which although is less shameful than it used to be, is still a reality. You should not consider marriage, which is for life, unless you are fully committed. If you are certain, then you should marry Amy; if not, then best not. If you do marry, you must accept that your differences in race and upbringing are not ideal. The big decision is for you, the fatherly advice from me.'

'The only advice I give,' Adam, my elder brother chipped in, 'is that if you marry, make sure it is what you both want. Don't get married because you think you should. Is she the one for you? You must be 100% positive. Also, and I'm not trying to sound negative or condescending,' which I knew meant he was about to be both negative and say something prick-worthy, 'but you're going to have to consider what's best for Amy and the baby, and not keep jumping on planes and going to the next project; you'll have to find somewhere permanent to live.'

'I'm very disappointed with you,' mum, who I'd been watching slowly get more and more agitated, suddenly blurted out. 'I have a mind to write you out of my will.'

'WHAT!' I exploded. 'You don't consider Amy a worthwhile wife for your son? Is it because she's African?' I stuttered, unable to believe what my mother had just said.

'You can do so much better,' she continued, at which point and for the first time in my life, I saw my father lost for words.

'Mum!' this from Adam, 'be reasonable.'

'I can no longer support your decisions,' mum continued standing up abruptly. 'There is much here for you to ponder. I pray that you make the right decision and come to your senses.' She left the room, leaving my brother, father and I speechless.

For the next two days I crashed on Jonas' couch, not wanting to stay under my parent's roof for one second more than I had to. I talked through everything with him over countless beers and a few bottles of whiskey, but I knew one way or the other I had to resolve the issue with my parents, or more pertinently, my mother.

Still brooding over the Sunday lunch altercation, I went home. The atmosphere was like ice. Clearly there had been much arguing while I had been away and no doubt some tears shed too.

'You did give us a surprise the other day,' mum started in an act of contrition. 'There are well established means of controlling these happenings,' she tried to joke.

'Firstly, mum, I don't understand the concept of you being disappointed with us or hurt, as the only way you can be either is if you envisaged my life more to your liking.' There was not even one-percent of my fibre willing to let her off the hook easily. 'From this, I can only conclude it is to do with Amy's ethnicity and skin colour? Would you have been, disappointed or hurt,' I spat out, 'if I'd married a Chinese, Indian or Brazilian? You knew my life is in Africa, so perhaps you thought I might fall in love with a white development worker or volunteer? I don't know if this is out of concern as mixed marriage can have difficulties, for Amy as much as me, or that you think that because Amy is African she is below your perceived social standing as a prospective mother-in-law? If it's not to do with material wealth and social standing, then the only conclusion I can come with, is that because she's African she is inherently inferior. This appears to be what Granny thinks,' this being after my talk with her the previous night. There was silence around the table.

'Dad, I'm sure you must have soldiered with Africans and Black English? I'm sure the colour of their skin didn't make them a better or worse soldier. More to the point, if you bled, it was the same colour blood, or if a soldier needed help, your response would not depend on if they were white or black. Humans are essentially the same, it's the circumstances that are different. Perhaps when you have been on holiday, you didn't have much interaction with locals who are business people, diplomats and civil servants etcetera, but kept exclusively within your predominantly elderly, white tour group?' I continued full of righteous indignation. 'If you had, you will know that everybody: race, creed, religion, or colour is the same, the only difference, access to opportunity. The mere fact I was born in the UK, have a British passport and credit cards, mean that I can literally make my life what I want. If you have an issue with Amy, who she is, where she comes from, and our relationship, then that is your prerogative. I was already thinking about marrying Amy, so for me this is not something out of the blue but rather brought forward. I'm happy to become a father, and yes, I'm happy to be marrying Amy and who has accepted my proposal. If you feel you can't come to the wedding for whatever reason, then that is your choice.' After some of the most heartfelt words I had ever uttered, I got up from the table and took my plate to the kitchen as a way to cool down. I had decided, that I would never step foot in my parents' house again if they didn't accept Amy.

'We don't require details of what went wrong,' my father said as I re-entered the dinning-room, 'but I am sorry that it did. However, we must live life as it is and not as we would have planned it—'

'If you're happy at becoming a father,' my mum interrupted, 'and marrying Amy, then we're happy for you. I'm not at all bothered by the fact that Amy is racially different from us, but we are a little sorry that she comes from a distant land, and it seems where you will likely settle. We would have liked you closer, but I fully understand why you see your future in Malawi. We shall of course see you from time to time, but not as often as we would have wished.' I didn't know whether Mum's tears were of the crocodile kind or real.

49. SIBLINGS

The wedding went surprisingly well. My parents came, thanks in no small part to Adam's intervention with my mother. Jonas was best man, and there were many of Amy's family and our Malawian friends. However, conspicuous by his absence, was the very same Adam. This was very hard for me to understand or accept.

'I hope all is well, though I'm not sure… I've not heard from you for a long time…' I sarcastically started the phone call with my brother, this being the first time we had spoken in six-months. 'I thought you might have been interested to hear how the wedding went, what we did on honeymoon, asked how your nephew, my first born child was. You and Jonas were the first people I told about Amy being pregnant, and later that we would be getting married. It was you who told mum and dad to support us and come to the wedding. There are few things in my life I would NEVER miss, no MATTER what, and your wedding would be one of those times.'

'I dropped you a message on Facebook the other night apologizing for not being in contact,' he petulantly replied.

'You're fucking joking,' I raged. 'The two reasons you gave, 1) that you couldn't afford it, and 2) you couldn't take time from work, were both lame. I assume, that between you and Sally,' that being his wife, 'you earn many multiples of what I and Amy do. I heard, you said, that you had better things to spend your money on.'

'That was in the heat of the moment. Sorry.'

'And your second reason… sure, they're busy times of the year at work, but I doubt if you took a couple of days holiday you would have got sacked… like you claimed. For you to then take a week's holiday shortly after my wedding doesn't add up.'

'I have supported and backed you over the years. I'm the one who gets the worried calls from mum when you're gallivanting around the world. I hope in time you will accept my reasons. You are my brother and I love you.'

'Although you might go to a 100 weddings you will never go to the wedding of your only brother; we both lost out!' I slammed the phone down. I didn't exchange one sentence, word or even syllable with Adam for another three months; I no longer had a brother.

That was then, and while I have now forgiven Adam and my mother, I don't think I will ever forget the pain.

50. GLOBETEL

Life continued on. Marriage had its ups and downs, our first child, Daniel was born and, I picked up enough contracts in Malawi to cover nappies and household essentials. I had a family, doing work I believed in, and after several years of struggles, and a very stressful last 12-months, things seemed to generally be going in the right direction. Overall, I was happy, but with a new family and plans to have a second child soon, having job security was becoming ever more important.

Then, out of the blue, I received an email which would change my life forever.

I'm recruiting for GlobeTel, a mobile network operator who is looking for a Microfinance professional for a project based in Tanzania. The requirements are:

> A high potential individual with the willingness to take on new challenges;
> Ability to strive in a non-structured, entrepreneurial environment;
> Highly self-motivated;
> Flexibility to travel 50% + of the time;
> Work experience in Africa.
> The salary is 6,000 USD per month, plus car, flights, pension, accommodation and school allowances.

If this is of interest, please forward your CV and cover letter.

Two weeks later, and after several phone interviews, I walked over to Amy with a grim look on my face, 'Sit down, my dear.'

'I hope it's not bad news,' she questioned with a worried look as she breastfed.

'No, quite the opposite,' I bust out smiling, not able to keep a poker face. 'Something very exciting,' I said waving the offer letter in my hand. 'But before you read this, I know the time we've been together has not always been easy, especially the wedding, but I think things are about to change for the better.'

'Tell me, tell me.'

'I applied for a job in Tanzania. It sounds absolutely ideal in terms of what I would like to achieve professionally. I have real potential to make a lasting impact. It also comes with a good salary!'

'What's it doing?'

'It's working for a mobile operator and helping them bring mobile financial services to micro finance clients. This is the corner we've been waiting to turn.'

REFLECTION #8—
THANK YOU MOTHER AFRICA

So, that's the end of my second and soberer—in every sense of the word—part of my life. There was still the adventure, but gone were my carefree days of assorted alcohol, skirt chasing and drugs, these being replaced with sleepless nights and changing nappies. True, I was doing this on the Dark Continent, and it's also true that when I say I didn't have booze, sex, or the occasional spliff, that's not factually correct—I still enjoyed a beer and a smoke, but life was now dinner-parties rather than lad's nights out. Likewise, I was still getting my fair share of what's between a woman's legs, though now it was spooning with Amy rather than with different and random ladies of the night.

After the subsequent consequences of leaving Steph three years earlier, and then the familial wedding challenges, financial and professional redemption seemed to be on the horizon. The job sounded great and the financial package would be exactly what we needed with the new baby. I was finally in a happy place. When I looked into the mirror the morning of my first day in my new job, I saw a content man. In fact, I was overjoyed and once again thanked Mother Africa for all she had given me. First, finding out who I was before I went to university, then meeting Amy and starting a family, and now a dream job.

So, what happened to so dramatically change my new found life of peace to one on the criminal edge? To get that answer, you'll have to read on.

51. BEING A PIGGY

Three months after starting my dream job, I had come to the realization that I was piggy-in-the-middle of office politics; this was a game that I neither enjoyed nor was very good at playing. It had become abundantly clear that my job was a newly created role which had been forced by corporate HQ onto the Tanzanian management. I reported to Ephraim and James, my duel Tanzanian managers, and Peter, who on paper was my direct line manager but who was in the regional office in Dubai. None of the three seemed willing to take responsibility for me or my role. I think they saw it as a poisoned chalice. I received little to no support and was always referred by one manger to the other two whenever a decision needed to be made; it was very disconcerting.

My dream had turned into a nightmare, when about five months after starting, I was called into Ephraim's office. 'You have three options. 1) resign and get your terminal benefits. 2) Resign and be a consultant to GlobeTel for six-months. 3) Resign and get a percentage of any future revenue you bring to GlobeTel.'

'I'm out of GlobeTel!?!' I uttered in shocked disbelief… though if truth be told, I had seen the writing on the wall for a while, my role having become untenable. While I expected my job to change, I was not ready for unemployment and once again having a very uncertain future, especially now that I was responsible for my growing family. Two weeks earlier, Amy had been confirmed as being three-months pregnant.

'I'm afraid so, there are no other options. You're just not generating enough revenue. It's not personal, just business.'

What horseshit! I was certain there was a lot of personal in this decision. Ephraim and I had been butting heads from the get go largely due to the ambiguity of whom I reported to. Admittedly, sales had been slow, but this was more due to the market's immaturity rather than a failing on my part.

'Why did I get offered the job in the first place?' I asked. 'The frigging platform is not even complete,' I sarcastically pointed out. 'How the hell am I meant to sell a half-finished service?'

'The management's decision is final—'

'And which leaves me like a goat with an empty stomach. During my interview, I told you I'd just signed a long-term consultancy contract.' This was a barefaced lie, but I had to try and negotiate better terms, 'but which I cut short to start here. GlobeTel can't just fuck with people's lives like this; you have to be reasonable.' My tone of voice had turned to a plea as I started to wonder, what in the hell I would do next. 'We might not have always seen eye-to-eye under the difficult circumstances, but I have been performing as well as can be reasonably expected; I assume that's why you rated me as a good performer on my annual appraisal.'

'That's life… shit happens.'

'Shit happens!?!' I shouted incredulously, 'Is that all you can say? That's just not good enough. This is going to screw me and my family on every level. My wife is pregnant with our second child and, we have just taken out a mortgage—'

'What's your point?' Ephraim interrupted. 'What you do outside GlobeTel is your concern and not ours. Our decision has been made; make yours!'

With hindsight, I can see he had a point—my personal business was just that, personal. However, seething with anger and worry in equal measure, I was not thinking rationally. 'There will be consequences if you unfairly fire me,' I menaced. This was an empty threat, though I had to say something.

'We are not firing you,' Ephraim re-iterated in a very measured tone. 'I invited you to resign.'

'What sort of loaded bullshit is that?' I was at a loss how else to reply.

'I have given you a fair set of options to choose from. You have 48 hours to make your decision.'

'You, James, and especially Peter, have all greatly under-estimated me and what I can do when I am very motivated. This is GlobeTel's loss; you need to make it right and give me twelve-months gardening leave so I can get my life in order.' This was the start of my negotiation. I stormed out of Ephraim's office in a daze. I knew twelve-months pay was unlikely but I would settle for six, halfway between Ephraim's offer—which the powers that be must have authorised—and my counter.

52. STRATEGY? WHAT STRATEGY?

To buy some extra time and work out what I would do post GlobeTel, I decided not to offer my resignation but wait and see what their next move would be. I didn't have to wait long. One week after the meeting in Ephraim's office, GlobeTel's management had hatched a plan. I was forced to redo my annual appraisal. Unsurprisingly, the second review now rated me as a poor performer and which in turn trigged a warning letter, and I quote, "Your work is unacceptable. You must show significant improvement within the next month or your contract will be terminated." What a stitch up; if I didn't resign they would fire me!

Reflection #9—
Doing the Ostrich

For the next month I continued my role to the best of my abilities while hoping there would be a change in management thinking, even going so far as to hope my lack of resignation might make them rethink and even applaud my stance. I now look back on that month, as, the putting my head in the sand phase of my life.

53. HUMILIATION

And so, one month after receiving my warning letter, my recent work was analysed by of all people, Ephraim, who, surprise-surprise, found that I was underperforming. Three days later, I was taken to a disciplinary hearing. The outcome of the Kangaroo Court was a foregone conclusion—I was apparently failing in a wide range of duties. Nevertheless, I handed the disciplinary committee a letter.

> As part of the evaluation process on my ability to perform my duties, I was given the task of preparing a pilot project to be delivered to Ephraim Nkwosie. Ephraim Nkwosie presented his findings at the Performance Improvement Evaluation meeting and gave me a score of 3.9 out of 10.
>
> Today I have presented my feedback to Ephraim Nkwosie's comments. I want the disciplinary committee to confirm that before making their final judgement that all documents were fully and impartially analysed.

The disciplinary committee refused to sign, the Chairman, Peter arrogantly dismissed my letter, my fate sealed when Ephraim "invited" me to resign. Five minutes after the committee's formal decision, I received the coup de grace.

> Ref—Termination of employment contract
>
> Dear Sir,
> I refer to the discipline hearing in which management determined the allegations of 'poor performance' against

you are valid. I therefore regret to inform you, that management has made the decision to terminate your employment contract for the reason of 'poor performance'. Termination is made with immediate effect. You will be paid all statutory requirements, salary, and any other payments legally due and owing to you as soon as you finalise all clearance required by the company.

Yours sincerely

As far as I could tell, GlobeTel had followed the labour laws, but I wasn't expecting to be humiliated. I was taken to my desk by a security guard and the Human Resource Director, and in front of my now former co-workers, many of whom were friends, I was ordered to hand over my Blackberry, car keys and fuel card, office laptop and security card.

As I was escorted out of the office premises in a state of shock, I was handed another letter.

Dear Sir,
Following the termination of your contract, please note the following:

➢   You need to leave your residence within 15 days.
➢   Your work permit will expire within 3 weeks.
➢   If you do not meet the above timeline, you will forgo your repatriation flight and shipping allowance.
➢   All school allowances and health insurance will stop immediately.

Yours sincerely
Human Resource Manager

It was brutally uncompromising. GlobeTel wanted me out of the company and country immediately. As I walked past the reception for the last time, I felt as if I had been accused of being a criminal... what irony considering what's come to pass.

54. Eminem

Driven home in a taxi, utterly demeaned, I was determined not to get lost in worry and promised to myself, never to feel such humiliation ever again, this as I started to analyse my situation and make a plan. Firstly, the conditions in my termination letter didn't give me sufficient time to get my financial affairs in order for life after GlobeTel. I figured that this was most likely standard procedure after an early contract termination of expatriate staff, the aim to scare the former employee out of country so as not to have time to start legal proceedings for unfair dismissal.

The taxi driver interrupted my musings when he turned on the radio. The DJ announced, "and our next song is Eminem's latest release, Not Afraid".

I'm an Eminem fan. I enjoy his heartfelt lyrics about the ups and downs of life. I'd not heard his latest hit, so for the next four or so minutes, I concentrated on what he had to say. As I let the meaning of the song sink in, I felt the chorus had been written specifically for me, and that like Eminem, I should not be afraid and, that I was not alone. I had Amy and could call on my friends for moral support. However, the line which had the most profound impact on my life was Eminem apparently telling me to make a stand. I reflected on other tight spots I'd been in and convinced myself, I wasn't afraid when I was a teacher in Tanzania aged nineteen. I wasn't afraid when I split with Steph and all the chaos that ensued. And I'd made a stand when I gave an ultimatum to my parents about coming to my wedding.

As the taxi pulled up outside my house—or at least where we would live for the next 15 days until kicked out—I came to a conclusion, that with my responsibilities I could not afford to be afraid. That I'd been in tight spots before and had found ingenuity, courage and balls to fight my way through the tough times. Now was the time to make a stand for the sake of my family, and, like Eminem, front up and not be afraid of an unknown future. Fuck'em! I decided. If those GlobeTel wankers think they can screw with my life… they assumed wrong.

Still in shock, but with a resolve stronger than I knew I possessed, I randomly remembered a poem my dad had written.

Live Like a Lion

Live like a man,
live like a lion,
live like a king.

Be proud of who you are
and what you represent.
To your pride
you are the figurehead,
the leader,
the clan's champion.
This is your life,
your fate,
your destiny.

As a king
you have huge responsibility.
Find your love,
your light,
your lioness;
together conquering the savannah.

Be a man,
be a lion.
Hold your head high
and let the crown sit well.

As I thought of my dad's words, and with Eminem's lyrics still in my head and heart, I now fully understood what it meant to be a father and head of your household—the ultimate responsibilities started and finished with me. With a surge of determination and clarity of purpose, I realized that I had to be a fearless lion who would do whatever was needed to protect and provide for my pride no matter what troubled times might ensue.

Arriving home, my first words to Amy, my lioness: don't worry. I'll do whatever I need for my family. We have been in tougher positions before and I will ensure that we're fine. I made a promise at the birth of my son that I would always provide for him just as my parents provided for me; I'll never go back on this word.

GlobeTel had calculated wrong, they had fucked with the wrong person; I started mentally preparing how to make my stand.

55. WHEN YOU NEED A LAWYER

My stand didn't start till the next day. The night of my firing I drank myself into a state of oblivion, this while trying to have a coherent conversation with Amy about our options and simultaneously watching a few episodes of Breaking Bad, Walter White, the meth-cooking impresario doing absolutely whatever he had to for his family.

Waking bleary headed the next morning, I knew that the first thing I had to do was talk to a lawyer and get advice on the legality of my firing; even to my untrained mind it seemed far from kosher.

As I no longer had my phone, GlobeTel having taken mine as part of their box of tricks to unbalance me, I opened my personal laptop and searched for an old email on which I knew there was the number I needed.

Finding the email, I borrowed Amy's phone and dialled. Ten rings later, 'Who the fuck is this?' The voice was groggy and sounded hungover.

'It's your friend in Tanzania.'

'Alright, mate?' His tone suggested he wasn't happy to be woken before midday.

'What are you up to these days?' I asked. 'It sounds like you're almost dead? Are you still putting toothpaste in people's ears?' This referring to the long standing joke between the two of us. I'd phoned Jonas in case you hadn't worked it out.

'Funny night all those years ago with those jokers in that London mad-house. Last night was massive.' Jonas informed me. 'I hooked up with a Scandinavian supermodel.'

If anybody else had claimed they were banging a cat walk queen, I would have called them a liar, but with Jonas anything was possible. 'Have you heard from Tony recently?'

'He's still in Columbia fucking whores and doing lines.'

'Are you still a lawyer?'

'I'm now a partner.' Jonas, a partner in a law firm and Scandinavian girlfriend, somehow didn't really surprise me… nor for that matter learning that Tony was snorting his way through South America. 'I'm still wasting most of my money on booze, drugs and gambling; you know me,' he added, and which was one the thing I always liked most about Jonas, and for that matter, Gillian, Lewis, Jim and Tony, their apparent ambivalence to their strengths and weaknesses, successes or failures, always laying everything out on the table, good or bad; there were few secrets between us. 'I really need a change from living at 100 MPH otherwise I'll keel over with a heart attack one of these days. Any suggestions?' he laughed aloud.

'Don't work for fuckers like GlobeTel,' I said with as much disdain as I could muster. 'My contract was terminated yesterday, or rather, six weeks ago; yesterday was the beheading.'

'Not good, not good at all. Did they do things by the book? You know, follow all the proper disciplinary process and procedures?' Jonas questioned in a soberer sounding voice.

'I'm no human resource manager or legal expert, but the termination process only started when I didn't leave, this after I'd been… invited to resign.' My last three words dripped with sarcasm.

'That sounds crooked.'

'Also, I had a second annual appraisal… one month after the first.'

'Sounds like they had it in for you one way or the other.'

'That's the truth.'

'I don't know all the ins and outs, but you should find a local employment lawyer who knows the Tanzanian termination process. Tell them your story, and maybe you will get unfair dismissal compensation. From what you've told me, it sounds like there were quite a few irregularities and you only need one small error from their side and you're quids in.'

'Cheers, mate, I'll get on it first thing. Jonas, just a quick thought, and if you're at a loose end and want a break from your chaotic life, how about you come here for a week or two? We can bang our heads together over a beer or ten and come up with an idea of how we can work together on something.'

'Not a bad idea, I really could do with a change of scenery; I'll think about it.'

56. GORDON

After the call with Jonas, I did some research on LinkedIn and found Gordon Wills, a part-time lawyer and full-time senior advisor for Employees Without Borders. If anyone should know about employment law, I reasoned, it should be him. Plus, I hoped, if he had a well-paying job then he was less likely to put his reputation in jeopardy by fucking me over and making an underhand deal with GlobeTel's lawyers. From rumour and supposition, such a scenario was an all too common an occurrence.

Before meeting Gordon, I researched Tanzanian labour law so as to be well-versed. 'I think there were a lot of procedural irregularities from the get-go,' I informed him. 'I had to write my own job description… two months after starting. In my letter of appointment, it was not clear who I reported to or what my performance would be measured against. I was asked to resign, and then swiftly had a second, contradictory annual appraisal, this just one month after the first. I specifically requested a justification, in writing, for this second appraisal but none was forthcoming. There is no independent evidence that I performed poorly; it was purely subjective and based on one person's word… that being the same person who tried to force my resignation. I never had any Key Performance Indicators or benchmarks with which an objective evaluation could be made. The termination process itself was flawed, as I should have been given two written warnings, not just one. And lastly, at my termination I wasn't informed of my right to refer my case to the Court for Mediation and Arbitration.'

'You have done your research,' Gordon laughed. 'It's an open and shut case. 1) You weren't given two written warnings. 2) There was no job description in your contract as prescribed by law. 3) The reasons attributed for your termination are not only invalid but non-existent. Whether your performance was spectacular or useless, they did not follow the law... end of story. Let me draft up an application to the Labour Court for Mediation and Arbitration and get this thing started.' I was impressed by Gordon's confidence in my case.

57. Coffee Date

As I was leaving Gordon's office, I decided to go to the Sheraton Hotel for a coffee and put down on paper some ideas which had been forming in my mind ever since I'd been unceremoniously marched out of GlobeTel's office a little over 72 hours earlier.

Paying my bill for a coffee and croissant, who should I bump into but Peter and who was with his Tanzanian girlfriend.

'Hi,' he cheerily said with not a care in the world, and which unlike me, I suppose he probably didn't have.

'Hi,' I curtly replied, wanting nothing more than to punch him in the face and wipe away his shit-eating grin.

'I've not seen a request for your flights and cargo back to Malawi.'

'Correct. I'm not being railroaded out of Tanzania. I'm staying. I'll work with the other mobile operators. Just because GlobeTel can't see the opportunity, maybe others will.'

'Three weeks is all you have, or so should I say, two weeks until you lose that benefit… it's very expensive moving country; I would get busy with those tickets if I were you.'

'That's the thing, Peter, you're not me and, thank God I'm not you. You have no idea of what I'm capable of. I'm not going to run from Tanzania because GlobeTel tries to frighten me. I can do anything when I put my mind to it.'

'Yes, you're not me; I have a job.'

'You're a slimy, back-stabbing wanker.'

'With a job,' he continued to mock.

'This is a warning, Peter, don't fuck with me or my family.'

'Whatever,' he nonchalantly retorted, as he put his arm around the waist of the petite woman.

'You do know he's married?' I queried the young woman.

'Yes,' she confirmed, as she seductively ran a hand over his chest.

'Is that the best you've got?' Peter smiled, turned and walked away, one hand pinching the ass of the Tanzanian, my words nothing but empty threats to him.

58. Fifty : Fifty

Two weeks after bumping into Peter, Gordon had filed a case for unfair dismissal on my behalf at the Court for Mediation and Arbitration. However, of more importance was that Jonas had come to visit. We were having a drink at T-Square Bar, a local bottlestore that served the best Mishikaki (kebabs) in Dar es Salaam. 'That one.' I pointed at his left hand.

'You're sure?'

'I can see it in your eyes.'

'Is that your final answer?' Jonas enquired as he shook his outstretched left hand.

'Yes.'

'Are you really sure?'

'Yes, I'm frigging sure,' I said raising my voice while taking a swig of beer.

'No change of mind?'

'NO!'

'Ok, the moment of truth.'

'This is not, Who Wants to be a fucking Millionaire, Jonas,' but I was starting to wonder if he was bluffing or double bluffing me.

'I'm just checking that you're sure.'

'Yeah, I'm sure. And before you ask again, yes, it is my final answer. Obviously, I'll be gutted and contemplate suicide if I'm wrong… just get on with it.'

After a further ten-second pause, Jonas reluctantly opened his clenched left fist to reveal a shiny 200 Tanzanian Shilling coin. 'I knew it all along,' I rose triumphantly from my chair after winning the fifth game of Fifty : Fifty in a row.

Fifty : Fifty had been devised one bored, drunk afternoon in the London houseshare eight years earlier. We had originally used 50p pieces. It was not a complicated game, and despite what everyone jokingly claimed about reading body language, eye movement, brain waves etcetera, it was a game of chance and an amusing way to pass time while supping on a beer. As the name suggests, there's a 50:50 chance of winning. A coin is placed in the hand of the winner who puts it behind their back, and then places their outstretched mitts for their opponent to guess which one the coin was in. If guessed correctly, you would win the 50p and get to guess again. If wrong, the roles reversed.

'Line'em up, Jonas. Another 50p, or should I say, 200 Shillings is coming my way.'

Jonas duly put a 200 Shilling coin in his hand, his hands behind his back and then gave false signals as to where the coin might be. When removing his pinkies from behind his back and placing them straight in front of me, Jonas asked, 'Hippopotamus,' as he waved his clenched right fist, 'or... Claire?' this as he punched the air with his left fist and referring to a slightly overweight lady that had been one of the infamous foursome many years earlier. For those who don't remember that anecdote, it was my birthday and I was knocked unconscious from the bowl of Jonas soup; we both chuckled at the memory.

'You're bluffing.'

'Maybe I'm bluffing, but then again, maybe not. Maybe I'm double bluffing or even triple bluffing. I know what hand you think I'm going to have the 200 Shilling coin in, so maybe I've put it in that hand so that you'd think I've put it in that hand and therefore you would choose the other. Or maybe, knowing that and you were thinking that I'm double bluffing, I've actually put it in my other hand... in a cunning triple bluff,' Jonas was not making much sense.

'I think you've put it in Claire... again,' I declared pointing to his left fist.

'Lucky, fucker!'

'As I said, my son, I can read you like a book. Line'em up, Jonas, it's going to be a free night on the beer for me. Off you go to the bar,' I smiled and pointed the way.

59. STRENGTHS, WEAKNESSES, OPPORTUNITIES AND THREATS

While Jonas was at the bar, it gave me time to think of what I would say to him on his return. Let me explain. After being fired from GlobeTel, and during those early dark days of unemployment, I'd started to form the genesis of a business idea. The Eureka moment came as I neared the bottom of a bottle of vodka... I should follow my own advice. More specifically, I saw potential salvation in following the business training manual that I'd written for Micro Finance Malawi.

I rolled a spliff, put on some Bob Dylan, opened the appropriate file on my laptop and then—in my inebriated state—jotted down a personal SWOT analysis. This was quite literally on the back of an envelope... the paper container in question being the one which contained my letter of termination. What delicious irony. This is what I came up with:

MY STRENGTHS	MY WEAKNESSES
➢ Business planning	➢ Limited start-up capital
➢ Client relationship building	➢ No steady income
➢ Networking	➢ Can't speak Swahili
OPPORTUNITIES	**THREATS**
➢ Find a job.	➢ Family expenses need to be paid.
➢ Business training	➢ GlobeTel stopping me from getting a job and / frustrating me in winning consultancy contracts
➢ Microfinance and digital payments consultancy	

The obvious choice was to go back to being a consultant, but I knew building a pipeline of clients doesn't happen overnight. And so, as I needed money quickly to keep bread on the table, I had to think of something else. I thought about running a bar as a plausible option, the main question then being, whether I wanted to be a bar manager or a pub owner. As a business owner, there was obviously a lot more risk but also potentially a lot more reward. I finally reasoned, if the walking, talking, drinking, whoring Alex in Kasungu could run a bar, anyone could. Plus, if I could find a good bar manager—and I had a number of friends who could fill that role—then I could build my consultancy business at the same time.

With the above in mind, I further analysed the bar owner option a bit more carefully. Turning to page 77 in my business training manual, the music changed from Dylan to Eminem, and I was reminded of his drink and drugs challenges. I jotted down some ideas:

> **Social**—people will always drink. Drink leads to sex. Drink, drugs, sex, rock and roll all go together—where is the ultimate business opportunity?
> **Technical**—the internet could or should be an option / opportunity somehow, but where and how?
> **Economic**—doesn't matter how the economy is going, people will always drink and shag. When things are going well, more drinking and more shagging.
> **Political**—Parliamentarians are the worst of the bunch for multiple mistresses. Could this be a demand I supply?
> **Legal**—as long as I keep the police on-side with free beers, then I don't think I will have any problems. I would need a strategy that would keep the police in my pocket rather than picking my pockets.

> **Cultural**—As per above, drinking and shagging is culture

The idea of being a bar owner while building up a consultancy business started to form. I did a second SWOT analysis:

STRENGTHS	WEAKNESSES
> Business planning > Consultancy will let me travel and network which will be important to bring clientele to the bar business. > I like drinks, drugs and girls; I know my market.	> Need a legal entity and all associated paperwork to at least appear above board; I currently don't have this covered > Limited knowledge of the narcotics business and no high level contacts > Limited start-up capital
OPPORTUNITIES	**THREATS**
> Build a chain of bottlestores; this business model doesn't currently exist in Tanzania > Drinks, drugs and sex—fun under one roof? > High end and exclusive, rather than down and dirty	> Lack of local language; I could be taken advantage of? > Police corruption… though this could also be an opportunity. > Amy will never condone this income model; I will have to work in the shadows of our marriage

Reflection #10— The Boss

Before I knew it, I was mentally developing a business plan to be a master criminal... and quite frankly it sounded exciting and a lot of fun. Besides which, I didn't know what other options I had.

I knew that if I wanted any chance of success then I had to urgently address my weaknesses. I would need a lawyer's help and it had to be someone I would have to quite possibly trust with my life. Jonas, with his technical proficiency in law, together with his knowledge of drinks, drugs, girls, and no serious attachments in the UK, nor being known in Tanzania, would be the ideal candidate. I was also certain that he couldn't have drunk or snorted all his earnings and would most likely have some money squirreled away for a rainy day. Jonas was the ideal business partner if I could convince him to join my endeavour.

Looking back, it is now easy to see the irony of what I was planning required a very similar skillset to the dream job advertised by GlobeTel, namely: a willingness to take on new challenges, an ability to strive in a non-structured, entrepreneurial environment, self-motivated and, experience of Africa. There really is a very thin dividing-line as to how life pans out.

60. YESTERDAY IS HISTORY, TOMORROW A MYSTERY

Coming back from the bar with two beers and two cloudy, coloured shooters, Jonas sat down and at the top of his drunken voice, shouted, 'red lorry, yellow lorry, red lolly, yellow lolly,' while lunging his clenched fists forwards, first right, then left, right fist again and then lastly left; the whole bar stared at us, not that we cared. The energy expounded, and my warm applause for this 50:50 classic, put a smile of satisfaction on his sweating face.

'It had to come at some time, didn't it?' I asked rhetorically.

'It's timeless,' he agreed.

'You only said it because you couldn't think of anything better,' I wanted Jonas to be in a good mood before I broached my plan of action with him. While Jonas had many attributes, he didn't understand what the eponymous TIA (This Is Africa) referred to, and he had limited business experience; these were the two key things I would bring to the table.

'Not true,' Jonas protested. 'Red lorry, yellow lolly never goes stale.'

'You have a point, but, you'll have to do better next time.' I pointed to his left hand.

'Ha,' Jonas, triumphantly reacted; I'd guessed the wrong hand. 'No more, who's going to be a fucking millionaire for you. Rack'em up, my son! This time next year, after non-stop 50:50, I'm going to be a millionaire,' this in reference to the UK's best loved sitcom, Only Fools and Horses.

'More like Rodders, you plonker.' I put a coin in my right hand, my fists behind my back and moved the coin from one hand to another. 'Criminal mastermind and die at 40, or boring life and die senile and incontinent aged 100?' I enquired, as I thrust my hands forward.

'Criminal mastermind every day. Live fast, die young is my motto.'

This was the reaction I'd been hoping for. 'On a more serious note, I have a proposal.' The next few minutes would quite possibly be the most life altering I'd ever made, including getting married, having a child, and certainly more than leaving Steph, job security and the cottage six years earlier, all of which now seemed a decision of relatively little consequence. 'As you know, I lost my job three weeks ago. In that time, I've done a lot of thinking. Firstly, I've been fired in my life twice and I'll not let my family's welfare be put into jeopardy ever again,' I dramatically paused. 'Taking everything into consideration, I have decided to start consultancy and business training in Tanzania, much as I did in Malawi—'

'I thought you would,' Jonas interrupted.

I'm sure he was wondering where this conversation was going, and so I continued. 'This will give me an income, an opportunity to network with influential people and travel, while hiring a manager to run a bottlestore.'

'What's the connection between consultancies and bars?' he justifiably wanted to know.

'There isn't,' I replied to a puzzled looking Jonas, 'other than the consultancy can act as a front for an illegal business. I'm not talking about a cheap bottlestore like the one we're in at the moment, but something super exclusive, that only the rich and influential go. Membership will be invite only. We will guarantee anonymity,' I informed him of my current thinking. Jonas stayed silent... for the first time ever. 'Why is anonymity important?' I dramatically asked. 'Well, all men want at least one of four things, one of four vices: drinks, drugs, gambling and girls.'

'I attest to that,' Jonas proudly boasted.

'I'm not talking about your run of the mill street hookers, but high-class ass. Tanzanian men dig snow pussy, and rich Africans will pay big money for sexy, free from disease dirty white girls who will do any deprived act demanded of them. This is the reason why networking with influential people through the consultancy side-of-the-business will be an important asset.

'Create the supply and use your network to induce demand?' He had connected the dots.

'Precisely,' I confirmed. 'To get to the financial goal I've provisionally set, I believe we need two years; I can show you the business plan tomorrow. I know I've not gone into much detail yet, but what I can say is that I can't do this by myself. I want you to be my partner. We share everything… 50:50… risk and reward. We need the best of both of our brains and to be 100% committed. What I will say, is, that for those two years, we'll have to do a lot of hard things, such as actually running financially viable businesses, both legal and illegal. We will have to commit multiple criminal activities, including hurting and potentially even killing people. We will require a lot of money, which for one I don't currently have.' I didn't go into further details as now was neither the time nor the place, but I had planted the seed of risk and reward into my friend's mind.

'I wasn't expecting that.' I didn't say anything. I kept my fingers crossed as I waited for what Jonas would say next. 'I knew you had something up your sleeve from the cagey way you've been since I arrived. How far have you thought this through?' Jonas asked, the tone of his voice indicating his distinct interest in my proposition.

'All the way,' I calmly, supremely confidently answered. 'In the business plan, I have written down all the roles and responsibilities, plus the considerable risks and rewards.' I repeated the phrase hoping it would stick in Jonas' mind. 'What I don't have is legal representation and a business partner. Amy must never know about this; I will protect my family through their ignorance. Whatever you decide, this must be kept between us.' Jonas nodded his head while deep in contemplation.

'I don't expect you to make up your mind now, but if you are interested, then over the next few days we can look through my business plan; I would welcome your input. If you want to be a partner, great, if not, I fully understand.' There was a long silence, both of us wanting to know what the other was thinking.

'Fuck it,' he finally said. 'Yesterday is history, tomorrow a mystery, it's what you do in the moment, baby. Life's a riddle and all that jazz.' I closed my eyes knowing there would be no going back. 'When you're on your death bed,' he continued, 'and if you've not had a few regrets, you've not lived; I'm in!'

61. LET'S GET THIS THING STARTED

The next day we poured over the business plan. 'You have most of the angles covered,' Jonas congratulated 'I like that you identified your challenges and knew you needed a co-conspirator. If you put that much planning into getting the partner you wanted, namely me, it bodes well. Appreciating your weaknesses is a rare gift in business, and indeed life. I have plenty of frailties but don't know if I would so openly admit them.'

'Honesty is going to be paramount.'

'Agreed. Let's get cracking.'

Activity 1—Set up legal framework for our businesses. 'We need to establish a multitude of third-party entities through a network of offshore holding companies and trusts, this so as to hide assets from tax authorities, provide legal protection from government seizure and lawsuits, and obfuscate any potential investigations into our laundering of illegal income,' Jonas explained. 'We need structures that remove us from any direct ownership of the businesses that we create. Our goal is to be as grey as possible to the tax authorities.' He went on, 'An offshore holding company funds the operations of its subsidiaries, so that the subsidiaries obtain the benefit of tax deductions on interest paid. If the holding company is situated in an offshore area where there is no income or corporation taxes, then there are no requirements for dividends to be paid. Thus accumulated profits are tax free and can subsequently be used to fund our investment requirements at our convenience rather than to meet tax deadlines.' It sounded good to me even though I didn't understand all the intricacies. 'It's a piece of piss,' Jonas summarized in his unique way.

Activity 2—Identify a fall guy... should the need arise.
There was a good chance that our criminal endeavour would
end in failure, quite likely arrest and possibly death. Our miti-
gation strategy was to identify a strawman. However, and there
was a very big however, the strawman would also have to be a
key person in our organization. If there were no problems they
would be an asset and thus need suitable attributes; we drew
up a wish list.

1. Enough of a dodgy background to turn a blind eye
   where needed, while still fully comprehending what
   we are trying to operationalize;
2. Someone not experienced in Tanzania criminality.
   There is a risk they could stab us in the back through
   defecting to another criminal network;
3. Someone who would not run to the hills with the first
   hint of danger;
4. In a worse-case scenario, someone whose silence could
   be bought, and/or understood the consequences if
   they ratted on us;
5. Ideally, someone with an armed forces or private
   security background, and who could help us procure
   weapons and personnel as the need arose.

We would willingly give a strong financial incentive to attract
the right person.

Activity 3—Identify a bottlestore to invest in. Jonas and I
realised that we had to start small, and then reinvest our profits into bigger and better enterprises. An advantage of starting small... was that small mistakes had small consequences.
This would allow us to fully understand our operational model
while keeping under-the-radar of both the law and other crim-

inals as we built up our business. Once we had sufficient capital, we would expand at pace.

Activity 4—Look and act legitimately. We had to establish a Tanzanian business with all the appropriate licenses, tax documentation, work permits, company seals, etcetera so that we were legally resident in Tanzania. This was Jonas' stock in trade and potentially an additional (legal) income stream. We decided to call the consultancy Tanzania Mobile Solutions (TMS) and which would specialize in mobile banking project management and business training... my expertise.

One advantage of having a legitimate consultancy business was that it could act as a conduit to pass illicit money through. We decided it would be best to set the consultancy up first, as that entity could then, for a fee, develop a business plan for the bottlestore. Indeed, our plan was that as the bottlestore business started to turn a profit, through both legal and illegal activities, the consultancy would be put on retainer and thus start the process of laundering dirty money.

Activity 5—Designate roles and responsibilities. It was essential for us to have absolute clarity on who was doing what at both the bar and consultancy, while at the same time making it as murky as possible to anyone who might want to investigate either business. It was decided, Jonas would be the legal face of the bottlestore business and yours truly in charge of all behind-the-scenes operations while also being the front person for the consultancy. This would play well to both our strengths. In effect, Jonas would be my Consiglieri. We agreed, so that no connection could be made between us, not to be seen in public together if at all possible.

62. A Business Plan... or Two

As Jonas registered the offshore holding company, I went to the Tanzanian Investment Centre to start the process of registering TMS. The benefit of going via the investment centre— rather than paying backhanders to corrupt civil servants—was that once all paperwork was done the TIC would fully legitimize us. Having a Certificate of Incentives would give much added credence to TMS. The only problem with the process was the need for a business plan. Making a business plan in and on itself was not the problem, indeed, it was a core service of TMS. However, we had to show that we would make a capital investment of $300,000, which as a consultancy was never going to happen nor was it needed; all I needed was a laptop. Fortunately, there was a loophole. The investment had to be within five years and not necessarily within the first year. I revised our business plan by claiming, I would invest my profits (after year 5) into a $300,000 office. This bending, but not breaking of bureaucratic rules, did the trick.

Jonas registered the offshore company in the British Virgin Islands, and named a few of his connections in London as directors, but with a clear understanding that it would be Jonas who would administer the company and take the profits. This was covered by small print in the company's Memorandum and Articles of Association. The holding company, and which would legally own TMS, was named LBT, a random set of initials, Jonas getting his inspiration from the Bacon Lettuce and Tomato sandwich he was eating when filling in the company registration paperwork.

REFLECTION #11—
AN EXPLANATION IS OWED

I think you deserve an explanation. I hear you asking: how did a generally speaking, law-abiding family man, who though he'd dabbled down the years with illegal activities (I'm specifically referring to drug use and prostitutes) suddenly decide at this stage in their reasonably respectable life, that they should risk everything and become a gangster? If I was in your shoes and reading my life's story, I would be asking this same question. In all honesty, I have no good explanation or reason. Maybe, it was the dam bursting of thirteen years of frustration coming out in a huge gush of what ifs and what the hells?

Yeah, I'd taken some risks before, but nothing like this. However, I saw this as a calculated risk, much like my previous ones had been. I'd calculated that leaving Steph would be the right option, and so it turned out to be. I'd calculated that marrying Amy, whatever opposition from my family, would be the best thing in my life, and so it has turned out to be. Plus, and this is the big difference... I'm not you. I don't know your life even though you have some idea of mine. But, you only know what I have told you, whereas I have missed out so many things that to you might think amazing, but to me were relatively run-of-the-mill and not worth mentioning. For instance, I didn't tell you that I had ran the London Marathon a couple of times, or cycled around Europe; I know what the mental and emotional demands of pushing yourself physically are. I didn't mention the number of part-time start-up businesses I've tried, and which although they failed or were never successful enough to go full-time, full throttle, I did know what running a business required and the challenges that would ensue. I haven't told you about the times I've been in police cells. I have not gone into detail of the countries I have travelled, the drugs I've done, or the girls (apart from some) I've fucked. These lists to me are insignificant life events, but to you any one might be a highlight of your life!

I'm not an ordinary person. I'm the 1%, of the 1%, of the 1% i.e. one in a million. 1% of Brits go to Africa, of which 1% stay, of which 1% marries an African. This is not to say that living in Africa is tricky, which by the way it is; I use a ratio of three-to-one for the hassle I expect compared to what I might otherwise expect in Blighty. So, if anyone was going to make a success of running a criminal enterprise in Tanzania, I rationalized, it was going to be me... as long as I could get a little bit of help from Jonas and other friends. Besides, what if I got hit by a car, eaten by a crocodile or diagnosed with a brain tumour, who would then look after my family if I hadn't fully provided for them?

Seeing as you know my predicament on the sandy beach, the rising waters getting ever closer to my face, then I would not fault you for pointing out, pride comes before a fall, that hubris has caught up with me. But, that would be missing the point, which is, however my life and this story might end, I dreamed big and had the conviction to go all in. Have you ever done that? Do you have the balls? Have you ever said: fuck you, world, I'm going to live on my terms! If your answer is, no, then my point is proved. If you answer is, yes, I hope you have a plan B for worse-case scenarios!

In summary, all I know, now more than ever, is that life rarely goes to plan. It is vital if you want to feel alive, to live in the moment to do what makes the most logical sense at any point in time... and for me that meant establishing and running a criminal enterprise.

63. THE TIPSY LION

Back to my story. While Jonas was registering LBT, I was on the lookout for a bottlestore, our first step into the world of criminality. Jonas suggested, 'The bottlestore needs to be busy enough that the accounts could be justifiably manipulated to show good sales while hiding actual revenue. By maximizing our costs through fake receipts and forged invoices, we can minimize our tax burden while still keeping notionally tax compliant.' Separately, through manipulating the tax system, we hoped it would also bring us into contact with likeminded people i.e. those who circumvented legal business practices. To achieve the duel objectives of tax avoidance and networking, we needed to find an accountant who could cook our books and be our interface with the Tanzanian Revenue Authority, this one more activity for our expanding to-do list.

After a week of looking at a wide range of potential bars and bottlestores to invest in, I shortlisted three which had potential and were in relative proximity to Mbezi Beach, a relatively affluent area to the north of the city centre. The location was important as it would allow us to interact with neighbours who might be clients for our planned exclusive den of vices.

Third on my list of prospective properties, was Beach View Pub. Beach View was situated on the busy Old Bagamoyo Road. It had good visibility from passing motorists and hence offered potential marketing opportunities. The owner, Davis Nkhoma, a fifty-four-year-old entrepreneur, had developed Beach View on a piece of land he'd inherited from his father. Davis had used artistic license in calling it Beach View, a more accurate name being Road View. Nevertheless, the

Beach View plot had a mini-supermarket, hair salon and the aforementioned bar, which while small had a large beer garden. Davis was open to the idea of selling a part share of his business, but he wanted to keep ownership of the land. From Jonas' perspective, multiple business premises meant multiple money laundering opportunities, but there was no interest in having an additional partner in any shape or form. Renting the whole plot would have been a good option, but that was more than we could afford.

Second choice was The Tipsy Lion, which was located in the middle of Kawe Market. The name alone gave it kudos in my books as it reminded me of my father's poem, Live like a Lion, and which had to a degree pushed me down this route of law-breaking in the first place. While Beach View had a relativity affluent clientele and an expansive top shelf of spirits and export beers, Tipsy Lion was defiantly a locals' bar. It sold the ubiquitous Tanzanian beers: Safari, Kilimanjaro and Serengeti, plus the ever present sugarcane spirit Konyagi. It had a BBQ space, two pool tables and blasted music 24/7. What The Tipsy Lion lacked in sophistication, it more than made up for in volume of customers.

My first choice was Diplomats, which unlike Beach View and The Tipsy Lion was hidden away. With a low profile and relatively expensive drinks and food, few Tanzanians went there, the main clientele being expatriates, either Mzungus or from neighbouring East African countries. Diplomats comprised a range of buildings which were used as offices, residencies and the bar. However, there was a major sticking point, the owner was only willing to sell the whole plot. He was asking $500,000 and we didn't have that kind of money.

Taking everything into consideration, and knowing that it would be easier to hide profit in a large volume rather than a high profit margin business, we opted for The Tipsy Lion.

Jonas used up the majority of his savings to became the new tenant of The Tipsy Lion. He paid $3,000 per month rent payable six-months in advance; we also bought sufficient start-up stock.

64. LA DOLCE VITA

Once-a-month there was a full-moon-party at La Dolce Vita, an upmarket restaurant cum hotel on the shore of Mbezi Beach. While Jonas was setting up The Tipsy Lion, I'd been tasked with identifying a bar manager.

I arrived just after midnight with the express intention of scoping out partygoers as potential recruits. The first person I met, however, was none other than Peter. 'Can I have a word with you?' he politely requested, as I was getting my first beer of the night having deliberately stayed off drinks all evening so that I would have a clear head.

'What's there to talk about? You fucked me over,' I replied as I puffed out my chest and got in his face. Whatever I'd planned about keeping unruffled, my emotions were still raw, especially when I saw Ephraim loitering in the background.

'I hear you're suing GlobeTel,' he said, as he calmly sipped his gin and tonic and put his arm around a girl, though not the same one I'd seen him with at the Sheraton.

'Too right, I am. You railroaded me out and there will be consequences. I told you about my problems with Ephraim and James from the beginning, but you did fuck all.'

'What did you expect me to do?' he quizzed, the arrogant grin on his face further riling me.

'You shouldn't have humiliated me.'

'C'est la vie.' The cunt was enjoying the conversation.

I took a very long sip from my beer while getting my rising anger under control. 'C'est la vie, indeed, Peter,' I smiled, while thinking about the plan that was underway with Jonas. 'Very well put,' I added, and which together with my lack of aggression seemed to rightly unnerve him. 'You've inspired me. And let me tell you, it's quite the change in direction. As I told you, anything is possible when you are motivated, and Peter,' I now had a big smile on my face, 'you arrogant pig prick, you've made me very motivated.'

'Whatever. You're pissing in the wind my friend if you really think you can take a multi-national like GlobeTel to court and win. Who's going to be your lawyer and how are you going to pay for them? We have an army of lawyers who will just waste your time and money; give it up,' he advised. 'You won't win at the courts and I'll personally make sure you are driven out of Tanzania if you carry on your shit. I have a lot of influence with immigration and police officials, and you've been in Africa long enough to know it's not hard to buy people. Fuck off back to the UK, Malawi or wherever with your African whore and bastard children.'

'You don't know me or what I can do. If you threaten me or my family again, you will only have yourself to blame for what comes your way. Remember, what goes around comes around and I'll fuck you up. I give you this warning once, don't cross me.'

'You're funny, you know that,' Peter laughed. 'You're a nobody! How dare you talk to me like that? I manage six countries and can do what I like. Fuck off!'

'Go fuck yourself, you piece of shit!' Under such provocation, I was not able to contain my anger any longer. 'You've been warned,' and with that I walked away quickly before I totally lost my cool; making a scene at the bar was not part of my plan.

'Fuck off, you loser!' Peter shouted to my back. I turned, gave Peter the finger and walked towards the beach to cool down, his and Ephraim's laughter ringing in my ears.

65. Chidi

Reaching the sand, I took some long, deep breaths, sat down and supped my icy cold Serengeti beer as I contemplated my run in with Peter.

After a few minutes, an idea started to form in my mind. While I was pondering my next moves, a stranger approached. 'Hey, man, what's your beef with the guy at the bar?'

'Sorry, who are you?' I demanded, surprised to be questioned so by an intruder, 'And what business is it of yours?' I added, annoyed at my reverie being broken.

'Only making conversation, mate. I saw that guy you were arguing with, and who seems to think he's the big man. I respect you for keeping your head when others would have lost theirs; I admire good judgement in heated circumstances'.

'Sorry, mate.' I was momentarily taken aback by his kind words. I offered my hand in apology and friendship to the stranger. 'I didn't mean to be rude, I'm just working through a few things. And you're right, that guy is a prick, but he'll get his comeuppance, you don't need to worry about that.'

'I'm Chidi. I'm Tanzanian, but as you might have worked out from my accent, I've been in the UK for the last fifteen years, or should that be, working at Her Majesty's pleasure; I was in the army for eight of those.'

'You still serving?'

'No. I had a rough tour in Afghanistan where I saw too many friends hurt and some killed; it was time to leave and come home.'

'Sorry for that, Chidi. The army can be rough,' I said aloud as I remembered my time in the Territorial Army and thought of a friend who had gone to Iraq and come back in a coffin. Looking at Chidi, I saw he too was thinking of lost brothers. 'What do you do?'

'Nothing at the moment, but I need to find some work, money and pussy… and not necessarily in that order,' he chuckled

'What sort of work are you looking for?' I asked, immediately seeing the possibility of Chidi being the manager of The Tipsy Lion.

'Being ex-army, there's always the private security option. I hear there's good money to be made.'

'Certainly.'

'But, I'd rather do something I can really get my teeth stuck into.'

'Chidi,' I started to say. 'I'm working on something which might be appealing to you. I'm sure your army background speaks for itself. How about we make this evening your interview?'

'Sounds interesting.'

'I will give you a mission tonight. We can discuss job details tomorrow… once I see how you get on.'

'I'm all ears, but I don't want to be doing any illegal shit.'

'Nothing illegal, just a little payback for the guy I had that altercation with.'

'If I do what you have in mind, what's in it for me?'

'Don't miss the bigger picture, Chidi. If you want me to give you $300 for this small favour, that's fine.'

'No, no; it's ok, boss, just asking. Let's hear your plan. If you're happy with my work we can talk contract issues tomorrow.'

'Good.' I was impressed the way Chidi had handled the conversation. 'You don't need to know what my beef with Peter is, only that I want you to get him in a compromising situation and record it so that I have evidence should I wish to use it at a later stage. There must be absolutely no inkling that I'm involved; I can't emphasize that enough!'

'I fully understand.'

'Here's the plan,' and I then went into detail of what I wanted him to do. After giving him my instructions, I finished by saying, 'I hope I don't need to mention what would happen if you and the car goes missing or you try to screw with me. If you are unsure about anything, tell me now. If you change your mind, just turn up tomorrow with the car and the money, there'll be no hard feelings.'

66. SASHA

The following day, Chidi met me at the agreed time. 'Great pictures, good video, wild party, beautiful girl; where did you find her?' I was impressed with Chidi's work, especially at such short notice.

'A little place I know.'

'Which place?' This while raising my voice. 'Don't mess me around… just give me the fucking details.' I was being a hard ass on purpose as I wanted Chidi to be very clear who was in charge.

'Ok, boss, it was the Escape Bar,' Chidi replied, slightly taken aback, just as I wanted. 'I used the $300 you gave me to procure the services of a girl to act as a honey-trap for our friend. I knew that on Saturdays, Escape Bar has weddings and so reasoned there would be girls dressed up and ready to party. I found Sasha… Peter was putty in her hands,' a big grin appearing on his face as if to imply that he too would have been. 'For the Rohypnol, I went to a bar called Jackson's in Sinza. Sasha partied like there was no tomorrow with Peter and slipped the Rohypnol in his drink. She then took a taxi with him to a cheap motel; I followed in your car. Undressed, Sasha snorted cocaine off Peter's naked and prostrate body, while all the time I recorded the action through a window. Once Peter was unconscious, Sasha took everything: phone, wallet, car keys and even his clothes. She was very professional and some-one I would happily work with again.'

'Very good. Was there any change?'

'The money you gave was sufficient; here's the change.' He handed me $50.

'Keep it.' I'd only wanted to know whether he was honest.

'I drove Peter's car to a garage where a friend changed the number plates, identification tags etcetera. Do you want me to sell it?'

'Good,' was my one worded, no-answer response... even though I was highly impressed.

'Sasha is ready to do more work and said she can find additional girls if needed.'

'Well done, Chidi; a good night's work. Sell the car, keep a $1,000 for yourself and give an extra $200 to Sasha. Tell her you will be in touch in due course and remind her to keep her mouth firmly shut. Give me the memory card from the camera and write down the details of all the people you used in last night's activities,' this I solicited with my hand out. 'I want names, phone numbers, locations, how to contact them, what their weaknesses are and, what they most value i.e. money, drink, drugs, women etcetera.' I wanted a database of people I could call on as and when needed.

After Chidi had handed over the memory card and list, but before we parted, I added, 'Bring the balance of the car sale here, tomorrow at 9am, that's when you start your day job as the manager of The Tipsy Lion.'

REFLECTION #12— REVENGE IS A DISH BEST SERVED COLD

Payback is a bitch, wouldn't you agree Peter?

67. It's Getting Real

For the next two-months, and with my bank balance fast depleting, I pursued my wrongful dismissal case against GlobeTel. However, the majority of my time was dedicated to helping Chidi get The Tipsy Lion up, running and turning a healthy profit. For this support, TMS received consultancy payments from Tipsy Lion for completing all the legal paperwork, doing a supplier analysis, writing a business plan, opening a bank account, and the 101 other things needed to become operational. All these activities could be justifiably invoiced... even if it was at inflated rates; this was our first act of money laundering.

Seeing Chidi in action, I quickly realised that he had the attributes to be an integral part of our plan above and beyond being The Tipsy Lion manager. With that in mind, I hired the 5'10, slim waist, generous bosomed and very striking Sasha and who had proved adept at influencing others, namely Peter. I gave her the job of managing The Tipsy Lion. As a useful addition to our enterprise, Sasha had recently graduated as an accountant from Dar es Salaam University, and thus we could offer this as an additional consultancy service line for TMS.

With Chidi's time freed up, I tasked him with finding other bottlestores and/or restaurants in the regional towns of Morogoro, Iringa, Tanga, Arusha, Mwanza, Moshi and Mbeya. He'd found at least one potential location in each town, all that was needed was to negotiate the rental price; I would backstop if needed.

With The Tipsy Lion running smoothly, it was time to meet Jonas to discuss our next steps. We met on the first Tuesday of the month at the Ramada Hotel, as while emails were fine for most operational matters we had to meet face-to-face to discuss strategy. When we did catch up, it was always in a hotel bedroom, not for some man-on-man action, but so no one could observe or hear what we were saying. 'Are we ready for tomorrow?' Jonas asked three months after making the momentous decision in T-Square Bar to work together.

'As much as we can be,' I replied, though not sure we really ever could be for what we were about to undertake. 'This is going to be the riskiest thing we've done, by far… but it's essential for my plan to work. Everything is set up as we planned, and we have no direct contact with the principles. Sasha knows how to react and Chidi's people are in place. We know who the Regional Police Commissioner is and what his weaknesses are. We have money in the bank and Chidi has located bars up-country for our expansion phase.'

'We have all the pieces in place, but are you personally ready for what we need to do?'

'While in the Territorial Army, I was told: that if you put your mind to something, even something you don't want to do, or something that's not natural to you, but you mentally walk through the scenario enough times, when it actually comes to doing the deed it will be second nature as you have already trained your brain to do the necessary. So, yeah, I'm as ready as I ever will be. How about you?'

'We have to do this, brother. We need the reputation and this is not something that can be outsourced.'

REFLECTION #13—
IT REALLY IS GETTING REAL

Up to this point in life, I had twice been confronted by extreme violence. First, in London when I got mugged on the bus. The second time, in Malawi, when five machete wielding thieves broke into Amy's house. I didn't take a backwards step either time and I wasn't about to start now. When I say, I'm going to do something, I will do it and don't give a damn about the consequences. And that meant I would do whatever I had to for my wife and son, there was not going to be anything or anyone who could stop me.

68. 12 PHASES

After meeting Jonas, we implemented my plan.

Phase 1—Forty-eight hours earlier, Chidi had told three thieves, Mkosi and his twin elder brothers, Mchumba and John: go to The Tipsy Lion bottlestore between 8pm and 9pm. There is a tall, thin girl with braids who is the manager and has keys to the safe in the office; there's bound to be at least 5 million Shillings in it. I'll also pay 1 million up-front and another 4 million should The Tipsy Lion be satisfactorily burned. Before you leave, make sure you set fire to the office and bar. This will rid the scene of any evidence, and I want to send those fuckers a message. The new owner doesn't know that The Tipsy Lion is protected by the Kawe brothers, but they will now. This is an easy 10 million Shillings.

The Kawe brothers were a figment of Chidi's imagination and had been invented to convince the three thieves they were working for someone high-up in the Tanzanian criminal underworld.

Phase 2—At 8:45pm the three balaclava wearing, machete wielding Tanzanians, walked up the steps of The Tipsy Lion. 'EVERYBODY ON THE GROUND!' the tallest of the three shouted, 'apart from you, bitch,' he was pointing his machete at Sasha. 'Open the tills and give me the keys to the safe.' Sasha, did as demanded and fled into the market.

While Mchumba and John tried to crowbar open the tills, Mkosi went to the office as instructed by Chidi. None of the three in their haste and excitement noticed the man in the shadows and who was wearing a tracksuit and reading a news-paper, their attention distracted by the attractive bar manager and the ease of the heist.

Locating the safe, Mkosi must have been more than a bit surprised to find it had a biometric lock, and thus the bunch of keys tightly held in his hands were useless. Disappointed, I expect he relished liberally pouring petrol over the office, bar and stockroom... just as Chidi had instructed.

The fire quickly spread throughout the building, though there was enough time for the now very annoyed three robbers to empty the tills and put as many bottles of spirits into their rucksacks as they could. Mchumba and John gracefully leaped over the bar and ran to their parked silver Toyota Corolla—number plate T378 BGD—in the smoke free air of the market.

Shorter and more rotund than his older brothers, Mkosi didn't jump over the bar, but waddled to the end and which gave the man in the tracksuit and baseball cap enough time to remove the 9mm semi-automatic pistol which had been pur-chased from one of Chidi's ex-army contacts two weeks earlier, aim and shoot Mkosi in the head.

Reaching their car, with the plan to drive to an acquaint-ance of Chidi's where they would lay low, Mchumba and John realized their brother was missing. When they looked back they saw Mkosi slumped over the pool table with half his head missing.

Phase 3—As soon as I fired the gun, I exited through the stockroom, took off my fake beard, removed my tracksuit—underneath which I had on running-shorts and a singlet—and threw the beard, baseball cap, sunglasses and tracksuit into the rubbish bin which I had earlier filled with petrol. I lighted a match to incinerate all evidence and started jogging down the main road.

Phase 4—Once Sasha had recovered from the adrenaline rush of the previous five heart-stopping minutes, she started asking questions of on-lookers. Who were the 3 robbers? What was the number plate of the car they were driving? My boss will pay big money for any information. Who was the man who shot the short robber and where did he go? Where are the police, they must know who the robbers are? The rumour mill had been started.

Phase 5—Nyka and Mary were friends of Sasha. They were in a nearby hair salon in the market at the time of the robbery. 'We were in the bar five minutes before the robbers came and talking about what style of haircut to get. I saw someone sitting in the corner reading a paper, but I couldn't see who it was,' Nyka informed those who were near her, this as she stood a distance away from the flame engulfed The Tipsy Lion.

'It was a Mzungu with a beard and sunglasses,' Mary would add, though wouldn't say anything about distinguishing features. 'He vanished into thin air like a ghost after shooting the shortest of the three robbers in the head.' This mentioning of a ghost was just as Sasha had instructed her.

'If I knew it was a white man, I would've asked him to be my boyfriend,' Nyka said to the sound of much laughter.

'We were talking when the robbers came in; I pissed myself,' Mary confirmed, even though at the time she was fifty-metres away.

'The next thing I knew, I heard this massive bang and a flash from where the Mzungu was sitting. When I looked in that direction five-seconds later, he'd vanished, just like a ghost, a fart in the wind,' Nyka concluded to the sound of more laughter.

The girls had been working on their script in the afternoon, knowing the more laughs they got, the more memorable and recounted their story would be, and at each telling a little more embellished. The myth of The Ghost had been born.

Phase 6—One day after the robbery, there were many stories and counter rumours circulating. Mary and Nyka, as the only witnesses to both the robbery and seeing The Ghost, had become minor celebrities. Few others claimed to be at the bar at the time of the robbery, shooting and fire, knowing, that any interaction with the police would likely end up meaning bad news for them.

When the police did start their investigation, they were immediately pointed in the direction of the two girls, who not only told the police about The Ghost, but also the first three digits of the number plate on the getaway car.

Phase 7—Shedrack, a Constable at Kawe Police Station, always had an eye out for how to make quick money, and most often unscrupulously. He was approached by Mohammed, another contact of Chidi's, to make an introduction for a contact of The Ghost to meet the Regional Commissioner at the Double Tree Hilton at 7am. Shedrack, was handed an envelope filled with photographs. He was told, 'The Ghost knows who Julius Mbogoye is, what he looks like, where he lives and who he fucks.'

The Regional Commissioner duly turned up at the requested time. Jonas met him. In disguise, I witnessed the meeting from a nearby table.

'Good morning, Commissioner,' Jonas started, as he shook Julius Mbogoye's hand.

'Good morning, Sir,' Julius replied, seemingly not expecting to be greeted by an impeccably dressed white man in a three-piece-suit. 'What should I call you?'

'Don't worry about my name, Julius, just know that I represent a client that was upset by the recent robbery and burning of The Tipsy Lion bottlestore on Tuesday evening.'

'I heard about that; we are making enquiries.'

'Let me be of assistance. The remaining two suspects are located at plot 167, Sinza Road. All my client asks, is that once you have arrested the robbers and have a confession from them, release them on Monday at 4pm.'

'Thank you for the information, but why should I do this? How can you be sure these are the guilty parties?'

'Our research is impeccable.' Jonas motioned to the envelope on the table which Shedrack had given to Julius, inside of which were compromising pictures of the regional commissioner with a young woman.

'Your point is made. But shouldn't men of power have fun at times? If my wife found out that I have a mistress, so what? She won't leave me.'

'The photos are just a small example of the detailed research we do… and the outreach we have. I hope we can work in a mutually beneficial partnership,' the undertones of not working together obvious.

'Sir,' a greatly unnerved Julius—someone who was rarely threatened and especially not by a white—started to formulate a reply, 'I will follow all proper police procedures and follow up on all information, including tip-offs that relate to this high profile crime. To make sure that all the paperwork is done properly and that my officers are not at risk at the time of arrest,' he added, showing only a minimal loss in composure, 'I request that my undercover division is assigned for the task.'

'How the police operate, I leave to your discretion.'

'Thank you. It's my recommendation that we use a force of eight officers and that surveillance equipment is deployed. This will ensure all escape routes are covered and that we will have the element of surprise on our side at the time of arrest.' Jonas nodded his head in ascent. 'Sir, you may not be aware, but our police force is poorly funded. To work at optimum efficiency and for a successful outcome, I request your help with the budget for such an operation.'

'I understand the nature and cost of police work in Tanzania,' Jonas answered back, knowing the bribery dance was about to begin. Together with my partner in crime, we had calculated that any money paid to coerce Julius now would be well worth it, as once he had accepted our blood money we would have a regional police commissioner in our proverbial pocket, all the more so since the conversation was being micro-video recorded from a pen-cap in Jonas' suit breast pocket... should we ever need such leverage.

'An operation of this nature,' Julius started to argue, then paused to do some mental arithmetic, 'from personal experience... costs approximately 4 million Shillings.' This was lower than Jonas and I had expected he would ask.

'Commissioner. When talking to a friend who has knowledge of such police operations,' Jonas started to counter, 'he suggested six undercover policemen should be sufficient, with an estimated budget of 3 million Shillings.'

'Maybe, your friend was working up-country where policing is cheaper and the criminals not so vicious? But I agree, maybe we can drop one officer. A cost of 3.5 million Shillings will be sufficient.' At this budget, Julius would probably pocket 2 million Shillings for himself. 1.5 million would go to various officers at the station to help with paperwork, and the raiding officers would get their usual windfall... the confiscation of whatever they could find in the house at the time of arrest.

'That sounds reasonable, Commissioner. Please have breakfast on us at the restaurant. An associate will be over with a down-payment, the remainder paid when the thieves are in our custody.'

'A breakfast at this hotel is very generous. Sir, will you join me?'

'Other business to attend, I'm afraid,' Jonas replied convivially. 'Julius, when you are holding the robbers, ensure that all the police men and women at the station, and indeed all prisoners, are well aware the reason for them being in custody.'

'Of course, Sir.'

'Good day, Julius.'

'Good day.' As Julius passed me, he gave a wink of satisfaction.

Phase 8—While Julius was being bribed, Sasha was adding fake inventory to the insurance paperwork. She claimed that 6 million Shillings had been stolen from the safe. Likewise, while there were full beer bottles in the inventory, and which there had been a delivery earlier in the day, with an invoice as evidence of the same, during the afternoon of the robbery, all the bottles had been taken to Chidi's house and replaced with empty ones at the time of the fire. We had receipts for brand new top of the line kitchen equipment rather than for the destroyed second-hand cookers. In total, the insurance claim was for $75,000 but worth only $20,000. If we had any issues with getting a signed letter for loss of property, then we hoped that a signature from the Regional Police Commissioner Julius Mbogoye, would help clear that particular hurdle.

Phase 9—As planned by Chidi, Mchumba and John were taking to the house in Sinza after the robbery, but what they didn't, and indeed couldn't have known, was that six-months earlier, when Chidi was still in the UK, Mkosi, their deceased brother, had raped Chidi's cousin. The set-up was Chidi's vengeance.

In the press conference after the arrest of the two from plot 167 on Sinza Road, Julius Mbogoye assured the assembled press, 'We tracked down the address of the robbers through analysis of the partial number plate details given by two young women who witnessed the robbery and which corroborated an anonymous tip-off. There's no doubt that Mchumba and James Nkhoma were the other robbers, they identified their dead brother in the police mortuary.'

Phase 10—Julius released Mchumba and James on bail at 4pm on Monday as instructed. He ensured there were no policemen in the vicinity to see the robbers being bundled into the side of a silver Toyota Noah with tinted windows. This was done by two of Chidi's ex-army friends, Watson and Terry, who'd each been offered a contract of $1,000 and an all-expenses paid weekend in Zanzibar for their unique brand of assistance.

Jonas and I had previously discussed what to do with the brothers as the connection back to Chidi had to be eradicated. It was a rubicon we all had to cross while at the same time giving us an opportunity for an uncompromising message, namely, that anyone who messed with The Ghost was doomed. We considered necklacing, but decided this was too barbaric and would take too long; extra time equalled added risk. Shooting them in the back of the head was another option, but this would have limited impact. Drowning, poisoning, and/or disappearing them would defeat the point of their gangland style execution.

Phase 11—Chidi had arranged that when the three security guards at the Esquire Flats construction site went for their dinner break at 9pm, they would leave the front gate unlocked. We found that it was so. Jonas, Chidi, Watson, Terry and myself, manhandled the sedated and handcuffed Mchumba and John through the front gate and up four flights of steps.

With a rope around their necks, Chidi pushed Mchumba over the balcony, Jonas pushing James into the abyss. We knew what we'd done was bad, but consoled ourselves in the knowledge that we had killed bad people who would be no loss to the world.

Phase 12—After rushing down the stairs and through the front gate, we closed the padlock and switched on a laptop which was connected to an outdoor projector, an image of a ghost icon appeared onto the wall behind the two swinging limp bodies in a ghastly shadow. With such a public slaying, there would be no mistaking that there was someone, or something called The Ghost, who would take the ultimate umbrage should anyone get in their way.

Reflection #14—
The Only Option is Forward

That night as I lay in bed, I reflected on how I had killed a man, a bad man admittedly, but still it was someone who was flesh and blood. I had broken one of the Ten Commandments and whatever I did with the rest of my life, I would not be able to undo it.

I justified my action, thus: I did what I had to do for my family. When I was pushed into a corner, I came out swinging and damn anybody who got in my way. I had a harder time reconciling how my life had so dramatically changed from when I previously lived in Tanzania as an idealistic volunteer teacher and when the joys of life were in front of me rather than harsh realities. I finally came to the conclusion as I drifted into a vodka induced sleep, there is no turning back, the only option is forward.

69. BUSINESS AND CRIME IS A NUMBERS GAME, IT ALWAYS HAS BEEN!

'We did it!' a very relieved Jonas said to me in Room 617 of the Ramada Hotel, the day after the night before. 'We really fucking did it!'

'Yeah. No turning back now. Everything, everything we planned went like clockwork,' I replied, as I puffed out my cheeks in blessed relief. 'We now have the urban legend of The Ghost and which we must maximize to our advantage.'

'And we have Julius by the short-and-curlies.'

'We shouldn't push that corrupt motherfucker too hard,' I cautioned. 'Let him think he's earned his money or that we are in his debt.'

'Agreed. What's our money situation?'

'We can put in a claim for $75,000 to the insurers. From two-months of trading at The Tipsy Lion and TMS consultancy, we have a profit of $10,000. I need some money for family things otherwise Amy will start to get worried. Of course, you need living costs and some money for having fun. Chidi, his ex-army mates and Sasha are all paid up.'

'Assuming we get the $75K reasonably quickly, we will have about $80,000 in the bank. We need to deduct $30,000 to get The Tipsy Lion operational again, and so have about $50K to play with.'

'Sounds about right,' I confirmed, though my mind was mentally absent as I considered for the umpteenth time, I murdered someone less than twenty-four hours earlier.

'Let's meet same-time-next-month to discuss our next round of investments.' Jonas seemed not affected one iota by the hangings.

'Sounds good to me.' We shook hands, took our leave and started preparing for the next phase of our two-year plan.

Later that afternoon, I met Chidi. 'Here's a bonus for you to share as you see fit with Sasha and your army friends,' I said giving him a brown envelope containing $3,000; it was very Hollywood. 'A great job all ways round. Well done.'

'What's next?' Chidi asked straight to the point, and to which I had now come to expect from him.

'First things first. We need the bars up-country that you identified to become part of our business; you need to make the owners... an offer they can't refuse,' this said in a very poor impersonation of Marlon Brando as Don Vito Corleone in The Godfather. 'Make them a fair offer based on local rents. You can offer them a sweetener should they need convincing. If that doesn't work, let me know and I'll make them an offer they can't refuse,' this time there was no humour in my voice, I was deadly serious.

'I'll get on it.'

'Secondly, I was impressed with Watson and Terry,' this in reference to Chidi's ex-army friends who had assisted us in the abduction and murder of Mchumba and James. 'Find out if they are available for some more work, specifically of the surveillance variety. If they're interested, and their rates reasonable, then there's a month's work starting immediately.'

'I'm meeting them this afternoon, boss; I'll give you feedback this evening.'

With a shake of hands, Chidi went to meet Watson and Terry while I phoned Sasha. I knew that as we moved into phase three, it would be important to have a woman on our management team. Under different circumstances this might have been Amy, but I refused to countenance her involvement on the grounds that if our best laid plans went awry, then my family must be insulated from my nefarious life. So far, Sasha had been kept at arm's length. I'd wanted to appraise her trustworthiness and operational efficiency before interacting with her more directly; she had passed all tests with flying colours. 'Hi,' I greeted her. 'You're as good looking as Chidi described. More importantly, your work has been exemplary and I will promote you to my management team.'

'Thank you, Sir,' she smiled to the news of her rapid promotion even though I could tell she didn't know exactly who I was. 'The work has been very interesting,' she said with a conspiratorial smile; I immediately liked her.

'You will of course get the associated benefits of promotion; Chidi will give you a bonus.'

'Thank you.' We shook hands, she with the devil.

'The first thing you need to do,' I wanted to get straight to business, 'is get The Tipsy Lion back up and running. Here's $20,000 cash to do the necessary.' I handed her a fat brown envelope... again, like in the movies. 'If you need more, inform Chidi. I also need you to identify someone who you can pass the management of The Tipsy Lion onto in a few months' time; I have bigger plans for you. Be very careful who you choose as you will be vouching for them.'

Sasha taped her chin deep in thought, 'I have a cousin who has bar experience and is known to find ways for extra income.'

'I hope I don't need to reiterate, that you will be held responsible for their performance; their screw up is your fuck up.'

'I understand,' Sasha replied confidently. 'I will get The Tipsy Lion back in business as soon as possible. I know a few painters and builders and will get them started tomorrow. Likewise, I'll contact our drink and food suppliers and inform them that we are back in business. I'll buy and install whatever kitchen and bar equipment is needed, plus order a new pool table. By Friday we can have the reopening.'

'Great.' I was very impressed with the way that Sasha took on the extra responsibility. 'Lastly, I need you to start identifying girls, who, like you, are bright and beautiful,' this said with a playful smile. 'They need to have a degree, wit and charm, and a personality that will allow them to confidently interact with powerful men. They should be trained professionals, whether that's business consultants, accountants, lawyers or human resource managers etcetera. They must have at least two years' work experience and not be straight out of university. Please, make a dossier of twenty girls and recommend ten to hire.'

'I'll work on it,' Sasha eagerly confirmed as I saw her mentally going through her phone contact list and little black book.

70. THE REGIONAL POLICE COMMISSIONER

While I was busy informing Chidi and Sasha of their new responsibilities, Jonas was following up with his various contacts. At the Sheraton, in Dar es Salaam city centre, he had coffee with Regional Police Commissioner Julius Mbogoye. 'Congratulations, Julius, you did a great job of catching The Tipsy Lion robbers. It was a real shame what happened,' Jonas' words laced with irony. 'I hope this will make the life of police officers that much easier,' to which Julius didn't initially understand. Jonas elaborated, 'Thieves will think twice before they rob a bottlestore... maybe the bar will be owned by The Ghost.'

'Thank you, Sir,' Julius replied, not knowing where the conversation was leading. I imagine, he didn't know much about our business with him despite a couple of his CID officers tracking my former housemate. 'The Tanzanian Police Force does it best to protect and serve. We assist our citizens however we can.' There was no irony in Julius' voice.

'Please sign this,' Jonas requested as he passed Julius our insurance claim, yet one more potential money making opportunity for the rotund policeman.

Jonas told me Julius had instinctively responded, 'I understand procedures... when there are hold ups, the boss can make things go quicker—'

'I want you to sign now, to save time later,' Jonas jumped in. 'Of course, saving time means saving money, and my client would be suitable thankful for your assistance in this matter.'

'You're right,' Julius, the worm had smiled. 'My officers are very busy and have too much paperwork. You know, as a boss, you should always look at how to make the lives of your underlings as stress free as possible... if that means less paperwork, I'm all for it,' he claimed as he scribbled his extravagant signature. 'My men are real police and not pen pushers; they like catching thieves.'

'Thank you.' Jonas, had no intention of giving the greedy Julius a penny.

'The other reason to meet today, is that my client would like to be acquainted with other talented men, such as yourself, who are at or near the top of their profession, whether that be cabinet ministers, principle secretaries, business men, judges or law and order. I'm sure through your network you know of such men.'

'Certainly,' Julius answered with a conspiratorial grin. 'On official duty, you do meet such gentlemen. Can I ask why your client wants to meet these gentlemen of high regard?'

'You can ask, Julius, but I won't tell you; attorney-client privilege,' Jonas stone-walled. 'However, your name will not be associated with the list you pass to me; it will be in strictest confidence.'

'Why ask me for a list when this information is openly available through the appropriate channels? Julius had asked, quickly adding, 'what's in it for me to provide such a list of reputable grandees?'

'Julius, my friend, this list will get you an invite to the most exclusive party going.'

'Ok, I'll write you a list,' Julius, now intrigued as he took a pen from his briefcase.

'You have five days to give me fifty names. Each person on your list must include any rumours you've heard about the gentlemen in question, and/or any ongoing police investigations they may be under. Your effort will more than be compensated.'

'You never said anything about dishing the dirt—'

'You are privileged to even be considered being put forward to join this VIP club. If you don't recognise the opportunity… I will find someone who does.'

'Ok, ok; I'll see what muck I can rake up. You'll have your list, but don't let this come back on me.'

'Julius, don't worry, this won't come back to bite you on the ass. What you should be more worried about… IS YOUR FUCKING ATTITUDE!' Jonas told me he'd screamed, spittle deliberately going in the face of the corrupt man opposite him. 'Don't ever threaten me or my client again, otherwise… well, let's not go down that road. Good day.' Jonas rose looking Julius in the eye, 'And tell your fucking CID officers to stop following me otherwise an accident might happen to them.' Jonas walked briskly away without a handshake or goodbye, leaving Julius intrigued, perplexed and worried in equal measure; he'd never been threatened in such a direct way before.

71. Woof-Woof

Jonas' second appointment of the day, was lunch with Danny Nyonda, the proprietor of the Tanzania Enquirer Newspaper Group.

'Danny, it was great to meet the other evening. A fun night had by all even if I lost far too much money at the casino.' It was of course no accident that Jonas had met Danny at the gaming club, it had been the first piece of surveillance work that Watson and Terry had been tasked with.

'Fun night, Jonas, fun night indeed. Who was that gorgeous girl I saw you putting your arm around?'

'To be honest, I can't remember… but she wasn't my girlfriend… or who I went to a hotel later with,' Jonas boasted. 'Though I am meeting her tomorrow evening.' This a lie.

'You're a dog.'

'Woof-woof,' Jonas told me he howled at the top of his voice.

'What do you want to drink?'

'My one rule, no lunchtime drinking,' Jonas lied again.

'So, you're a lawyer, Jonas?' Danny, wanted to confirm once the fruit juices had arrived.

'For my sins, yes! I'm sure you've heard plenty of lawyer jokes but this is my favourite. Lawyers think lawyer jokes aren't funny; non-lawyers fail to understand they're not jokes!' This got a big belly laugh out of Danny. Jonas continued, 'I've been a lawyer for ten-years, mainly in London, and where any money I earned, swiftly went on wine, women and other enjoyable delights.'

'I could see the other night that you have quite the eye for exquisite things, especially beautiful girls.'

'Funny you say that, and though I know we've not known each other for long…' Jonas said as he leant conspiratorially towards Danny. 'Before I carry on, I need to ensure I have your complete confidence.'

'That's very cloak and dagger,' Danny joked.

'No laughing matter; do I have your complete confidence?' Jonas asked in his most lawyerly voice.

'Sure,' Danny replied more seriously, never knowing where a good story might come from.

'In the coming months, a very exclusive, invitation only bar will be opening. It will be for the high-fliers of Tanzanian society: judges, MPs, law officers and… newspaper proprietors.'

'I look forward to my summons,' Danny grinned.

'There will be 100 invitations only. It will be a club to discuss business and enjoy pleasures of every imagination.'

'I look forward to it,' Danny re-iterated.

'Irrespective of who you are or who you know, each member will need to bring a little something extra to the table. Members will be expected to scratch each other's back.'

'It sounds like the Masons.'

'Similar goals, but much, much more fun.' Jonas paused. 'Let me get to the point. As editor-in-chief, I'm sure you know many influential people and hear many rumours. What I can say, is, that if you were to write a list of fifty names and any rumours that you may have heard about that person, then my partner would be very thankful.'

'Well, I don't know about that,' Danny, clearly surprised at the audacity of such a blunt request. 'Confidentiality in my game is what reputation is built on. If a source doesn't have confidence in my ability to keep my mouth shut, I'll quickly have no more sources.'

'I fully appreciate your predicament, and if you don't want to be invited…' Jonas shrugged his shoulders unperturbed, this indicating the list was a pre-requisite for membership.

'I'll think about it.'

'Let's meet for drinks on Friday at the casino,' Jonas suggested, now that business was out of the way. 'If you bring the list, perfect, and as your friend I strongly recommend you do. But if no list, I understand. Either way, drinks on me and girls on you.'

'Cheers to that.'

'By the way, if you hear anything more about The Ghost, do give me a heads up. My client is very interested in this story, myth or whatever you want to call it. It has certainly caught the imagination of the public, first the shooting and then the revenge hangings. Are you doing any more articles?' Jonas innocently queried.

'Of course, it's our most popular story; it has so many newsworthy ingredients.'

'An editor's wet dream, I'm sure.' Jonas shook Danny's hand. 'See you Friday.'

72. FRIENDS IN THE RIGHT PLACES

Jonas' third and last meeting was with Asupya Nkhonde, the Managing Director of General Alliance Insurance (GAI), the carefully selected insurers of The Tipsy Lion.

'Good afternoon, Sir,' Asupya greeted Jonas.

'Thank you for seeing me at such short notice.'

'We do our best for our esteemed clients.' Tipsy Lion was a very small client for GAI, but The Ghost was big business and any association could be worth its weight in marketing gold and hence the granting of an immediate meeting. We had banked—quite literally—on the notoriety of The Ghost related slayings to get a quick insurance pay-out.

'Getting down to business, please find all documentation related to the bottlestore and the claim we are making.' Jonas handed over the paperwork. Asupya's eyes were drawn to the Regional Police Commissioner's signature.

'There was a pause of thirty-seconds,' Jonas later told me. 'I could clearly see that Asupya was making a calculation, though what at the time, I didn't know.'

'In my experience of such destruction,' Asupya calmly announced, 'a claim of $75,000 might be on the conservative side. I will ask one of my best investigators to make a thorough inspection first thing tomorrow. Without seeing the damage to the property, or loss of stock and equipment, it's obviously very difficult for me to speculate... but from experience, I would expect the figure to be closer to $125,000.'

'I was not expecting this turn of conversation from the smiling insurance man,' Jonas later informed me. 'Indeed this had been my first real surprise since your initial proposition when playing 50:50.'

At the time of this meeting, Asupya had not been on the short list of invitees to our soon to be opened exclusive bar, but Jonas reasoned, that as our business grew, more "accidents"—I use quotation marks on this occasion on purpose—might happen. Asupya could be a very useful contact if ever we had a shortage of cash.

'Thank you,' Jonas had thus replied. 'It's great to know that your best investigators will be looking into our claim. Of course, we appreciate the expediency and size of any pay-out; I'm sure there will be other business opportunities that my client will put your way.'

'All business is greatly appreciated at GAI'

'On a personal note,' Jonas cryptically added as he went with his gut feeling, 'you may receive an invitation to a private members' club… please don't mention it to anybody.'

'I'll be sure to have your claim processed as soon as possible,' Asupya appreciatively deadpanned.

73. AN OFFER THAT CAN'T BE REFUSED

As Sasha had promised, by Friday The Tipsy Lion had been repainted and a new kitchen installed. She had restocked and hired new staff (Nyka and Mary) rented a pool table and put up new signage and lighting.

While Sasha was busy at The Tipsy Lion, Jonas doing his lawyerly work, I gave the VIP lists supplied by Julius and Danny to Watson and Terry and tasked them with starting a surveillance operation on all the names.

With activities in Dar es Salaam moving smoothly, I got ready for a trip up-country, ostensibly this was for consultancy work but in reality to see the bottlestores that Chidi had identified.

'You're going away, again?' Amy asked.

'Yes, and I'll be leaving at 3am, so that I can be up in Mwanga by 9am to do a full day's work at the bank before moving onto other meetings; I'll be away for ten days.' It was true, that indeed on Monday I would be going to Mwanga Community Bank to start a small consultancy helping them update their mobile banking policies and procedures. However, that work would only last two days, the other eight I would visit the bars Chidi had identified. 'At least I'm home this weekend. Let's go to the Chinese restaurant tonight and, tomorrow to the beach.'

'I hate it when you do long journeys, especially when you leave so early in the morning.'

'I don't like it either, but I have to do what I have to do.' If only Amy really knew what I would be up to.'

I left at 3am as promised, but instead of going direct to Mwanga, I went via the coastal town of Tanga which had been identified as a strategic location due to its close proximity to Mombasa. It was an ideal location into the Kenyan market as and when we were ready to expand operations outside Tanzanian borders.

I reached Summer Park at 8am, though why this booze den, as local bars are termed in the vernacular, had been given such a name, I was at a loss. There was no park of any shape or size, just a dingy nightclub on the beach front, which even at this early time of day had patrons. I couldn't tell if they were starting the day's drinking or still going strong from the night before. I didn't need to go inside Summer Park to know what it was like or what amenities it had... I had been to plenty similar. The fact that it seemed to be busy 24/7, and that Chidi had recommended it, was good enough for me.

Leaving Tanga, I drove four hours to Mwanga. After successfully doing my consultancy work at the bank, that evening I drove the fifty-kilometres to Moshi, the principle town in Kilimanjaro Region and where Chidi had identified the Kilimanjaro Lounge as the bar with the greatest potential.

Kilimanjaro Lounge was a franchised bar on the top floor of The Kilimanjaro Hotel; they weren't shy with promoting the great tourist draw that was omnipotent everyway you went in a thirty kilometre radius. While the views of Mount Kilimanjaro were indeed spectacular, the hotel itself didn't live up to the same billing, indeed, on a charitable day I would've classified it as rundown. Being as such, I was surprised that Chidi had given such an endorsement, though it did make me very curious. Walking in and spending twenty minutes as an ordinary punter, I realised, that with a lick of paint to the bar, and strongly suggesting to the owner to do likewise with the hotel, there was no reason why we couldn't turn this location into a favoured spot for tourists and expatriate volunteers alike, both of whom seemed to throng around the town. I calculated, with plenty of Mzungus this would draw in the locals of both genders, boys to distribute narcotics and female prostitutes.

After spending a night at the more upmarket Keys Hotel, and drawing up a list of activities which I emailed to Chidi, I drove to Arusha, the third largest city in Tanzania. While Moshi was packed with volunteers—one of whom I had been fifteen years earlier—and/or tourists wanting to climb Mount Kilimanjaro, Arusha, seventy-five kilometres to the west had a very different vibe. It was increasingly cosmopolitan and largely built on tourists visiting the Serengeti and the Ngorongoro Crater National Parks. There was also a relatively large East African community due to the town's proximity to the Kenyan Border, and a number of business minded Europeans who had lived in Arusha for many generations. The last major group of foreigners were those who worked at the Arusha International Conference Centre, which amongst other roles, had hosted the United Nations investigation into the 1994 Rwandan Genocide.

The Rugby Club, eight kilometres outside the city, was down a very potholed road. It was a favoured spot for the local expat community on Friday and Saturday nights, and especially match days. However, I wasn't going there, but rather to the Jamaica Inn, a popular spot run by a ruby faced, foul-talking Frenchman who had a 24/7 policy. While some of the clients would undoubtedly be potential members of my soon to be opened exclusive bar in Dar es Salaam, I saw potential of the Jamaica Inn becoming a franchise for the north of Tanzania. However, now though was too early. I made a note that Chidi should find somewhere more suitable for our immediate purposes.

After a number of consultancy related meetings in Arusha, I drove to Mwanza, located on Lake Victoria, the second largest city in Tanzania. In recent times, it had become a boom town, this largely due to the mining sector which had grown very fast in the last two decades. I stayed at the Tilapia Hotel and which I'd heard was the watering-hole for many of the international miners and who had plenty of money but few options where or how to spend it other than alcohol, drugs, women and gambling; my type of clientele.

Chidi had identified the Picadilo Bar located 100 metres from the Tilapia Hotel. It was close enough to entice the miners and their money to the aforementioned vices. Chidi hadn't been successful in persuading the owner that we should be the new tenants; I was there to lead the negotiation. 'Nice bar,' I said to a pretty waitress who smiled seductively at me. 'Can I talk to the owner, please,' I asked pleasantly.

'Who shall I say is asking?' she probed in a flirtatious tone. I contemplated the invitation, though expected I would have other plans that evening.

'You can give Patrick Mwangi this.' I handed the waitress an envelope to take to the owner.

She returned three minutes later, with a look of concern on her face. 'Please go up those stairs,' all thoughts of lifting her skirt for me now far removed. 'He's waiting for you.'

Knowing of the threats I'd written in the letter, I was ready for an ambush as I walked up the stairs. 'What do you mean by coming into my bar and threatening me?' Patrick was glowing with anger. There were three heavily built men standing behind him; they looked like they were probably his brothers.

'It's not a threat, just a statement of facts,' I replied. 'My associate made you a fair offer; I insist you accept.'

'I'm not selling or renting to anyone; FUCK OFF!' he shouted, as his three brothers brought the baseball bats they'd not so subtly been hiding behind the tree trunk-like bodies into open view.

'You might want to reconsider,' I convivially suggested, as I took out my wallet and pulled out a business card which I passed to Patrick. 'I work on behalf of the person who goes by the moniker, The Ghost; I'm sure you've heard of him.' Patrick turned over the business card and saw a logo of a ghost. Of course, I knew anyone could have printed such cards, but I just needed to put enough doubt in his mind to buy some time.

'I'll come back in twenty-four hours. You will present terms that I find acceptable to lease this premises for two years.' Patrick and his brothers were left open-mouthed by my confidence in them agreeing to my outlandish demand. Before they had a chance to reply, I walked back down the stairs.

That night I threw a Molotov cocktail at his Toyota Prado, this to ensure Patrick would be under no illusions as to the seriousness of my threats. I'd done this in full view of three witnesses, one of which was the attractive girl who'd taken my envelope earlier in the day.

Walking calmly back into the Picadilo Bar the next day, I went up the stairs to see Patrick. 'What will the rent be?' I asked Patrick, who, it is fair to say, was between a rock and a hard place.

'The Picadilo has a great name, a good reputation and very profitable. If you want to change it, that's your choice. I take home $7,000 a month after tax, but if you can give me the same monthly income from sitting on my arse watching football, you have a deal.'

'I like your negotiating balls, Patrick. I offer you $4,000 and not a penny more; take it or leave it.'

'$6,000.'

'$4,000. This is business.'

'Let's meet halfway, $5,500?' This sum, I could tell, was more out of hope than expectation.

'The Ghost can't be said to be unfair, he will go up to $4,500,' I offered wanting to conclude the negotiation and move onto other business.

'Ok, but only for two-years?' Patrick reluctantly agreed, though in reality he had little option.

'Two-years is fine.' I knew after that time, whatever happened to the Picadilo would no longer be my problem. 'We will pay at the end of every quarter; that's non-negotiable.' Truth be told, we didn't have the cash flow to pay rent in advance.

'I will be out of pocket for the next three months' Patrick, quite reasonably complained.

'Not my problem; live within your means!' I advised, as I brokered no argument. 'A lawyer will be in contact,' this in reference to Jonas. Rising, I made my way to the exit not bothering to shake Patrick's trembling hand.

REFLECTION #15—
SUPPLY AND DEMAND

Back in my car, I thought about the words I just articulated, it's just business, these being exactly the same as those Ephraim and Peter had said to me in my last doomed days at GlobeTel. The irony that it was now I doing the nonchalant threat was not lost on me.

Finished in the north, next it was to the southern towns to finalise rental agreements.

As I drove back to Dar es Salaam and my family, I considered it had been a successful tour. Bars in Tanga, Moshi and Mwanza had been successfully negotiated, and together with the yet to be identified location in Arusha, it seemed that all northern hostelries were primarily targeting the more well off demographic. On the other hand, Devil Pub, Coconut High and 999, the bottlestores respectively in Mbeya, Iringa and Morogoro, in central and southern Tanzania, were closer in drunken ambiance to The Tipsy Lion and Summer Park. The different types of bar followed my strategy of identifying big spenders in the northern cities, whereas the southern towns' boys and girls could be found for a low price and would willingly sell drugs, commit acts of violence or prostitute themselves; by bringing the two worlds together I was creating supply and demand.

74. The Dirty Dossier

While I'd been making offers that couldn't be refused, Watson and Terry had been conducting surveillance on the list of 100 VIPS that Jonas and I had compiled. Their mission had led them to following, his Honour Judge Nyarko to Miriam's Massage Parlour where he received a rub and tug—a massage and hand job with a happy ending to those not familiar with the term.

Watson entered Miriam's Massage parlour five minutes after the judge had left, and while having a massage found out that the judge was a regular visitor, his usual time, half-past-three on a Thursday afternoon.

'We must come again next week,' Watson advised Terry. 'I'll hide a micro-video-camera in the room after my massage.'

'You get all the tough assignments,' Terry said with grin. Next on their list was Joel Mandala, the owner of three of the most prestigious hotels in the capital and the first self-made entrepreneur to have a private wealth above $100 million. There were whisperings, that ministers of both the political and religious variety, had beaten him to that landmark. Mr Mandala was born into rural poverty forty-four years earlier, and had hustled and bustled his way to his first $1,000 by the age of fifteen. From that early start, his income doubled on a six-monthly basis before it took off into the financial stratosphere five years earlier with his purchase of his first hotel. His wealth and business acumen had been noticed by politicians, who had plenty of the former, wealth, but precious little of the later, sense. Joel would give advice on how to invest their often corrupt earnings for a 10% service fee.

It was for myriad reasons why he was one of our top VIP targets. Fortunately for us, he had a weakness for drugs, notably Speed. Though intrinsically there is nothing wrong with taking drugs for recreational usage—I'm not a hypocrite—it did however lead him into a few indiscretions. Watson and Terry tracked Joel's chauffer driven, ostentatious, marine blue Rolls Royce Phantom to the Ramada Hotel, where over a two-hour business lunch, and using a directional recording microphone hidden under a table napkin, Watson and Terry recorded him offering a bribe for an oil and gas contract to the Minister for Natural Resources. He was added to Watson and Terry's surveillance report and which now made for titillating reading. In no specific order, they'd found out:

> ➢ Joel Mandala—bribes and drugs
> ➢ Judge Nyarko—prostitution
> ➢ Chief Inspector Phiri—paedophile
> ➢ District Commissioner Mrema—bribery
> ➢ Chief Inspector Mrope—adultery with multiple women
> ➢ Minister for Prisons—buggery of a male minor
> ➢ Minister for Internal Affairs—bribery and fraud…

And so the list went on.

75. Don Tony

As Watson and Terry were compiling their dirty dossier, Sasha identifying girls for phase three and, Jonas ticking off items on his list of activities, I started phoning my contacts. I was hoping to recruit an eclectic mix of talents into my inner circle, and while this undoubtedly would create new dangers, I had little choice if I wanted to keep to my two-year timeline. My first call was to Columbia. 'Alright Tony, how're things?' Bearing in mind his recreational activities and penchant for Cocaine, I imagined he might have contacts with the drug cartels.

'Long time, long time. What are you doing these days? How's Africa?'

'Very good. Amy and the kids are fine. I've started a business with Jonas.'

'No ways. What's he doing there, or should I say, what are you two up to?'

'He's doing his lawyerly thing and helping foreign investors set up business.'

'I should visit you boys sometime.'

'Yes, you should. Jonas loves it here, especially the women. A night of excess with quality ass and drugs costs no more than £200, or so he keeps telling me.'

'Still the same madman,' Tony laughed. 'I remember him complaining how he would blow £2,000 on a night of drugs, a few bottles of Crystal champagne and paying a quality hooker £500 an hour.'

After a few more entertaining minutes catching up, 'I have a business proposition for you,' this the main point of the phone call. I briefed him about what Jonas and I had been up to and what our plans for the next 18-months were.

'That sounds very interesting.'

'I'm guessing you still dabble in the drugs game?' I wanted to see how Tony would respond; he didn't say anything. 'I need a supplier,' I continued, the conversation moving from repartee to business, 'and I'm not talking about some local toe-rag who wants to make a quick buck, but businessmen who can supply quantity.'

'You mean, buy from a cartel?'

'Yes.'

'Are you taking the piss?'

'Straight up. Jonas and I are currently setting up the logistics for a national drugs distribution network. Most of the finance is in place for the initial shipment; in another few months we can front an initial order of $1 million.'

'Fuck, me!' Tony was genuinely surprised. 'What are you boys doing over there? I know you smoked a bit of pot when we shared the house, but never any Charlie. I didn't think that would be your game.'

'That was then and this is now. Charles Darwin, on his theory of evolution, said, "It's not the strongest of the species that survives, nor the most intelligent that survives. It is the one most adaptable to change," and I have adapted to my changing circumstances. This is business and drugs just happens to be one of our products of choice.'

'What do you mean, one of your products?' Tony probed.

'I'm building a business around drugs, alcohol, prostitution and gambling,' I then paused, the silence lasting a-full-thirty-seconds. 'I didn't know if I could follow through on my plan.' I tried to lighten the mood of the conversation. 'But here we are, having the conversation I envisaged when I put my proposition to Jonas.'

'Ok.' Those two letters and the tone of his voice, indicating that he finally understood I wasn't pulling his leg. Tony took a few seconds to collect his thoughts. 'Are you shitting me about the $1 million order?'

Getting $1 million was a problem. We had $200,000 cash in the bank but most of that had been earmarked for the initial rent and furnishing of our national expansion of bars and the opening of our super exclusive, The Blue Label Bar. We hoped that the launch of The Blue Label Bar would raise $500,000 through membership fees, and then we would dupe some of the VIPs who were looking for a quick return to invest in a Ponzi scheme that Jonas had been working on over the previous three-years. 'Ways and means, Tony, ways and means,' I causally replied. 'Of course, any introductions would be well compensated.'

I honestly didn't know what he would say next. Twenty seconds later I found out. 'How about you set me up with a house, a girl, a plentiful supply of alcohol and we'll call it quits; I need to leave this shithole anyway.'

'I'll take that as a, yes,' I said relieved he was coming on-board. 'I'm sure we can sort you out with a nice pad and as much pussy and booze as you can manage.'

'Give me a week and I'll see what I can do in regards introductions.'

'Good man, Tony. I'll call next Thursday.'

76. THE BIGGEST BASTARDS

Our strategy to attract VIPs to join as members of our yet to-be-opened exclusive bar, lay in building the myth of The Ghost, the notional owner. We'd assumed, VIPs would want to mingle in exclusive surroundings that were associated with The Ghost. It was a very big assumption, and as Jonas reminded me on more than one occasions: assumptions are the mother of all fuck-ups.

While The Ghost had already achieved a certain level of notoriety, to reach our strategic objectives we needed to turn the urban myth into a national legend; this was no easy matter. 'We kill lots of scumbags,' was Jonas' offhanded suggestion.

'It took a lot of planning, time and money to set up The Tipsy Lion robbery; plus, do you really want more murders on your hands?'

'Not really,' he conceded.

'It needs to be something short, sharp and leave an indelible, but favourable image on the public.'

'How do we get the average man or woman on our, or should I say, The Ghost's side, other than wasting scumbags?'

'Well, Jonas,' I started to reply, an idea popping into my head, a proverbial Einstein moment if you like, 'TIA.'

'What the hell is, TIA?'

'This-Is-Africa.'

'Go on,' Jonas encouraged me and having no idea what I might suggest.

'The three types of people your average citizen hates most in Tanzania in descending order are…' I did a drum roll with my fingers on the table top. 'At number three, agricultural traders.'

'Who the fuck are they?'

'People who buy crop from the farmgate at well below market price, knowing that the farmers are desperate for cash.'

'How do they do that?' he asked, not familiar with the market inefficiencies which dogged much of the agricultural sector on the African continent.

'Ignorance and lack of information on the part of the farmer, who even though they instinctively know they're getting screwed are cash-strapped and need money immediately and not in one month's time when the price might have doubled. Its great business by the trader and who's also often a money lender. They lend to the farmer and are repaid through an in-kind payment i.e. the farmer's harvest. This keeps the farmer stuck in the poverty trap.'

'They sound like bastards to me, cunning bastards admittedly… but bastards all the same. Who is number two?'

'Number two is the local government party official. They wield an inordinate amount of power in the village. They decide which villagers get subsidies or allowances, and inevitably their decisions are to their benefit. Their rule the village with an iron fist but with full support of the ruling party who calls on them at election time. I'm sure there are some good ones, but most are bastards.'

'And numero uno?'

'The most hated bastards are the police, or more specifically, traffic cops. They are like a bad fart that hangs around and no matter how much air freshener you use the smell won't go away. Their day consists of looking for bribes. Whenever there is an actual crime to investigate, they are nowhere to be found. They are often in cahoots with the villains. This—'

'For example?' Jonas cut in.

'I'm glad you asked. When we were looking for a house to rent just after arriving in Tanzania, Amy found a place that we liked. Naïvely, we were bluffed by a fake landlord and which cost us nine-months of rent—$6,000. Long story short, a friend pretended they were also looking for a house to rent; a viewing was set with the fake landlord. We paid the police to come with us to arrest the arsehole. It ended with a dog and pony show at the cop house, with police officers busy on their phones, presumably warning the fake house owner not to turn up. Lo and behold, the arsehole didn't come and their SIM card immediately stopped working. We had to write off the loss to life's rocky journey.'

'Ah, yes, life's rocky road. So, what's the plan? I know you've been thinking this through over the last however many months, so don't tell me you don't have one.'

'That's why I wanted that corrupt dickhead Julius in our pocket from an early stage.'

'What do we need to do?'

'One month before we send the invitations to the Blue Label Bar,' the name for our super exclusive bar in reverence to Johnnie Walker, 'we put our plan into action.' I went onto explain what I had in mind.

77. Membership

One week later, it was the night before the storm. 'We can't stay if you don't have work,' Amy complained, as indeed she'd been doing increasingly regularly over the past weeks.

'I have various consultancy contracts in the pipeline.' This was indeed true, TMS was picking up work and helped in no small part by Sasha ability to offer accountancy services to small and medium sized businesses.

'But how many? We always seem to be short of money,' she accurately pointed out. 'Are we going to have enough for hospital fees when I give birth? Or for the next lot of rent?' She asked with a very worried look on her wrinkle free face.

'We'll be fine,' I assured her as if I had not a care in the world. The irony of her questions was not lost on me as it was my double-life which was finishing all our income and what little savings we had.

'How? Don't you think it would be better to go back to the UK and get a job there?' She suggested for the umpteenth time.

'No, I don't think that would be the best option.' I needed to make a justification for why we should stay. 'First, I have the court case against GlobeTel. If I win, and which is looking promising, it will financially change everything for us. We could use the money to start building a house in Malawi or as a deposit for a home in the UK; we could even decide to try our luck in another part of the world. Secondly, my income would be drastically cut if we went to the UK as I would have to start paying income tax; being self-employed I can minimize my tax exposure. Rent and most living costs would be much higher, especially running a car. Car tax and insurance alone are crazy expensive. Then there are the utility bills… there's no need to pay for heating in Tanzania. And there's no council tax either.' As I was the breadwinner of the family, I had to make the case on a purely financial persuasion; I admit, I spread it on a bit thick.

'I still think it would be better,' she persisted.

'And do what? A job where I commute an hour each day to an office I don't want to work in with people I have nothing in common with other than the carpet I walk on,' I said thinking back to Jim's classic quote. 'Childcare is so expensive that there will be little financial benefit if you work. We won't have house helpers. What happens if I get a contract and am away for a couple of months? You'll be looking after the kids and do all the cooking, cleaning, ironing, etcetera by yourself; it will be very difficult for you, for us.' I could see my arguments were not winning her around. 'Let's see how things are in a few months.' I had twenty months in mind. 'If things are not looking up by then, yes, maybe we should think about moving. But at the moment, and taking everything into account, I still think Tanzania is the best option… for now.'

'Right,' she sullenly replied and walked into the bedroom closing the door loudly behind her.

'I'm going out for a beer,' I informed her… I was actually going to meet Jonas.

78. The Devil is in the Detail

'Are we ready?' Jonas asked. 'Tomorrow is the start of our most critical month.'

'A lot of moving parts,' I agreed, 'but we're ready,' I confidently confirmed while pulling a couple of sheets of paper from my rucksack which detailed our forthcoming operational activities. I handed them to Jonas.

Drugs import and distribution

➢ Tony flies to Columbia tomorrow to meet his contact, Miguel Hernandez and who has organised a sit-down with Diego Gomez, the number two in a cartel.

➢ The sales pitch is: the East African market is so far an untapped opportunity and distribution will be run by businessmen who have an existing network.

➢ Our negotiating tactic will be: while Tony is meeting Diego, we do what we have to with the traffic police officers. We ensure we get maximum publicity by leveraging your relationship with Danny, the newspaper proprietor, and give him exclusives for his cooperation.

➢ Tony estimates it will take three weeks from making payment to receiving the first shipment of goods.

➢ Watson, Terry and Chidi are identifying a suitable mid-ocean rendezvous point for the exchange. They have already leased a fishing boat and will manage all logistics for first cutting and then moving the drugs to the bottlestores in the regional cities.

Bottlestores and marketing

> ➤ While Tony is in Columbia, we open the regional bottlestores. Rent has already been paid. We still need to buy stock, hire managers and promote the new bars.
> ➤ Once the drugs arrive, the bottlestores will act as our distribution hubs.
> ➤ When marketing the bars, we will brand them with the logo of The Ghost.
> ➤ Sasha will print t-shirts and other Ghost related marketing merchandise, and which will be sold once the newspapers start running daily stories about The Ghost.
> ➤ Sasha is looking for a drinks supplier who can brand a high energy, highly alcoholic drink: The Ghost. She is also negotiating with a national drinks distributor to sell the drink in as many bars, restaurants and shops as possible.

'The site for The Blue Label Bar has been identified,' I informed Jonas once he had finished reading. 'It's a secluded double-story house on the beachfront. It has two outhouses, a swimming pool and a double garage. The only potential challenge are the four neighbours, though Watson and Terry have found out that, one is a holiday cottage and another a love nest; both are visited irregularly. The third is where Judge Mandala lives. The fourth house is rented by a Mr Patel who runs a small import export business. I propose we give Mr Patel an honouree membership and on his first night get him high, drunk and hammered and then blackmail him into silence.'

While Jonas nodded his head in appreciation at the level of detail I had gone into, I reflected, I have become a true criminal mastermind, a real life Don Corleone.

'Once The Ghost has moved from myth to legend,' I continued, 'we send out this invitation letter to the VIPs.'

Dear xxxxxx,

On Friday the 25th of April, you are requested to attend the opening of The Blue Label Bar. It will be the most exclusive member organisation in Tanzania and where you will be able to network with your peers. We are only inviting 100 VIPs. You have been shortlisted due to your position of power and influence. For example, should (add the details from Watson and Terry's dirty dossier) ever come to light, then either The Ghost and/or a fellow member will be able to assist you.

The Blue Label Bar is so named, as blue is the most exclusive of the Johnnie Walker brands. As the name suggests, it will be where all your business and recreational demands can be met... legal or otherwise. We will provide a full range of professional services, such as accountants, lawyers, lobbyists, business advisory etcetera.

Please find below the terms and conditions of membership.

Yours sincerely

The Ghost

Terms and conditions of membership

Membership

1. Membership is for life. Only under exceptional circumstances can membership be relinquished.
2. Due to the exclusive nature of membership, under no circumstances, whatsoever, are you to inform non-members of The Blue Label Bar's existence. Should it be found out that a member has told a third

party, they will automatically be stripped of their membership. Members may decide under secret ballot if there should be further repercussions.

3. You may not question the membership status of others unless you have special grievance. Should a member ask for another to be excluded and this is denied, the enquiring member will be excluded.

Fees

4. There is joining fee of $5,000 and a quarterly fee of $5,000. This is to be paid in advance into an offshore account. Banking facilities will be available at the launch party.

5. New members can be recommended. They must be seconded by at least two other members. There is a non-refundable application fee of $10,000. The Ghost will authorise / veto all applications.

Activities

6. Any agreement made between members while at The Blue Label Club can be notarised by the in-house lawyer who is on call 24/7. If a member does not keep to their part of the agreement, they will automatically relinquish their membership.

7. While many services will be complimentary, depending on the specific requirements of the member there may be additional charges and which will be negotiated with the Blue Label Bar manager. This includes the use of professional services, such as lawyers and lobbyists, or the procurement of narcotics, girls or boys etcetera.

8. The Blue Label Bar will be open 24/7. There is a complimentary bar, restaurant, swimming pool, sauna, jacuzzi and gym.

9. Personal trainers are available. They must be requested 12 hours in advance or a regular time slot agreed

10. There are casino services 24/7. Members can request special games, but must give a minimum of 12 hours' notice and details of all players. There is a 10% house fee.

11. The Blue Label Bar will on occasion hold special evenings of utmost decadence; there will be special house rules for those nights.

12. Management has right of veto on all decisions.

Jonas sat in silence for a few minutes after he had completed reading my documents, this something highly unusual. 'I like it. I like it a lot!'

79. TURNING A MYTH INTO A LEGEND

At 7am on Monday 25th March, and as Tony boarded the plane to Columbia, Watson drove to Summer Park in Tanga, Terry drove to Kilimanjaro Lounge in Arusha, Chidi flew to Mwanza to open the Picadilo, Sasha went to Mwanza, Jonas drove to Korogwe near the Kenyan border and I drove to Mikumi in the centre of Tanzania.

During the four-hour drive I thought back to all that had gone before to lead me to this place and time. I also contemplated what I was about to do. How, I asked myself, had I gone from a care-free volunteer to a ruthless killer? I knew the answer, it was the same justification I gave every time I looked in the mirror, whatever it takes for my family. I knew that was not a sufficient excuse, and what I'd already done would be totally inexcusable to the majority of people… but I was committed, and going forward was the only option on the path I had trodden.

As I got closer to my day's objective, I imagined the following day's headlines, but first, the deed had to be done. Whatever doubts or misgivings I might have had, there was no chance to turn back.

Reaching a certain bend in the road, I expected I would see traffic police sitting under the same mango tree they always did. I knew they would be waving their speed guns at passing motorists, and which for all intents and purposes could have been recording themselves at an excessive speed earlier in the day, as the camera didn't show: 1) the vehicle that was apparently going over the speed limit, 2) where the car was at the apparent time of speeding, or 3) a calibration sheet. The supposed evidence would never hold up in a court of law... but police and driver never expected it to go that far. If a rotund policeman had your driving license in their pudgy hands, as a motorist your dilemma was, 1) argue, 2) pay the fine, or 3) haggle over the cost of the bribe. It was a no-win situation and the reason why traffic police were so hated.

At 10:12am, and checking that there were no pedestrians or drivers in sight, I purposely drove at 45 KM/H as I approached the bend that I knew so well; sure enough, I was pulled over.

The policeman in his starched white uniform self-importantly waddled up to my car with an arrogant swagger. He waved his fat finger at me. 'Did you not see the 50 kilometres per hour sign?' This while showing me the speed gun which read 75 KM/H.

'Sorry, sir,' I replied while biting my tongue. 'That must have been the car in front; I was only doing 45 KM/H.'

'No, it was you. Did you see a sign that said you could go faster than 50 KM/H?'

'There was no sign.'

'Exactly. Even if there is no sign, the law of the land states: that the speed limit in a built-up-area is 50 KM/H.' I had not yet reached the collection of nine huts which apparently constituted a built up area. 'This is not America.' He didn't pick my British accent. 'You are in Tanzania and must obey our laws. You will pay a fine; follow me.' He didn't expect any resistance from a Mzungu.

I followed the sparkling white fat behind to the police car where his Sergeant was lounging, his feet on the dashboard and little pieces of paper with speeds and monetary amounts lying carelessly on the ground.

'Boss, this man must be fined for two offences. First, for travelling over the speed limit, and secondly, for going faster than 50 KM/H in a built up area.' I'd experienced this tactic of a double fining countless times.

'Pay up or we shall confiscate your car,' the Police Sergeant dismissively ordered as he looked over the top of the news-paper, barely even catching my eye. 'Each offence is 30,000 Shillings; you must pay 60,000.'

'I've just topped up my fuel; I only have pocket change left,' I answered with my usual haggling strategy as I wanted to ensure the policemen were worm infected apples. 'I have to get to Iringa for a meeting and can't leave my car here.'

'What can we do? How can we help you? The Sergeant innocently enquired as if he was my best friend in all the world. 'You broke the law, twice,' he re-iterated while taking a sup from his beer bottle.

There was a long pregnant silence, as I stared at the police-men hoping they would say something that would absolve them. 'Give me 20,000 Shillings and you can go,' the Police Sergeant glibly suggested. In other circumstances, I would try to negotiate this down to 5,000 Shillings, but the two police-men had made their choice, their words had sealed their fate.

'I'll get the money.' I sluggishly walked to my car which was parked ten-metres away. Pretending to take out my wallet from the glove-box, I actually took out two business cards and put them into my trouser pocket.

I walked slowly back to the policemen who were sharing a joke, both of them perspiring in their tight fitting uniforms that were stretched over protruding bellies. I could feel the cold weight of the semi-automatic handgun with silencer in my left trouser pocket and with one last glance to check there were no passerby's or approaching cars, I walked to within three metres of the policemen and swiftly pulled out the handgun. I shot the standing policemen square in the forehead, and before he had fallen to the earth, I shot the lounging sergeant, first in his stomach and then his forehead. In less than two seconds, I had rid Tanzania of two corrupt policemen. I didn't feel overly guilty.

Looking around, I was relieved there were still no motorists or pedestrians in sight. I bundled the hefty dead traffic cop into the backseat of the police car, and then from my pocket took out the two business cards, placing one on the chest of each policeman.

No more police corruption!
No more police bribes!

I pulled out my smartphone and took a few photos and a ten-second-video of the dead policemen and then closed the door of the car. I got back into my vehicle and sped off into Mikumi National Park where I threw the handgun, its serial number already filed off, into a creek.

By 11am and safely parked on-the-side of the road, I uploaded my photos and video to an email I'd drafted earlier. I also attached the photos and video Jonas had emailed me, and which showed an equally grizzly scene from what he'd done to three corrupt policemen near Korogwe. Satisfied, I sent the email to Danny.

80. THE CARTEL

Wednesday's headlines disappointed; there was no mention of either shooting. Nor on Thursday. Perhaps, I thought to myself, Danny has been intimidated by the police to keep quiet? However, on Friday the 29th there was only one story on the front page.

The Ghost slays five corrupt policemen... in two locations... 400 km apart... at the exact same time.
Tuesday the 26th March will be remembered as a day of infamy for Tanzanians. This was the day when someone said, enough is enough. They took the law into their hands in an effort to end police corruption.

An anonymous policeman from Mikumi Police Station, confirmed, "At 11:20am we received a call from a member of the public, who told as they had found two dead policemen in a police car. There were business cards on their chests. A colleague went immediately to investigate and found the report was accurate." A policeman at Korogwe Police Station confirmed they had received a similar report at 10:45am.

For three days, the Police Service remained tight lipped, just as The Ghost had suggested might happen in an email sent to our office at 11:00am on Tuesday the 26th March.

Dear Editor

45 minutes ago, five corrupt traffic policemen were killed after asking for a bribe for a nonsensical motoring offence. Enough is enough and today we put an end to

police bribery and intimidation. Attached are photos and videos of the dead policeman. Do your homework and confirm these deaths, as the Tanzanian Police Force may try to cover the murders up. With this single act, no longer should Tanzanians have to accept police and state intrusion, coercion and corruption. From now on, every time a police officer asks for a bribe, they will be dealt with swiftly.

The Ghost

Why have neither the Ministry of Internal Affairs nor the Police Commissioner made an official comment for three days about the slaying of their officers? Are they worried, the status of police officers being considered untouchable, being so openly and violently questioned? The lack of information from the authorities raises many more questions than gives answers. We will keep asking until we get those answers.

Seeing the newspaper article which had been copied verbatim from my email to Danny two days earlier, I immediately sent Tony an SMS.

> Check out the Tanzanian Enquirer website you northern monkey!

The article was also Sasha's cue to collect the 10,000 t-shirts and distribute them through our network. The selling of t-shirts would not be a major new revenue stream in and on itself, but it would bring extra foot traffic into our bottlestores and enhance the implicit connection between the bottlestores and The Ghost brand. This linkage would be reinforced through our selling of The Ghost high-energy drinks.

81. BOGOTA

Though I was not in Columbia, Tony later described his meetings with the cartel. It all started when he felt his trouser pocket vibrate from a notification of an incoming SMS. He opened the message. Checking the website, he must have been excited to read what had happened in Tanzania.

'Gentlemen,' he'd started the conversation, 'we're here to talk business. I told you there would be a story which would grab your attention and which highlights the seriousness of my partners. When I said it would involve a ghost, you laughed about African black magic, witchcraft and other such things, but if you go to the Tanzanian Enquirer website you'll see it's no joking matter.'

Diego and Santiago typed the web address into their smartphones; they were not expecting to be met by such a headline. Tony told me with a big smile, 'It was great theatre.'

'This Ghost is making a name,' a clearly surprised Diego spoke first.

'Indeed, he is. This is all part of our criminal corporate branding. We have eight bars in our network which are our distribution hubs. Shortly, we will be opening the most exclusive bar in East Africa. It will be invitation only, with members including Judges, Cabinet Ministers, CEOs and Police Commissioners… we have dirt on all them. Any problem that we might encounter in the future, though we're not expecting any, will be easily resolved. You will of course receive complimentary membership.'

'You have your bases covered,' Diego congratulated Tony.

'We have; there's no risk to you or your men. All we need to do is agree on a rendezvous point in the Indian Ocean off the Tanzanian coast. We have an initial order of $1 million and expect this to increase to a monthly order of $10 million within three months. We are looking to exit all associated business operations within 20 months, at which time, if you or one of your contacts would like to take over our business of import and distribution of narcotics in East Africa, plus buy significant capital assets, you will be given first refusal.'

'One step at a time, my friend. You must understand, any deal less than $2 million is not worth our time let alone the risk.'

'We fully appreciate the need for your own business case,' Tony calmly replied having expected such as reply. Together with Jonas, the three of us had formulated a reply. 'We ask you to give us credit of $1 million on which we are happy to pay $200,000 interest per week. Our second order will be for $3 million, and at which time we will repay $500,000 of the loan principle, plus the accrued interest. Our third order will be $5 million, and we will repay the remaining loan interest and principle. We understand the risk that you are taking, but we hope the prospect of $2 million interest will show you how much we respect a partnership with you.'

'That's not the way we do business, its money up front or not at all.'

'If I told you that in our business model, we expect over the next 18 months to buy $250 million product from you, would that change your mind?'

'No,' Santiago responded immediately.

'When I said, $250 million, that's only 50% of our expected order. Assuming you make a conservative margin of 40%, then you would have a profit of $200 million, plus of course the initial interest on the loan.'

'On those figures, why not borrow $1 million from someone?' Diego quite reasonably wanted to know.

'Of course we could, and I'm sure the VIPs would jump at such an opportunity, but management have discussed and prefer to build a mutually beneficial business relationship with you based on trust from the get go; this small loan shows trust from both sides.'

'No, it shows trust from our side. Where's the show of trust from your side?'

'Firstly, we exposed ourselves to you as being the team behind The Ghost. Secondly, we have been upfront about our business model and exit strategy. Lastly, you have the opportunity to enter new markets and take over our existing infrastructure and a distribution network when we exit.'

'Assuming we go ahead and you give a loan with an interest of $3 million and not $2 million, what are your provisional operational recommendations?' Santiago asked, now seemingly satisfied.

$3 million was more than we'd been hoping for, but it was not a major problem in the bigger scheme of things. More importantly, it started to build a bond of trust between us and the cartel with no need to involve third parties. '$3 million is ok, but I ask that we make the repayment over a three-month timeline and in one full payment rather than instalments so that it doesn't affect our cash-flow for other operational activities.'

'Fine,' Diego finally came to a decision after a long conference between the pair. 'You have a clear business model and attitude; we appreciate that in partners. To operations... what, where and when should our contact meet yours?'

'We'd like to meet your courier 200 kilometres south-south-east of Mafia Island.' There really is such a place. It's a marine national park, a paradise... rather than a bad pun and unlikely fiction! 'Two of our operatives will charter a private yacht and rendezvous with your contact at midnight for the exchange. They will continue to the Tanzanian coast and meet a third operative who will have transport ready to take the product in-land for cutting and distribution. We expect product to be on the street within seventy-two hours of the exchange.'

'How soon do you need product?' Diego queried.

'Within the next two-to-three weeks.'

'The night of 22nd April,' Santiago suggested after checking his calendar and doing some mental arithmetic. Give us a down payment of $200,000 and we can get the ball rolling.'

'If you can give me the bank details, my partners will do a wire transfer and the money will be with you in less than forty-eight hours.' Jonas, Tony and I, knew this is where everything would hinge. We thought there was a 60:40 possibility that once we had transferred the money we would not see the delivery in three-weeks-time, and possibly Tony ever again. It was a risk we had to take, no more so than for our friend. There was no way round asking the cartel for the loan as our finances were stretched very thin what with getting everything operational in Tanzania.

'Of course,' Diego addressed Tony, 'you will stay at our pleasure until we confirm the money has been received.'

'Naturally,' Tony coolly replied, no doubt with butterflies in his stomach; he was the cartel's insurance. 'It's a pleasure doing business with you,' he however declared, hoping the reassurances that Jonas and I had given him multiple times would turn to reality.

82. THE BLUE LABEL BAR

Three weeks later and with all bottlestores opened, ghost t-shirts and drinks selling like fatted geese and, confirmation that the cocaine shipment was due for collection the following evening, I was confident to start with the last part of our expansion phase, the launch of The Blue Label Bar. As such, Chidi who had earlier changed the number plates, tax and insurance discs on the 2nd hand Toyota Noah, one of the most common cars in Tanzania, hand-delivered the 100 invitations.

Finishing his day's work, Judge Warioba, who Watson and Terry taped discussing fixing the outcome of a trial, first in favour of the defence... and then the prosecution, went to Africana Bar for a drink with friends, this before meeting his teenage mistress. As he was leaving, he was somewhat puzzled to see an envelope under the windscreen wipers of his Land Cruiser Prado. The immediate questions that must have come into his mind, I assume, were, how did that get there? Who put it there? And, why was it put there? No doubt, his questions only increased when he opened the envelope and saw the invitation to The Blue Label Bar opening night and membership rules. More surprising though than any of those questions, must have been how someone had apparently found out about his proposition to rig a trial two weeks earlier... or at least that would have been my reaction.

83. The Rendezvous

While Chidi was busy handing out invitations, Jonas had given Watson and Terry the go-ahead to charter a yacht and make their way to Mafia Island where they would spend the night before proceeding to the rendezvous point to meet the cartel's courier.

After an early lunch of a cheese and tomato Panini, they got in their dinghy, rowed back to the yacht and set the auto pilot to 200 km south-south-east of Mafia Island. Thirteen-hours later, and thirty-minutes after the planned rendezvous time, the cartel's speedboat arrived at the agreed GPS point. Exchanging $800,000 cash for 200 kilograms of uncut cocaine, the two boats went their separate ways into the silence of the night. Keeping radio silence, Watson steered the yacht to a small beach on the Tanzania coast where I met him.

'How did it go?' I asked in a low voice.

'Like clockwork. The South American boys were very professional.'

'Good stuff. Let me load the cocaine into the car and I'll meet you back in Dar es Salaam this evening to start cutting.' In less than 24 hours, cocaine with a street value of $5 million was cut, mixed and en-route to my bottlestores.

84. CURIOSITY KILLED THE CAT

Whatever questions had gone through Judge Warioba's mind since he'd received the mysterious letter, he nevertheless came to The Blue Label Bar on the aforementioned date with his chequebook. He followed the directions given on the invitation letter to the lane leading to the bar. Looking at the CCTV images, I could see the judge was surprised to see lightly armed security guards patrolling the road near the entrance and that he didn't have to show any identification. Regarding the latter, I had made sure that all staff knew all the VIPs by sight... and also their peccadillos. I imagine the judge must have been thinking, if these people know about my offer to the prosecution and defence teams, then they must already have my identification details and car registration—he was correct.

The judge looked at a guard who pressed a button on his tablet which registered Warioba's entrance to the secured compound. The guard then spoke into his walkie-talkie to advise the more heavily fortified gate to the inner sanctum, seventy-five metres up the road and where the security guards would do a vehicle check, ostensibly to check for bombs in and/or under the car, but in reality just as a show of reassurance to the VIPs that they were indeed about to enter very rarefied, secure and exclusive surroundings.

Through the CCTV cameras, I watched the judge enter the premises, surprise on his face as he recognized some of the number plates of fellow members. The next thing that caught his eye, was a fellow judge and a cabinet minister frolicking in a jacuzzi with four scantily clad young women. 'Fun can be had,' the cabinet minister shouted to the judge on seeing his friend, a smile spread wide on his face. Warioba then went to the bar, where he would have seen that it was expensively furnished and had a fine range of wines, spirits and imported beers. There was an adjacent lavishly fitted-out fumier for cigar smoking.

While the judge was taking in his surroundings and looking around to see who else he might recognize, he was approached by 24-year-old Julie. She had a light complexion, short hair and a slim waist; she was an MBA. 'Judge Warioba, can I get you a double Martini on the rocks with a slice of lime?' She asked, and who like the guards had been given profiles of all the members. I wanted all the VIPs to be impressed by the attention to detail we'd put in, including how they liked their favourite drink. The flip-side to such attention to detail, was the VIP would be under no illusions what would happen if they broke the house rules. I actively wanted them to think, if they go into that much research to find out how I like my drink, how far do their tentacles reach?

'Thank you,' the flattered judge replied. Soon after Julie had given him his Martini on the rocks, the judge had come to a decision. 'Where do I pay my $10,000 joining and membership fee?'

In our cash flow calculations, and which were vital for our negotiation with the cartel, Jonas and I had planned for a 90% attendance and 70% payment on the first night, with the other 30% to be paid in the coming week; this was the only way our sums would add up. Thus, we were pleasantly surprised when all but Police Chief Inspector Mrope of the many mistresses, didn't come to the opening night, and of all those that did, 85 made payment. We were immediately $920,000 richer and which would cover 25% of our next order from Columbia, the other 75% coming from sales of the first shipment. It had been a very intense six months, but my plan was very much on track.

85. LAWYERS

Over the next twelve-months business boomed and it was soon time to fine tune my exit strategy. On a parallel front, having won the unfair dismissal case at the Court for Mediation and Arbitration, I assumed GlobeTel would pay up and that would be the end of that particular headache. But, apparently not, this as I read GlobeTel's appeal to the High Court. Though it was GlobeTel's legal right to appeal, all involved knew it was a tactic being used to, 1) slow down the process of restitution, 2) frustrate me, 3) bite into my financial resources, but most importantly, 4) set an example and deterrent to any other would be disgruntled former employees who considered taking GlobeTel to court for labour related issues. While financially any settlement in my favour was now not the imperative it had been 18 months earlier, the principle of justice made me want to continue fighting. The irony of taking GlobeTel to court for not working within the labour law, while simultaneously breaking multiple rules was not lost on me.

'Just because you won at the Court for Mediation and Arbitration, it's only the battle and not the war that's been won,' Gordon informed me. 'GlobeTel's lawyer even told me,' he continued, 'that even if you win at the High Court, they'll take the case to the Supreme Court; are you ready for the long haul?'

I was surprised as to why GlobeTel were being so obstinate, but not to worry; with my new source of influence at The Blue Label Bar, I was confident I could expedite the case. It was just a question of getting the right person, to ask the right question, at the right time and, most importantly, into the right set of ears… and which after all was the principle value proposition of being a Blue Label Bar member! 'Thanks for your efforts. Let's hope the High Court doesn't take long to come to a conclusion.'

'Indeed. How's your family and business?'

'I can't complain. The consultancy is going fine in spite of GlobeTel's best efforts to sabotage me. It's clear they put out the bad word,' I informed Gordon, and which in truth was now my main motivation to keep pursuing the case. 'I was doing some research for a client who wanted me to engage on their behalf with GlobeTel; they refused to meet me and which cost me the contract. If they think I'm just going to disappear, they miscalculated.'

'Good to know you're keeping your chin up. How's your visa?'

'Fine,' I monosyllabically replied, as I started to wonder, why all the questions?

'Where do you live now? Do you have an office?' Gordon persisted his questioning.

'I live near White Sands Hotel and recently opened an office in Mwenge.' Why all the probing questions? I asked myself again. 'I'd better get going,' I told him, my sixth sense starting to feel uneasy.

86. THE PIGEON HOLE

When Judge Warioba next visited The Blue Label Bar, and which had become a thrice weekly event, he saw a note in his pigeon hole. The pigeon holes were a row of locked boxes with a small opening for letters or notes to be inserted (hence their name). Each compartment had the initials of the member on their respective box. It was an easy, cheap and confidential way for members to anonymously communicate with each other… though as I had a master key, I could read all correspondences and which I did on a daily basis.

> Dear Judge,
>
> It has been noticed that your judicial brethren, specifically Judge Nkhoma, is taking longer than might be anticipated on certain cases which deal with appeals from the Labour Court for Mediation and Arbitration. So employers don't use this as a tactic at the expense of aggrieved former employees who have less resource to fight a long court case, please can you recommend to your fellow Honours to expedite these cases.
>
> Your friend and fellow member.

This was the first note that the judge had received and which I think was a reasonable request. I presumed members liked the idea of anonymous requests, knowing that they could also ask for a favour as and when needed. It's quite some power base to be able to call on 100 influential members to scratch your back.

I knew from information that Watson and Terry had gleamed, that the judges next unofficial monthly get together at The Sheraton Hotel happened to be later that week. While Judge Warioba knew that his two fellow judges were also members of The Blue Label Bar, he wouldn't have known that they had also received the exact same note, thus, I was very confident my request would be proposed and my case duly expedited. Knowing what had gone on behind the scenes, I was delighted to hear from Gordon that my case had indeed been rescheduled for two-weeks-time and not several months down the line as it had originally been.

87. FACEBOOK

Some days after I'd met Gordon, I received a Facebook message out of the blue from Belmont. He was GlobeTel's fixer. I'd had built quite a good friendship with him when I first started in Tanzania. He had assisted me with finding a house, getting a local driving license, a social security number, a work permit and, introduced me to some of his friends outside of work hours.

> I have some bad news. It seems you have started to seriously worry GlobeTel's management with your court case. Peter thinks you have no chance of success, but nevertheless asked me to make sure you lose or are forced out of the country. Peter knows you were on GlobeTel's work permit after you were fired and he told me to set the Immigration dogs on you. Sorry to land you in the shit, but you know how life is... what else can I say or do? I know I won't get paid better elsewhere and, if I do this, Peter said he would personally give me a cash bonus. This message is just to forewarn you.

I'd bumped into Peter a number of times over the previous eighteen-months, none had been particularly cordial affairs. I was sure he desperately didn't want me to win the case as any pay-out would have to be authorized by GlobeTel Head Office, and though it was a relative drop in the ocean for them, it would nevertheless not be good for Peter however he tried to spin it. I thanked Belmont and reassured him that I knew he was in a no-win situation.

After sending my reply on Facebook, I called Jonas. 'Things are running smoothly and we just need to keep going for a few more months and then we can move into the exit phase.'

'Yeah, man, we've done the hard 80% and just need to keep our nerve. We run all operations as business as usual and, open The Fun House as planned.'

'I'm in agreement,' I concurred. 'Something might have come up.' I took a brief pause. 'Peter is planning a move against me in regards my ongoing court case. He's ordered the GlobeTel fixer to cause me immigration troubles.' I then summarised Belmont's email.

'Let's not panic,' was Jonas' first words after thirty seconds of silence. 'Why are those wankers not prepared to pay up and move on?' he rhetorically asked. 'I'll double-check, but I'm 99% certain sure that you are allowed to legally stay in Tanzania if you are taking a former employer to court. Give me a few days to work through all the legal ins and outs; worse-case scenario, we call in favours through The Blue Label Bar.'

'For now, I'll play with a straight bat and spend a few nights in police cells, but I will need you to be the cavalry and get me out of dodge quick-smart if needed; in prison, anything can happen… I could get stabbed.'

'Don't worry, mate; I have your back.'

'Ok. Let's not involve anyone from The Blue Label Bar unless a last resort. Let Peter think he's getting one over on me, but assign Watson and Terry to do some extra surveillance on him in case he tries any other dirty tricks.'

88. The Best Laid Schemes o' Mice an' Men, Gang Aft A-Gley

Peter was not the only problem that Jonas and I had to contend with. While supply from the cartel was smooth and Tony was managing the relationship skilfully with frequent visits to Bogota, bringing that much cocaine into the market upset competitors. Plus, the mere logistics of distributing cocaine—which now had a street value of $3 million per week—had its inherent challenges. It had been Chidi who had called the meeting. 'The police are really cracking down on our dealers, not just in the capital but all over the country. I'm not confident our street boys will keep their mouths' shut. They might let slip information which leads back to one of the bottle-stores… and who knows after that.'

'Where do you think this pressure is coming from?' Jonas wanted to know.

'My best guess, the Mwanza Playaz Gang. We know they import through the Kenyan border and have been doing so for over ten-years. They must have contacts high up at border control and the police. If we are eating too much of their market share they will try and put us out of business. I think the recent heat is a warning shot.'

'You think it'll lead to war?' This from me.

'I wouldn't bet against it, unless we can come to some sort of agreement with them.'

'Do you know how much they distribute?' Tony, who had flown in from Bogota overnight queried.

'It's difficult to be accurate, but I estimate around $2 million a month,' Watson answered. 'But this is just a guess.'

'They're small fry,' Tony pointed out, 'we supply ten-times that.'

'Do we know who their supplier is?' I asked. Everyone shook their head. 'If we start a fight then we're not earning. Tony, get in touch with the cartel and see if they can do anything their end to slow the Playaz supply.'

'On it, boss.'

'Chidi and Sasha, I want you to go to all distribution points and check if there are any leaks. If you have any suspicions, fire the managers and replace them. Watson and Terry, see if you can find out anything more on their distribution chain, from import to the street. Work with our Kenyan contacts if you need to. Jonas, talk to Julius and order him to find out who is causing us heat from inside the police. I'll talk to some financiers and see if we can't up our order to $5 million a week... so we can start a price war and take their remaining market share. We have good product and good operations; let's not make this an issue. We send them an unequivocal message that Tanzania is our sandpit, and if they want to play, they go through us.'

89. A RAT?

That evening I had a drink with Jonas. 'Could it be someone from within who's aligning with the Playaz and double-crossing us?'

It was a great question and one which truth be told, I hadn't really considered, I had faith in all my team. 'Who?'

'I'm just putting the question out there; we have to consider all possibilities.'

'You're absolutely right. Any suggestions?' I asked.

'No, but we must look at each and every one carefully. I would start with Watson and Terry as Kenya is their former playground.'

'Chidi as well?'

'We have to check. Besides, what do we really know about him other than what he told us about his army background? Things seem to come very easy for him, maybe too easily?'

'He's killed with us!' I couldn't believe Jonas doubted him. 'Maybe it's someone closer to home, Julius? He's a slimy sod who would sell his grandmother if it in anyway benefited him. He knows we have the dirt on him, maybe he's looking for a backup option for a partner?'

'I'll get Watson and Terry to get more background on him?'

'I thought they were potential suspects?'

'They are, but we can't let them know that. We have to proceed as if we have no suspicions.'

90. Ring Ring

Two nights later, and while having a sleepless night thinking about the challenge the Mwanza Playaz were putting down, a potential rat in our crew and, the ongoing annoyance that was Peter, the front door bell rung; it was 3am. Though I knew this moment would come, I'd decided not to forewarn Amy. If I acted stupefied, then she would be genuinely shocked, scared and surprised. This was important so as not to give the police and/or immigration officers any inkling that I knew what was about to go down.

'Who the hell is that?' I angrily shouted after the bell had been wrung for the fifth time.

'Probably some drunk at the wrong house,' Amy replied, as she walked over to the curtains as annoyed as I was pretending to be. 'What the hell?' She now sounded a little frightened. 'It's the police,' she informed me, this when she saw blue and red lights flashing. 'What do those idiots want at this time in the morning?'

Two minutes later, and after letting the police through the front gate, Amy's question was answered. 'Show us your passport,' the police commander demanded.

'What for?' I sounded incredulous. 'I have a business permit.'

'JUST GET YOUR FUCKING PASSPORT!' Was shouted in my face.

'Ok, ok,' I said meekly stepping back as I put on an Oscar winning performance of someone shitting their pants. 'My children are asleep. Wait outside. I'll be thirty-seconds.'

'You two,' the police commander pointed at two heavily armed junior officers, 'go with him.' As I walked inside, I heard the officer-in-charge, say, 'I'm counting,' this before letting out a big belly laugh.

'Here.' My voice was bullish and inflicted with utter displeasure at being woken for such a bullshit frivolity as I gave my burgundy document, opened at the business permit page, to the commander.

'I have a letter which states, you left GlobeTel's employment in May last year, and yet it seems you used the same permit for another six months rather than leaving the country; you were here as an illegal alien.'

There it was, Peter's masterplan to get me thrown out of Tanzania. 'No. I took GlobeTel to the Court for Mediation and Arbitration for unfair dismissal, and thus was legally allowed to stay here on that permit,' I informed them, indicating I now understood what all the hassle was about. My show of bravado was primarily for Amy's sake.

'No, you weren't,' the commander confidently informed me. 'Arrest him,' he then ordered the two policemen who'd followed me indoors.

'Don't worry, Amy,' I tried to reassure my wife. 'Call Gordon and get him to meet me at the prison. If you can't get hold of him, call Jonas. Just tell the kids that I left early for business and I'll be back in a few days. Don't worry, everything will be fine.'

'Ok, Sweet. I'll also phone the British Embassy.'

'I'll be fine,' I said over my shoulder as I was manhandled into the back of the police pickup truck by the three policemen and two immigration officials.

'So, guys,' this as we drove to the police station, 'I hope GlobeTel are paying you a lot of money for this nonsense. You know and I know, that I'm legally allowed to stay in Tanzania if I have a court case against my former employer; don't you think that was one of the first questions I asked my lawyer? How stupid do you think I am to put my family at risk?'

'SHUT THE FUCK UP,' the policeman holding an AK47 shouted at me, his halitosis full blast in my face. As much as he was trying to intimidate me, I thought I detected a tinge of guilt in his tone of voice, or at least I did until he jammed his weapon in my gut full force.

91. BUSINESS ANALYST

I had no choice but to go along with the charade for the next few days until Gordon, Jonas or the embassy came to my rescue. So, once in the filthy cell which I shared with fifteen other sorry souls, and with plenty of time on my hands, I meditated. Peter, this is what getting personal means and it's my move next!

Having silently vented my fury, I moved as far away from the putrid bucket toilet which had a crack in it, the raw sewage seeping onto the floor. I had to find a way to be constructive, this the best way to pass the time. Knowing I was going to be stuck in prison for the next few days, and without all my usual day-to-day operational interruptions, I decided, I might as well use my time to analyse where things stood in the business and plan the next steps for my rapidly expanding criminal empire.

I tried to recall the introduction in my training manual, thinking that would be as good a place as any to start my analysis.

> Taking the analogy of a human body, the heart is the most important organ as it pumps blood (carrying oxygen) to the rest of the body. Sales are the 'heart' of any business, as it is the only part of a business which generates money / pumps blood to the rest of the body / business. With no heart / sales, the body / business will stop functioning.
>
> Marketing is the 'Brain', as it coordinates all the functions of the body / business. If the brain is not functioning, the body will still just about function, as the heart can still pump blood, but the actions of the limbs / rest of business will not work effectively or efficiently.

Accounts, operations, Information Communication Technology and Human Resources, are the 'limbs.' All need to work effectively for the business to work to its maximum capacity.

I started to analyse my business:

1. **Sales**—all revenue streams are doing well. The only real question I have is, what is my motivation to keep going other than the undoubted adrenalin rush? It was a rhetorical, though highly insightful question.
2. **Marketing**—The Ghost is the brand, but it needs to keep the public's imagination.
3. **Accounts**—Sasha knows what she's doing. Financially, I'm making more money than I can think what to do with, or rather, the value of the business is quickly accumulating in both fixed and liquid assets, especially the offshore account.
4. **Human Resources**—a good team, especially Jonas. My lieutenants: Watson, Terry, Chidi, Sasha and Tony are all dependable and trustworthy.
5. **Information Communication Technology**—keeping things quiet on internal communications, though I need to increase surveillance for the exit strategy.
6. **Logistics and operations**—I'm running a fairly tight ship with little leakage, but now need to open the Fun House and decide how to deal with Peter.

REFLECTION #16—
BECOMING DON CORLEONE

Once I'd mentally worked through all that needed to be done, I contemplated how I'd turned from volunteer to master criminal. I knew I hadn't planned for this life, and I certainly hadn't given up my life in Essex with Steph for such ill-gotten riches but rather with the express intention of using my business experience to help those most in need. I knew I'd lost my way, though I still had clarity on my end goal even if this meant through a criminal enterprise. The end justifies the means, I tried to convince myself... though failed. I knew darn well that what I was doing was wrong even if in principle it was for the right reasons. The real reason why I kept going, digging even deeper into the recesses of my soul, was the rush. I couldn't be weaned of the narcotic of adrenalin. I didn't even want to try and stop as I was having far too much fun. If that makes me sound slightly psychotic, so be it; label me as you like.

In regards having a rat on the good ship Crime, nothing of significance turned up in my private investigation. I had used a third party that no one knew about, not even Jonas. All my main friends and allies were clean and trusted as far as I was concerned. I had instinctively thought it most likely a disgruntled low-level runner that had switched allegiance and I remained of that opinion. I didn't consider the whole Mwanza Playaz episode bothersome, though perhaps I should have. It was good that Jonas had an open mind to pose such introspective questions as I was becoming somewhat blasé with the apparent ease that our detailed planning afforded. If I had taken Jonas' lead in this regard perhaps I wouldn't have ended up in a hole on the Indian Ocean coastline!

92. Masters-of-the-Universe

Two days after being arrested and, with no help from the embassies or Gordon, it was Jonas who got me released, this after having a word with Julius, our "friendly" Regional Police Commissioner.

As I was leaving the police station, I received a warning from the Officer-in-Charge, 'GlobeTel have big pockets and my men are hungry. I would leave the country my friend, or have deeper pockets.' I was not overly concerned by the threat.

'I've been having a think over the last few days,' I said to Jonas once freed from the rotten smell of the cells. 'We have four priorities: bring The Ghost out of retirement, start to make a dossier of all things GlobeTel, fast track the opening of The Fun House and, I need to give an old friend a call to start preparations for our end game.'

'I've been thinking the same. I'll bring the team together on Monday,' Jonas confirmed. 'We should meet outside of Tanzania, somewhere we can talk freely.'

'Where do you have in mind?'

'Nairobi. Watson and Terry are already there.'

'Nairobi it is; book the tickets.'

'Will do. Enjoy the weekend with the family and forget about the last few days,' Jonas advised. 'Things are moving in the right direction and we have much fatter fish to fry.'

'That, we certainly do,' I fully agreed, 'though I'm not letting Peter off the hook,' I continued the piscine analogy.

Once home, I looked through the latest set of accounts that Sasha had prepared. I saw that we were getting close to our target of $50 million cash-in-the-bank, the agreed amount we needed for the final phase of my plan. To be honest, I was amazed how much we had made in such a short space of time. Drugs import and distribution made up the majority of our income. It is unbelievably profitable if you have control of the whole value chain, I thought super smugly.

Satisfied, I phoned my university soulmate. 'Gillian, how are you doing? I hear on the grapevine that you're no longer a teacher but a stockbroker?'

'Indeed. I learnt how to be a hard ass in the classroom, but it's much more fun busting balls of little pricks who think they're mini-gods.'

'And it's going well?' The glamourous photos she'd posted on Facebook of her penthouse apartment and cavorting with handsome men while swilling champagne seemed to confirm that it was, but I asked all the same.

'Things are going very well,' she laughed loudly down the line. 'Teaching just wasn't for me, this life is.' She didn't expand further the reasons for her career change, though did open up some time later that she'd been physically assaulted by three kids at her school after which she'd resigned. She'd become a successful broker, before then establishing her own firm, this as her way of taking back control from males; she was very successful at it. 'Are you still in Africa doing consultancy work?'

'Yes, or at least some of the time.' I paused, not wanting to tell her the whole story straightaway.

'Come on, spit it out; I know there's something you want to tell or ask me,' she perceptively enquired.

'Yeah, you're right… there's a $100 million question.'

'That's real money.' I could tell she was interested in whatever I was selling. 'Where did you get that sort of mullah? What are you doing?' I could see dollar signs light up in her eyes. That size of money would excite anyone and especially a broker.

'We would like you to invest in African telecoms on our behalf.'

'Who is, we, and, our?' she immediately picked up. 'And what the FUCK?? Where did you get that sort of money?'

'I'm doing a bit of business with Jonas and Tony. I'll leave it at that for now.'

'Ok, I'm not here to question where your money comes from, it's none of my business.' She then paused, before continuing, 'I'm asking now as a friend, are you sure you know what you're doing? I hope you guys are not getting in over your heads.'

'It's all good, Gillian, don't worry, but thanks for asking.' I was genuinely appreciative that she was thinking about her friend and not the commission she would surely be making if my plan worked. 'I need a bit more time, but will be in contact in the coming months; just be ready.'

'Sure thing. Say hi to Jonas and Tony. Are they as nuts as ever?'

'Roasted and salted,' I laughed.

93. BRAINSTORMING

'I hope you all had a good weekend,' I said at the start of the Nairobi meeting. 'We're here for two days and while we shall enjoy ourselves, this is also a formal planning session for the next six months. In the short term, we have three priorities: Bring The Ghost out of retirement, make a dossier of all things GlobeTel and, fast-track the opening of The Fun House.' Apart from Jonas, the others had no need to know about my strategy of bringing Gillian into the team or what her involvement would be.

'Let's split into two groups and do an analysis of where we are at the moment. Both groups need to come up with plans for each of the three priorities. Watson, Tony and Sasha go with Jonas. Chidi and Terry, you're with me. We'll meet in two hours and share ideas.'

Jonas took a roll of flip chart paper and Magic Markers and led his group to a table in the left hand side of the King George bar, while I went with Chidi and Terry to the right corner of the room.

'So, lads,' I started as team leader, 'what do you think our current strengths and weaknesses are?' Twenty-minutes later, we finalized on:

STRENGTHS	WEAKNESSES
1. Existing distribution network	1. Not a business that's easy to delegate
2. Small core team of many talents	2. Never know what Tanzanians might do to screw you over
3. Association with The Ghost	3. Family members are unaware of what's happening
4. Diverse though complimentary range of revenue lines	4. Overstretching the amount of activities
5. Leverage and influence through The Blue Label Bar	

OPPORTUNITIES	THREATS
1. Open more bottlestores / distribution points	1. Columbian cartel stopping supply
2. Resurrect The Ghost and sell new merchandise	2. Implicitly dangerous / illegal activities
3. Open The Fun House	3. GlobeTel / Peter upping the ante
4. Start Jonas' Ponzi scheme	4. Mwanza Playaz or other new competitors entering the drugs market

Two hours later, and back in the bigger group, we compared notes. Over the next four-hours we finalized operational plans. Jonas and I would plan how to bring The Ghost out of retirement. Watson and Terry would put a dossier on GlobeTel and keep a closer eye on Peter and Gordon, the latter having gone suddenly and very suspiciously quiet. Sasha and Chidi would prepare the opening of The Fun House. Tony would continue to be our man in Columbia.

94. POINT TAKEN

With the day's business completed, we went to Black Diamond Bar and Nightclub and where we drank, danced and made merry to the early hours. All, except the ever spritely Sasha, were feeling the worse for wear as we boarded the plane back to Dar es Salaam the following morning.

Landing and then proceeding to the Ramada, I wrote up in detail the plans we had sketched out in Nairobi. In the evening, I met with Jonas to talk things through one last time. 'We have a solid crew. Once we execute the exit strategy, we need to sort these guys out big time for all the risks they have taken.'

'I'm in total agreement, they have been good… so far. The money will also make sure they keep their mouths shut.'

'Point taken.'

'It's going to be critical how we manage the cash flow while investing with the help of Gillian to build our share portfolio.'

'Certainly.'

'I know you will do it anyway,' Jonas smiled, 'but in this instance, and with so many moving parts, I think a project plan will be very beneficial. There is so much that could go wrong with either bad timing or activities being out of sync; we need to be careful and not overlook anything.'

'Agreed. One mistake and everything we have worked so hard for could go up in smoke—'

'And quite possibly with us in the middle of the flames,' Jonas interrupted my thought process, this to my slight annoyance.

'Point taken,' I replied for the second time in as many minutes, though this time slightly testily. Later that evening,

I asked myself, does Jonas think I'm getting sloppy? It was a good question, and I certainly needed to keep on my toes to make sure the plans didn't go awry. But in all honesty, up until then, almost everything had gone to plan. I concluded: I was on top of my game and that Jonas was overly worrying.

95. STRATEGY

While Jonas and I were planning how to resurrect The Ghost, and to set up entities to buy shares with Gillian's help, Watson and Terry started to plan how they would uncover institutional malpractice at GlobeTel. 'We thought of GlobeTel as the human body with the six areas that you mentioned in Nairobi,' Terry started.

Isn't that a little fillip for my ego, I thought as I smiled at my two loyal ex-squaddies, the pair having taken note of my business training.

'We reckon, at each level of the organisation they must be doing dodgy things, and other than your history with Peter we need to find other juice,' Terry continued informing me.

'I like your idea of splitting the company into general management and the six areas,' I magnanimously complimented them.

'We will also look at issues of corporate responsibility, investor relations, regulatory compliance, and all things legal; we are bound to uncover a few skeletons.'

'I like it.'

'We will start by tracking down other disgruntled former employees and find out what happened to them; what were their grievances and did GlobeTel threaten them.' Watson had taken over their presentation.

'I'll do some digging at the labour courts and see if I can get one of the GlobeTel human resources team to become my girlfriend, my inside girl so to speak, and who will be our unwitting mole to spill all the beans.' Terry was very confident in his ability as a ladies' man.

'Sounds like a plan,' I congratulated them. 'Remember, at the end of the research, surveillance and interviews, you need to present a report of all their misdoings in a very presentable fashion. We will keep some of the information for ourselves, but we might also choose to release some of the findings through our media contacts.'

'When we get to that stage, I reckon we might want to call on Jonas to chip in, he's a lawyer after all.'

'Point taken, Watson,' I now remember saying, though at the time I hadn't realized I'd also said, point taken, the previous evening when discussing plans with Jonas.

96. LOCATION, LOCATION, LOCATION

Chidi and Sasha agreed terms with the landlord for his double storey office and beer garden, and which with some revamping would be made into the Fun House.

'We will turn the ground floor into a nightclub,' Sasha explained when I visited the site.

'The upstairs will be where the real fun is had,' Chidi said with a big grin on his face.

'We need to do some redecoration and add a bar and swimming pool, but otherwise there is not much need for structural changes; the existing offices are about the right size,' Sasha continued.

'Agreed, but I think we need to differentiate between the nightclub and bar downstairs, and the Fun House. It will also be important to have separate entrances,' I advised. 'Implicitly, the two businesses are associated, but we have to differentiate for our punters.'

'I see where you are coming from,' Chidi, nodding his head. 'Customers might go to the nightclub or bar first and then go upstairs to The Fun House.'

'Exactly.' I confirmed.

97. Resurrection

Three weeks later, with the GlobeTel file starting to be filled, and the redecoration of the offices into the nightclub and Fun House well on its way, it was time to resurrect The Ghost.

'Lads,' I addressed Chidi, Watson and Terry, 'are you ready?'

'Yes, boss,' they replied in unison. The plan was to attack the Kawe Police Station, the shit stinking hell-hole where I had resided for three miserable, though quite productive days.

Parking our cars 100-metres past the police station at 3am, the four of us circuitously snuck back making sure all the while to keep in the shadows and out of view of any passerby's on the main road.

We had practiced this manoeuvre over the previous two nights, each knowing where to go and what to do. But unlike on the two dry-runs, we now each carried two twenty-litre jerry cans of petrol. Chidi went to the vehicles parked to the left of the police station, and Terry to the cars parked on the right. Watson went to the administration block, while yours truly crouched below the windows of the main building. While Watson, Terry and Chidi poured petrol onto vehicles and buildings, I used a white spray paint to quickly write, NO MORE, on the ground and draw the shape of The Ghost logo. My work finished, I propped my two cans of petrol under the windows of the reception area and put a scrunched up news-paper into the top which would act as a crude timing device. When I saw that the three others had done the same prepa-ration to their jerry cans, I gave a hand signal for all to ignite matches and throw them onto their respective petrol trails.

Our arsonist work done, we ran back to the car and within thirty-seconds of the police station going up in flames, we were each driving towards the highway and our respective homes.

Sasha had booked into Entertainment Hotel 200-metres from the police station earlier that day. As I and the guys were lighting our matches at 3am on the dot, she hit the record button on her camcorder to document the blaze.

After five minutes of filming, and having seen us drive safely away, she stopped recording, downloaded the film onto her laptop and emailed the film to journalists, editors, newspaper proprietors and TV producers with an accompanying statement.

> The public has had enough of the corruption and incompetence of the police, yet it seems the warning they received one-year ago has been forgotten. This is a reminder to the police, that you are vulnerable. You must respect the public and not take advantage of them. You are meant to serve and protect, not enrich yourselves.
>
> The Ghost

The film and email statement featured prominently on TV, radio and social media the next day, under the somewhat predictable headline, The Ghost returns to haunt the police and pun laden varieties of the same.

98. The Fun House

A month after the police station fire, Peter was in Dar es Salaam on one of his bi-monthly three-day business trips. I'd been reliably informed by Watson, that he'd spent the morning at Coco Beach where he'd been drinking coconut juice in an effort to cure his hangover; he'd been followed by Terry to La Dolce Vita till the early hours the night before.

That evening, Peter with GlobeTel senior management, decided to visit the newly opened Fun House to see what all the fuss was about. 'You have to sign this form before you enter,' came the voice from beneath a bushy moustache; it was our bald headed, 21 stone barman cum bouncer Ngake. The GlobeTel managers all signed the paperwork and handed over the $20 entrance fee. If they had taken the time to read the terms and conditions, they would have seen that whatever happened in the Fun House would be live-streamed onto the internet and, that "actors" would forgo all rights to future earnings. When I had read the same sort of disclaimer many moons ago while on my dentistry holiday in Prague, it just made me even more curious as to what lay within!

'In for a penny in for a pound,' Peter was recorded on the CCTV camera as saying to his colleagues as he passed Ngake and entered. At the top of the stairs, the friends were ordered to leave their bags and clothes in a locker, undress fully and, put on a white dressing gown; the excitement of patrons futhered increase at this point.

Leaving the sanctity of the dressing room, punters would enter the bar area. We had made a number of unique refinements from what would be found in most drinking establishments. The first thing the customer would see were twenty-or-so girls in bras and panties, others wore not a stitch of lingerie. Next, clientele would see a pole in the middle of a dance floor, clearly for pole dancing by the aforementioned scantily clad women. However, the show stopper was a glass fronted elevated swimming pool behind the bar which more often than not had a naked girl paddling in it, quite often with an amorous and aroused man paying her very close attention. It had been known for fucking to happen in the watery confines. This was not only allowed by management but actively encouraged.

Being brought up as a Catholic, when I had entered the Fun House for the first time ten days earlier, a big grin immediately came to my face and the words, Sodom and Gomorrah, came to mind, just as they had that unforgettable night in Prague. Looking at the CCTV camera screen, I could see Peter had an equally large smile on his face as he walked over to the bar and ordered a very over-priced whiskey.

Seeing Peter with a look on his face of what have I got myself into? Samantha, a tall, light-skinned girl, approached him. 'Hi, darling. Which girl do you want to fuck?'

Peter pointed to a full figured girl with braids. Samantha motioned for Jazz to approach. 'Which room do you want, sweetheart?' Jazz flirted. 'There are ten rooms, each with their own theme: mountain-top, romance, dungeon, lake, castle—'

'Dungeon,' Peter quickly made up his mind, his decision being caught on our hidden microphones.

Two-minutes later, and with the full bodied Jazz leading the way, Peter entered the dungeon. 'You must shower first… for cleanliness,' Jazz informed my former boss.

Peter de-robed, entered the shower and was shortly followed by Jazz, who getting on her knees expertly put a condom on with her mouth. 'Make sure you let the cameras see the action,' Jazz advised as she led Peter out of the shower and into the bedroom where she pointed out the five web cameras which were live streaming onto the Fun House's website; Peter was about to make his first foray into the world of being an internet porn star.

By now, you may be a little confused as to how we made money from the Fun House, after all we weren't charging the men to go with the girls as is the general business model for prostitution the world over. Let me explain. The business model, Jonas and I had devised, had four income streams. The first was through the entrance fee, a more than reasonable $20 and which guaranteed as much time with the girls as the punter wanted in one-hour slots. The second revenue stream, the vastly over-priced drinks at the swimming pool backed bar; a fruit juice was $10 and anything alcoholic was over $15. We made it a condition that the customer would have to buy at least one drink an hour when at the bar. We thought the customer would still think this was good value for money considering they didn't have to pay for going into a room with one of the gorgeous girls. Any drinks the customer bought for a girl, the money would be split 50:50 between her and management. Any tips a girl was given as the punter was re-acquainted with their clothes, was theirs to keep. Our third and principle revenue stream, was through subscription to our website showing live sex with ordinary amateurs. Our last revenue stream, was selling merchandise of both the Fun House and The Ghost brands, and which included, if the customer so wanted, a DVD of their performance.

True genius, had been Jonas' reaction when I'd first explained the concept to him many months earlier, though in truth, it was a replica of the business model of the place I had visited in Prague during my dental trip where, as a single man, I'd had a particularly enjoyable night of depravity.

Peter was a useless porn actor, his first performance lasting a mere thirty-seconds. Seeing his thrusting hips on the flat screen TV was just too much of a turn on for him, as indeed it was for many first-timers... myself included. On his second outing, and despite being constantly re-positioned by Jazz so the web cameras could get the best angles, and being told multiple times, keep your leg down it's restricting the viewing, Peter lasted a more respectable half-an-hour.

After an enjoyable time with Jazz, Peter rested in the sauna before going for a skinny-dip in the glass fronted swimming pool behind the bar and where he got chatting to the very attractive, petite Romanian Lori; she was the co-star of Peter's second film.

More than sexually satisfied, Peter returned to the bar and considered the last three hours of this once in a lifetime experience, though I expected he was already thinking when he would next return.

'The drink is on the house, from management,' Samantha, who had shimmered over to my former boss, said, as she put the glass on the counter, pausing a few seconds as she'd been instructed. 'Peter.'

'Pardon,' he spluttered into his drink. 'How do you know my name?' He'd been clearly caught off-guard.

'From the form you signed on entering,' Samantha replied, just as I'd told her to. This was not true; Peter had used a pseudonym. 'These DVDs are also for you,' Samantha continued while handing over the disks.

'Thanks.' I assume he was starting to wonder how Samantha knew his name and, why he'd been given the DVDs of his time in the mountain and dungeon rooms for free when it clearly stated that they cost $10. Peter would now be under no illusions that there were recordings of his sexual shenanigans. I wanted him to question himself, how such artefacts could be used in unfriendly hands. Pleasantly, a furrowed look came on Peter's face as he took the DVDs. I expect he was probably starting to if not regret his presence at the Fun House, at least starting to have reservations.

Five minutes later, Ephraim returned to the bar with a big smirk on his face. He sat down next to Peter; he'd purchased his DVDs. When Ephraim went to the gents, Peter was given another free drink from Samantha, but this time he was also handed a letter. I admit, it was very satisfying seeing him confused and unsure what game was being played with him.

Curiosity finally got the better of the cat and Peter started to read.

Peter,

You've enjoyed tonight, though what your wife and two children would think if they ever saw the DVD, I don't know; naughty boy. I'll make a deal with you, you never come back to Tanzania again and I won't email the DVD to your wife… how about it?

I know this will make your life difficult, what with you being the regional manager and all that, but you're a resourceful man as shown by you making other people's life difficult, most notably, a mutual acquaintance and former employee of GlobeTel.

If you accept this deal, then I ask you to sign on the dotted line below and give the letter back to the lovely Samantha as well as your robe and locker room key… and leave, now. If on the other hand you don't accept my deal, then I will ask the doormen to forcefully remove you from the premises, naked, and make a call to the police that you were causing problems with the girls; I'm sure a few nights in prison wouldn't be fun; I should know.

A difficult decision, and so I will give you one more drink on the house for Dutch courage and five minutes to make up your mind. After that, one way or another, you will be leaving highly embarrassed, but which all things considered, I feel is only fair considering you don't mind humiliating others when ejecting them from premises.

Yours hysterically,

The Ghost.

I watched Peter mumbling and heard through from the microphones, 'Holy shit, holy shit, what the hell is this? Who have I wronged? How the hell could they be connected to The Ghost? What's The Ghost got to do with this place?'

Beautiful! I had a supercilious smile on my face. Revenge really is a dish best served cold.

I gave Peter a few minutes more than the five I'd promised; I was interested to hear what he would say to Ephraim who had returned to the bar while eyeing up the lingerie wearing beauties.

'In business, all is fair in love and war; it's never personal,' Peter said beseechingly to his colleague.

'What the hell are you on about?' Ephraim, who was far more interested in Samantha, absentmindedly replied.

'I've never had a personal grudge against anybody, except maybe…' Peter remembered. 'But that's impossible, there was no way that little shit could have anything to do with this.'

'With what?' Ephraim was still very much in the dark about what Peter was on about.

'There's no way he could have some connection with The Ghost, not that anyone even knows who The Ghost is—'

'What?' Ephraim interrupted Peter's ramblings.

'I know lots of people. I have many conversations and speculation over drinks at dinners with cabinet ministers and the like; no one has an inkling about the identification of The Ghost.'

'It's most likely mistaken identity or some misunderstanding.'

'But if it was mistaken identity, how the hell did he know about my wife, my two kids and my name?' Peter asked in an increasingly worried state.

It was at this stage of utmost anxiety that I told Samantha, 'Go back to Peter with Ngake and two other bouncers hovering behind you.' I was masochistically looking forward to what dire option Peter would choose.

'What's it to be?' Samantha, all sweetness, enquired.

'What is this? What have I done? I've never done wrong to anybody,' Peter squirmed.

'It's make up your mind time,' Samantha coldly re-iterated. 'You have one minute before these gentlemen escort you out and I call the police.'

'Ok, ok.' Peter knew he had no choice but to leave and hoped he could get into Ephraim's car before too many people saw his nakedness. I'm sure with great misgivings, he picked up the pen and wrote.

I don't know who you are or what I've done wrong?

He signed the letter as requested then sheepishly handed his locker key and robe to Samantha. He told Ephraim, 'Get your bloody car, quick,' this as he made his way to the exit. At this stage, I left the office and quickly went down the fire escape stairs.

Walking out of the Fun House, Peter was greeted by a posse of Sasha's friends whom she'd earlier told to take pictures of Peter and post them on Facebook; I didn't care if this turned a few people away from entering the Fun House for fear of similar treatment, as we had more than enough money and could more than afford to lose a few clientele, though I actually thought, that all publicity was good publicity and, this would further publicise the now notorious Fun House. In business parlance, it was a win-win.

'Hi, Peter, fancy seeing you here… naked?' I had a mischievous sneer on my face; I just couldn't resist to see the expression of shock and horror on his face and witness his total humiliation.

'It must be a coincidence,' he mumbled in utter confusion. 'It just must be.' Back at the hotel, I was sure he would try to regroup and think what the hell he would do next, as never coming back to Tanzania was an impossibility for him, or at least that is what I would do if I was in his shoes and needed to buy some time to formulate a plan.

99. Sweet as a Nut

'Sweet as a nut,' Jonas said once I had gone back into the Fun House and through to the office where we had been enjoying champagne while watching Peter through the CCTV cameras and listening in on him.

'We now have even greater leverage over him with these DVDs,' I happily pointed out.

'He's confused, surprised and terrified, or at least I would be. Next time we ambush Peter, he will spill the beans on GlobeTel.'

'That's the plan,' I confidently agreed. 'Things are coming together nicely. We have two more months to get all our ducks lined up and then we start our exit strategy. Talking of which, how is the share purchase coming along?'

'I have my man in place with the accounts opened. We just need to start funnelling the money to Gillian to buy the shares for us, slowly for now, and then in a great rush as we count down to zero-hour.'

'Great. How about the other operations?'

'Chidi, Sasha, Watson, Terry and Tony are all doing a great job. We are making about $5 million a month profit from just letting everything roll as it is. As long as there are no hiccups, especially on the drug import and distribution side of things, we should be up to our target of $100 million within our two-month timeframe.'

'That's pretty much as we hoped. Have you started to make plans for your future life?'

'No, have you?' Jonas asked. 'It's been such a rush over the last two years I haven't even started to think of what to do afterwards.'

'GlobeTel will bring down a lot of heat on us once we are through with them; you do know that, don't you? They will use all their many resources to try and track us down.'

'Certainly. We will need to be completely off the grid for some time.'

'We need new identities.'

'Point taken,' I agreed. 'Talking to Tony the other day, he's started final negotiations with the cartel on buying our business and to organize transportation out of Tanzania.'

'I'll task Watson and Terry to organize new IDs for all of us, including your family,' Jonas promised.

'We're going to need to be extra careful as we get closer to the sharp end.'

'It's all in hand, we just need to keep our nerve and follow through with our plans. There's nothing that can go wrong,' Jonas confidently predicted. 'We've got to where we are from good planning and then executing. We must keep following the idiom: Proper Planning Prevents Piss Poor Performance.'

100. Transcript Number 1

Three days after Peter's humiliation he was safely back in Dubai, but what he didn't know, couldn't have known, is that while in Tanzania, Terry had broken into his flat and hidden a few listening bugs, thus when he got a call from my lawyer, Gordon, and which I admit was quite a surprise to me, I could read the transcript at my leisure.

GORDON: You might have heard, but all appealed labour cases to the High Court have been expedited… including your unfair dismissal case.

PETER: Thanks for the heads up, Gordon.

GORDON: I'm not going to commit professional suicide and throw the case. A word-to-the-wise, there's no way GlobeTel can win. It's a slam dunk for my man, and which I told your lawyers from the get-go; you should have settled.

PETER: It's the principle, Gordon. GlobeTel can't let an ex-employee go to court for unfair dismissal, otherwise all employees we fire will do the same; we had to make an example.

GORDON: You better start thinking of a plan B then, as there's nothing more I can do to slow down or stop the case.

PETER: You've done what I've asked. You've been well compensated. Put up a weak case at the final hearing and I'll take care of the rest.

GORDON: I have another ex-GlobeTel client starting a case next week.

PETER: GlobeTel must be a gold mine for you at the moment.

GORDON: The good times are rolling. Seriously though, you should give me a consultancy to sort out your human resource policies and procedures so that they follow labour law.

Reading the transcript, I could see that I was pushing Peter into a corner. I had been in that position nearly two years earlier and had come out fighting; I expected Peter would do likewise. With that in mind, I dispatched Watson to join Terry and keep round the clock surveillance on him.

The next update I got from my two ex-army employees, was that they had followed Peter to The Exchange Bar in Nairobi. There he met Judge Nkhoma of the Tanzania Courts. I had read transcripts of their previous discussions about the progress of my case, the judge brazenly saying on their last phone call: before I commit to throwing the case in GlobeTel's favour, we must meet face-to-face.

If I was in the judge's shoes, I would also want to meet in person so I could size up the man I was dealing with and see how much money I could squeeze out of GlobeTel. As with any negotiation, it's best to do it eyeball-to-eyeball.

'Good to finally meet you, Judge,' Peter, shaking the offered hand. Watson and Terry were sitting at an adjacent table and recording the conversation.

'Please call me, Shaka; all my friends do,' the judge coolly replied.

'Can I get you a drink, Shaka?' Peter, knowing full well that he was now in a game of poker and wanting the judge to do all the running in the conversation.

'So, to business, Peter,' the judge wasting no time now that he had a whisky and tonic in hand. 'Let's not beat around the bush. You want me to put a ruling in GlobeTel's favour against the respondent, is that correct?'

'Correct,' Peter confirmed. 'I'll be straight with you, Shaka. It's not strategically in GlobeTel's interest to let highly paid expatriate staff, or for that matter any employees to start claiming unfair dismissal. If he wins, this could open the floodgates to other disgruntled former employees claiming against us; it will cost time and resource to fight them all. We want to cut this case off at the knees so to speak.'

'You mean, make an example?'

'Yes, judge.' Having set the tone for the parlay, both took a brief pause in anticipation of the upcoming negotiation.

'GlobeTel didn't follow proper disciplinary procedures. This is clear from the Court for Mediation and Arbitration ruling.'

'We beg to differ,' Peter, quickly responded, before taking a gulp from his draft beer and shovelling a handful of salted peanuts into his mouth. 'All I'm asking, is that you see that there is enough flexibility in the Court for Mediation and Arbitration ruling for it to be overturned.'

'And if I do that, what's in it for me?'

'We will pay you the same amount of money we would have had to pay out if we lost. To reiterate, it's not a question of money for GlobeTel, but of setting a dangerous precedent.'

'You're giving me 75,000 reasons to rule in your favour?'

'Yes. We can pay this into any nominated account from head office so that there is no traceability from Tanzania operations. If need be, we can set up an offshore account for you.'

'I already have one,' Shaka nonchalantly informed the man opposite him, and for which I presume was used for other such corrupt transactions. 'Thank you for being candid with me, Peter, I will let you know my decision by the end of the week. Now that business is out of the way, let's enjoy ourselves at this fine pub. The prawns are brilliant and go very well with any South African White Wine; I personally recommend the

KMV Cathedral Cellar Chardonnay 2013—it's quite exquisite. Next door is a nightclub where you can find beautiful girls; you'll enjoy.'

101. TRANSCRIPT NUMBER 2

I was slightly disappointed there wasn't any negotiation—
Judge Nkhoma accepting what Peter was offering. Nevertheless, I now knew what I needed to do to further ratchet up the
pressure; I went to work.

Two days later, I received another transcript from Terry,
this also originating from Peter's Dubai flat.

PETER: Judge, thank you for the very enjoyable evening
in Nairobi.

JUDGE NKHOMA: I'm glad you had fun. I've been review-
ing the Court for Mediation and Arbitration ruling and the
affidavits from both GlobeTel and the respondent. The risk is
too high for me to rule against your former employee.

PETER: What do you mean?

JUDGE NKHOMA: You did not follow the correct procedures at any part of your employment process with this
person. There is not enough doubt for me to overrule the
original ruling. It would be professional suicide and my fellow judges would ask too many questions if this ever went
to the Court of Appeal.

PETER: Is there nothing I can offer that would change
your mind?

JUDGE NKHOMA: I will be frank with you, Peter, I do
understand your situation and the labour laws as they currently stand are heavily in favour of the employee. I truly
sympathize, but I have political ambitions and can't afford
any questions being asked about my impartiality; I'm sorry,
but you'll have to think of something else.

After reading the transcript, I felt invincible. However, you might be wondering why Nkhoma did such a volte-a-face… well, I left a little detail out. After reading the transcript of Peter and the Judge's meeting in Nairobi, I wrote a letter to Judges Warioba and Banda and deposited it in their respective Blue Label Bar pigeon holes.

> Dear Judge,
>
> It has come to my attention, that one of your brethren, Judge Nkhoma is making large strides in the world of the judiciary; I believe it would be beneficial for The Blue Label Bar for him to become a fellow member.
>
> If Judge Nkhoma becomes a member, he must restrict himself to any negotiations and/or contracts with fellow members, and this includes any ongoing discussions that he may or may not be currently having with third parties.
>
> I look forward to his nomination within the week.
>
> Yours sincerely
>
> The Ghost

Do you now understand why I felt all powerful and that nothing could get in my way, much less stop me?

102. Savannah Lounge

Ten days after Peter's phone call with Judge Nkhoma, I was sitting at the bar of the Savannah Lounge, reading a book and trying not to think how the next two-weeks were going to play out. I'd gone through all the possible scenarios of our exit strategy many times, and it was now starting to mess with my dreams. I needed a complete break, an evening to ease my brain and reduce my stress. I thought, what better way than to sit quietly, have a few cold beers and do some civilian watching—individuals who were not involved in my sordid world—I was becoming increasingly pompous.

An hour after arriving at my usual haunt, a noisy crowd of university aged friends entered; I was reminded of my halcyon days.

'What a lovely bunch of coconuts, Christina.' the tallest of the boys addressed the barmaid as he walked through the doors of the bar.

'Can I put my banana between your peaches,' another of the boys joked.

'Cheeky young men, these coconuts are strictly for Darius's attention.' Christina playfully replied. 'And Afandy, Darius is the only one going to play with my peaches, and I'm the only one going to suck his banana.' everyone laughed.

'May I enquire what the house specials are tonight?' the one named Afandy flirted.

'Well, my dear, tonight and tonight only, double tequila is 5,000 Shillings and the special is the Savannah Lounge pineapple passion'

'What the fuck is in a pineapple passion?'

'Pineapple—'

'Yeah, duh.'

'I haven't finished yet.' Christina gave Afandy a peeved look for the interruption.

'Easy, coconuts.'

'Cheeky. As I was saying,' Christina tried to carry on, 'the pineapple passion consists of: pineapple, obviously, Afandy, but also Malibu, orange juice and Blue Bols; trust me, it's as lovely as I am.'

'Sounds a bit sweet for me, and I'm sweet enough. Four double tequilas please, Christina, and one for yourself.'

'Here you go, lads,' Christina said three minutes later as she brought the drinks over to the table where the friends were sitting. Don't get as hammered as last night.'

As I sat quietly observing the banter and reminisced about university and London house-sharing days, I noticed a gentleman enter. 'Guinness, please,' he ordered from the effervescent Christina.

'Would you like anything else?'

'No, thanks.'

'I've not seen you here before,' this as I offered my hand to the gentleman that went by the name, Nkhonde; I had become bored reading, slow drinking and seeing others enjoy themselves; I needed to chat.

'I'm just in town for the night on business,' he convivially told me as he relished his first hearty gulp of Guinness. 'Someone recommended here as a good place for a few drinks.'

'It gets fairly lively later on, if that's what you like.'

'That sounds promising.'

'What work do you do?' I asked while finishing my beer.

'I sell stationary. It's not the most exciting job in the world, but it pays the bills and I have my independence.'

'That's the main thing… as long as you have a bit of money left over for a few beers.'

'Cheers to that.' We clinked glasses. 'I've been an entrepreneur ever since leaving school. Sometimes I have good months, at other times…'

'Not so good,' I completed the sentence, to which he nodded his head in agreement at the challenges of being self-employed; we were kindred spirits.

'Can I get you a drink?' he offered when he noticed my empty glass.

'Thanks, I'll have a Guinness. I'm just going to the gents.'

Back from the gents, I saw the Guinness freshly served on the bar counter. 'Cheers, Nkhonde.' We clinked glasses again.

103. PRIDE COMES BEFORE A FALL

Eight hours after meeting Nkhonde, my body had almost given up the fight against dehydration. After regaining consciousness and some amount of lucidity, I realize that I'm buried neck deep in sand.

I looked around to try and get some sense of where I might be, but only see a golden horizon. There was no human life, not even fishermen pulling in their nets or readying their dugout canoes on this stretch of beach. Next I started to think logically how I could have ended up in such a predicament; I came up answerless. I tried to recall all that had happened before I blacked out, the last thing I remembered, something about: coconuts, peaches and bananas; I had no idea what that could mean. I started to become increasingly anxious as I saw the incoming tide was no more than fifteen metres, or thirty minutes away. I shouted, HELP! HELP! OVER HERE!

'It will do you no good, my friend,' a voice said from behind my head. Due to my immobility I couldn't turn around and see who the pronouncement belonged to. However, from these few words, I deduced I was starring death in the face… assuming it was not an elaborate prank by Jonas and Tony, I wouldn't put it past the pair!

The mysterious gentleman was standing just a few feet behind me, his shadow looming over me. I estimated it was early morning. I eventually figured out, I must have been drugged. I thought, most likely by the cartel double-crossing me, but why, I was not sure; we'd been good business partners. Maybe Tony had fucked-me over? More likely the daft twat did something stupid to annoy the Latinos. I hadn't a clue what had happened.

The shadow started to move and after an agonizingly long time the face to the voice came into view. It looked vaguely familiar but I couldn't immediately place it. 'What brings you to my attention?' he rhetorically asked in a cocksure and arrogant manner. 'And why, oh why, have I been tasked to kill you?' He was puffing a cigar, from the smell wafting on the sea-breeze, I instantly realized it was one of my best Cubans… a present from the cartel. So, it is them! I came to the conclusion.

'Good question, I don't know why anyone would want to harm me.'

'You must know something. I was paid $10,000 to bring you here and I'll get the same again in two-hours' time when I take a picture of your dead body. I suggest you think quickly of a good reason why I should set you free or enough information that my client would be willing to let you live; what's it going to be?'

'Well, it would help if I knew who your client was and what I'd done to upset them.'

'I'm sure you know as much as me, besides, there is no way I can give you that information. You'll have to rack your brains and see if you get lucky with your analysis.'

His arrogance was infuriating. I desperately started racking my brains, but had no idea who might have ordered my watery death, not that I didn't deserve it, my law breaking and hubris finally catching up with me. 'The Latinos?' I guessed, but got no response. 'The Mwanza Playaz?' I probed, but only to further silence from my captor, the only sound the lapping of the fast encroaching waves. 'Jonas? Sasha? Tony? Terry?' I desperately blurted out hoping beyond hope for some facial tick of recognition which I could use as the starting point for a negotiation. 'Watson? Chidi? Gillian? Peter? Ephraim? Belmont?' Nothing. This guy was the consummate professional.

'Why? Why did you do it? You are very rich, so rich in fact,' he eventually started to lecture me, 'you have what we call in the business, Fuck off money, that is to say, there is nothing that you couldn't say, fuck off to. Work for someone else, fuck off. Worry about not having enough money for your family, fuck off. Being in debt, FUCK OFF.' This last one he shouted as if he was really disappointed in me. 'Why then did you end up in a hole in the beach with hungry crabs licking their lips?'

REFLECTION #17— BUGGER—PART 2

And so, dear reader, this is where you found me at the beginning of my story—neck deep in sand, my assassin enjoying the taste of my stogie, the sweet aroma wafting on the sea breeze, as I, King Canute like, wished the sea would come no further up the beach while I contemplated my imminent demise.

104. MY ASSASSIN

'I don't know you and I don't know who you're working for,' I said to the gentleman as I tried to engage him in repartee while praying he might show some compassion, not that I deserved it for my many misdeeds in recent times. From his general disposition, I wasn't hopeful for being let of the hook. 'Similarly, you don't know who I can influence. How about, you tell me something that you really want; I guarantee I can make it happen.' It was my only, my last possible gambit.

'You have influence? I'm led to believe you're a business consultant?'

This reply indicated to me that he wasn't working for the cartel... unless he was bluffing. I wondered, how much has he been told about me and what does his client know about my double life? Maybe this has nothing to do with being The Ghost, the cartel or drugs, and is something completely unrelated or a case of mistaken identity? I really had no clue.

'Yes, I run a consultancy,' I answered, all the time thinking, what I should or shouldn't reveal. 'I get to meet a lot of influential people and I've built good relationships with a great many of them.'

'Give me an example.'

'Perhaps, you're looking for money or a new life? I can make anything happen, nothing is impossible.' I prayed that he would ask for something, anything; I was confident I could fulfil it however outlandish.

'Nice try, but you need to come up with something better in the next twenty-minutes; the tide's coming in quick.'

Indeed, the water was approaching fast and now only two

metres from my head. I watched the crabs scuttling by and who seemed to be giving me a curious look, as if to ask each other, I wonder what he tastes like? 'Try me,' was my short and simple riposte. I hoped beyond hope that he would question who the better paymaster was. 'If I fail to impress you, I die. If I fulfil your request, then we have something to talk about.'

'I have a brother in jail who was wrongly convicted of murder. You arrange his release within the next twenty-minutes and we can talk.'

'Not a problem,' I replied more confident than I felt. 'Let me use your phone and you will get a call from the Attorney General. I will do this to prove that it's in your interests for me to be your friend, dead or alive, rather than an enemy. If I get your brother released, tell me who put a bounty on my head, I'll then owe you a favour which can be called in at any time of day or night from anywhere in the world; how does that sound?'

'Reasonable. I hope you know what you're doing. What number should I call?'

'0756890536. You'll speak to a person called Jonas. Tell him the situation and then let me give him instructions.'

After my assassin had spoken to Jonas, it was my turn, 'Jonas, I'm in a sticky situation.' Sticky situation being our code to indicate a dire emergency. 'You need to immediately contact the Attorney General and tell him to call this number within the next fifteen-minutes. If for any reason you can't get hold of him, contact Judge Warioba or Regional Police Commissioner Julius.'

'On it,' Jonas tried to assure me, concern in his voice. 'Hang in there.'

'Sounds like you do know people.' I'd impressed my executor, the first hurdle crossed as he took the phone away from my face. 'You're not who you seem to be.'

'As I told you. Can you start digging a hole higher up the beach,' I cheekily requested. While I waited for the phone to ring, I started to contemplate the highs and lows of my life. I thought back to school, university, drinking benders in London and on the Kho San Road in Bangkok where I'd had wild sex with two LBFMs (Little Brown Fucking Machines) and which if politically incorrect is descriptively accurate. I considered how life had morphed from being a husband and father to my double life as The Ghost, where I was running a drug empire and the owner of Fun House and The Blue Label Bar. Would I be granted entry through the pearly gates of heaven and greeted by St Peter or cast to hell and be Satan's bitch?

It had been an interesting life full of anecdotes. I'd been to many parts of the world; Monday-to-Friday, nine-to-five was not my style. Sure, there were regrets, things I missed out on doing, routes I should have followed, decisions I should have made, and women I wished I hadn't slept with; but overall I wouldn't change a thing.

I reflected on the crossroads of my life, the two biggies largely influenced by songs, namely Lynyrd Skynyrd's FreeBird and, Eminem's Not Afraid. It only seemed right that another melody should be my farewell tune and I couldn't think of anything more appropriate than, My Way by Frank Sinatra. And so I started to sing this classic at the top of my voice, my rendition greatly bemusing Nkhonde.

My musings and atrocious singing was thankfully interrupted by the sweet, sweet sound of a phone jingle. Nkhonde answered. I heard just one side of the conversation.

'How do I know I'm really talking to the Attorney General?… I want to speak to my brother… He's in Dar es Salaam Central Prison… Ok, in ten-minutes… I'll wait.' He put the phone back in his pocket.

'Are you, what they call—a riddle wrapped in a mystery inside an enigma?'

Statement of Relief #3

As precarious as my position might have seemed in my preamble, I never said I was recounting my story from the other-side... like in some fictional books. I was in a hole, quite literally, but not yet dead.

105. Brothers

'Now that the wheels have been put in motion, your brother is as good as free. I can arrange for a vehicle to collect you from here, wherever here is.'

Five minutes later, the phone rang. Again, I only heard Nkhonde's side of the conversation. 'Hey bro, is this really you?... What was the secret word we had as children?... NO SHIT!... What have you been told?... It's all under control... You'll be out in ten minutes... Pass the phone back to whoever gave it to you... Yes, my brother needs a car. He's not to be followed... Good, you can talk to this fellow.'

'Who am I speaking to?' I asked as Nkhonde put the phone next to my sunburned face.

'The Governor of Dar es Salaam Prison'

'You have been instructed by the Attorney General to release the prisoner. Make sure your car is immediately available to him; you will be adequately compensated.'

'Who the hell are you?'

'Just do what I request.' I gave no entry for an argument. 'Let me speak to the prisoner.'

'Hello.' This a voice at the other end of the line.

'Hello, Nkhonde's brother,' I said loudly while looking into the eyes of my kidnapper, finally remembering who he was or at least claimed to be; Nkhonde remained as cool as a cucumber.

'I'm about to drown, and if I do, you and your brother will be tracked down and die a very slow miserable death. Reassure your brother that you are safe, that you are about to leave the prison and, that you have been given the keys to the Governor's car. When you are out of Dar es Salaam, make sure you are not followed and then call your brother who will give you directions where to meet him.' Instructions given, I pulled my head away from the phone indicating that I had nothing more to add.

The brothers spoke for another minute and then the phone was put back in Nkhonde's trouser pocket. 'Very impressive. I would like to be in a position where you owe me a favour. How about I dig you out of your hole and you jump into the one higher up the beach?'

'It's much better to have me as a live friend than a dead enemy.'

'Once my brother arrives, I'll tell you what I know about my client and inform Jonas where he can find you.'

Two hours later and much to my gratitude, the phone rang. Nkhonde gave his brother directions to where we were and then there was silence once again. 'Who gave you the contract?'

'Let's wait until my bro gets here; I don't want any surprises from your friends. I will write the information on a piece of paper and put it under that rock.' Nkhonde pointed to a large flat stone. 'I'm going to give you an injection so that you can't see my brother or know which direction we leave. You will be unconscious for six-hours and then delirious for four days. The antidote is in two parts, the first I will leave next to the note to ensure you don't die. The second, which will bring you out of your delirium, I will give instructions to Jonas where he can find it four days from now. If there is any attempt to find me or my brother in that time, or for any reason our exit from Tanzania is not successful, you will die of toxic shock. I'll make this very clear on the note and hope that Jonas is good at following rules. I will write details of the person who ordered the hit on you, but you and Jonas will have to do your own detective work to find out where the original instruction came from.' Nkhonde walked over and injected me with the venom; I blacked out.

106. THE END GAME

'Finally you're back in the land of the living.' This from a relieved looking Jonas. 'Everything is going like clockwork, well it had been until you were kidnapped. But we're back on track and into the last seventy-two hours till we finish what we started a little over two-years ago. Soon we will start new lives. You have to tell Amy what you've been up to.'

'Slow down. First, what did you tell Amy about my disappearance?'

'That you'd been called away at the last minute for a market research contract in the villages; this explains why you couldn't communicate with her. I don't think she bought my lie.'

'Ok. What's been happening over the last few days?' Hallucinating and bed-ridden, I was at a complete loss.

'I read Nkhonde's note—'

'I bet that was interesting.'

'And then gave you the anti-venom injection. The long and short of it... your kidnapping leads back to GlobeTel, most probably Peter. I don't know why he has such a hard-on for you? I'm sure all will be revealed when you meet him tomorrow.'

'Meeting, Peter? Tomorrow?' I was very surprised... though pleasantly so.

'I told him that he needed to be at the Fun House at 10pm; I didn't give him any option to say, no.'

'What else?'

'Gillian is lining up her team to do some major buying and selling on Friday. Tony is in final negotiations with the Columbians.'

'Sounds likes everything is going to plan. What do you need me for?' I joked.

'You're Verbal Kint!'

'What are you on about?' I didn't have a clue what he was referring to.

'You're the man with the plan... you know, Kevin Spacey in The Usual Suspects. Verbal Kint / Keyser Söze sets the whole scenario up just to knock off the Turkish guy who was going to give evidence against him; pure genius!'

'Oh,' I replied, my mind still too frazzled to get the Hollywood reference. 'I'll take that as a compliment.'

'Mate, we've been through thick and thin over the last few years, but we have not deviated much from your two-year plan that you first proposed in T-Square Bar while playing 50:50. I thought you were mad, but what can I say, we've almost pulled it off.'

'Not yet we haven't,' I cautioned, well aware of how close to death I had been a few days earlier.

'Who would have guessed your crazy plan would mostly come to pass and we would have a fortune close on $100 million and which is about to sky rocket.'

'Does everyone know what needs to do done? What have you told Sasha, Watson, Terry and Chidi?'

'I've told them nothing other than to continue business as usual. We keep them in the dark until they are contacted by our lawyer in Switzerland giving them a bank account number with many millions of dollars and a letter explaining all.'

107. AN INTRIGUING PROPOSITION

Tony met Diego and Santiago in Bogota. 'Gentleman, it's been 18 months doing business with you,' he recalled the meeting had started. 'I said at the beginning of our relationship that we were going to be in this for a limited amount of time, and that time is now upon us.'

'It's good business, yes? Why stop?' Santiago asked.

'The drugs business was only ever a means to an end; we are now near that final point. Cash in the bank, plus the value of our business which I give you first refusal to buy, when combined, reaches the monetary target we were aiming for.'

'You're happy to give your business up, just like that?'

'There's a $100 million price tag.'

'That's a very high price.'

'Not when considering the margin we make on every shipment. We calculate that it will take you six-months to get your investment back. You will have the fixed assets and an expanding distribution network into Tanzania, Uganda, Burundi and Rwanda. I should be asking you for $150 million, but we want a quick sale.'

'We decline your offer,' Diego informed Tony.

'That would be a shame. We've done business for some time now and you can trust me. The value we have put on our business is not only on expected future income, but also on the extensive amount of influence we have across East Africa; it's more than a fair price.'

'$60 million seems more reasonable,' Santiago started to negotiate. As an opening offer, this was higher than we'd expected.

'$60 million is on the low side. I have an alternative proposal.'

'Let's hear it, but no screwing around.'

'Respect, please. If we were messing with you, we wouldn't be having this very serious conversation.' Tony had become good at playing hardball.

'We hold you in high esteem, Don Tony,' Diego, was slightly taken aback by Tony's bullishness.

'Take your time before you answer.' Tony paused for effect. 'The reason why we are selling our going concern, is that all the money is going to be invested in some shares. I can't go into details, and will only say, we expect a significant return in a very short period of time. And so I offer you the following. You buy at the agreed price of $100 million, lend us a further $300 million for seven days, after which we will give you the $300 million principle back... and $100 million in interest.'

'The net cost of buying your business will be zero?'

'Precisely!'

'How are you managing that?' Diego was intrigued. 'If we're making 33% in that short space of time, how much are you making?'

'The how, is for us to know. The only question you have to ask yourself is whether you trust us; I hope you do.'

'You English fellows always seem very relaxed, but there are some cogs ticking away aren't there, my friend?' Santiago continued after a quick discussion with Diego, 'When and where do you need the money?'

'Like where a good clock is made and safe banks can be found, Switzerland. We need the money in the next twenty-four hours.'

'Northern English man, we've done good business together, so let's keep being friends and make another big amount of money.'

I've fucking done it, Tony told me he suddenly realised when the two Columbians agreed to his proposition.

'My good friend, Don Tony, I know your type well. Once you've smelled big money, lived on super yachts and fucked the most beautiful girls in the world, you can't go back to a quiet life… you can't live without the adrenalin! We will do business together in the future.' At that they shook hands and Santiago ordered the housekeeper to get champagne, caviar, Cuban cigars and two girls each to celebrate.

108. DTW1

In the West Wing of the twenty-sixth floor of a recently opened office in the City of London, Gillian was giving an early morning briefing to her DTW1 traders. She affectionately called these employees, her phone troopers; she'd been inspired by Jordon Belfort, the Wolf of Wall Street.

'You champagne guzzling bitches and bastards,' this her customary opening to any internal meeting, 'over the next two days, that's sixteen-hours of trading for the dim-witted, we are going to make more money than you can imagine.' There was a huge animal roar from those assembled. 'You are going to buy every share you can find for mobile operators in Africa. The industry dynamics are going to change shortly and we are going to be at the forefront of exploiting it for our personal financial gain. You are going to make your clients rich and yourselves even richer. The quarterly results are coming out today, and as ever for mobile operators in Africa, they are making huge profits. Whatever the price, whatever the mobile operator,' Gillian paused for dramatic effect, 'BUY, BUY, FUCKING BUY.' she shouted. 'What the fuck did I say?'

'Buy, fucking buy,' the office rumbled.

'I CAN'T HEAR YOU,' Gillian shouted back in her best impression of Gunnery Sargent Hartman in Full Metal Jacket.

'Buy, fucking buy.'

'I still can't hear you.'

'BUY, FUCKING BUY,' the phone troopers screamed,

'That's it. I want to see your ears glowing red, your mouth dry like sandpaper and your fingers raw. Tomorrow, we are going to go doubly hard buying and selling, and after that… I have a little treat for you.' It was normally every two or three months that the employees of DTW1 had a little treat. No one knew where the party would be, or when, but all knew there would be much excess and that the top broker would get a £250,000 cash bonus; the next few days was going to be trading on steroids.

109. No Joke

As Tony was enjoying the attentions of two Columbian linge-rie models, Gillian working her phone troopers into a state of frenzy, and Jonas was getting preparations ready for the evening meeting with Peter, I had a chat with Amy, a discussion that I had been putting off for as long as possible. Frankly, I was dreading it, knowing my revelations could quite possibly end in divorce. 'Amy, how do you fancy going to Fiji on holiday… tomorrow?' I didn't know how else to start such a conversation that would revel my secret life.

'What are you on about?' Amy smiled, thinking I was being playful. 'We have a BBQ on Saturday with our friends?'

'I've cancelled it. I've told our guests the kids are sick.'

'Why would you say that?' Amy was understandably con-fused. 'We've spent a lot of money on the BBQ, which by the way, is money we don't have; our bank account is almost empty,' she reminded me.

'That's what I need to talk to you about.' I paused not sure how I could explain my double life. 'I've been working on a few business things over the last months and we will never have to worry about money again.'

'What the hell are you talking about?' Amy, was now very angry. 'Jonas claimed you had to rush up country for a con-tract even though it was only small money.'

'You know Jonas, he tells the odd white lie every now and then,' I said trying to laugh my sudden disappearance away.

'Oh, ok. I know what happened, you were fucking a girl and Jonas was covering for you.'

'No! Nothing like that. Admittedly, I've done many things I shouldn't have, but no girls were involved.'

'I don't believe you. WHAT'S HER NAME?' Amy shouted, and then slapped my face.

'There's no girl, I promise. I've had to keep things from you over the last two years, but it was for your and the kids' safety.'

'My safety? You're not making sense.'

'When I was fired from GlobeTel, I had to make a decision, do I sink or swim; sinking was not an option.' The conversation had to come to a conclusion, so I took a deep breath. 'I made a solemn oath when each of the kids was born, and to you on our wedding day, that I would do whatever was necessary for our well-being.' I paused knowing how I had taken that promise in the eyes of God to an extreme. 'I've been running another business with Jonas, and which has involved in no particular order: bars and nightclubs,' I took another deep breath, 'prostitutes, extortion, gambling, drugs and guns.'

Amy's jaw dropped, but no words came out for nearly a minute. 'That's not a funny joke. Where's the punch line?' she finally enquired.

'Look me in the eye, Amy, this is no joke. Over the last two years, I have amassed $100 million and that is going to be multiplied many times in the next twenty-four hours.'

'You mean, 100 million Tanzanian Shillings?'

'No, 100 million United States Dollars. Look at me, Amy,' I reached for her hand, 'when I said Fiji that was just a random suggestion. You can choose where we go. A Gulfstream jet will pick us up from a private airstrip at 4pm tomorrow afternoon. You can tell the pilot where we should fly to—New Zealand, Canada, Brazil, where ever you want…'

'Stop teasing me.' She looked shell-shocked, probably wondering if this was some elaborate wind-up. 'Tomorrow, I'll drop the kids to school in our old beat up Toyota Noah, with its cracked windscreen, squeaky breaks and broken bumper… not go to a private island paradise in a Gulfstream.'

'No, Amy, tomorrow we are starting a new life… and we will have new names. Here are our passports,' I handed over the aforementioned documents so she could see in black and white that this was no joking matter.

It took her some time to open the passports, knowing that if there was any other name than the one she had been born with, then everything that I'd just alleged was in fact true. After a few seconds of getting over the shock of her life to see her picture… but with a different name, she slapped me again, even harder the second time. 'Who the hell are you? I thought I married a family man, who was funny, clever, hard-working and useless all at the same time. Someone who took financial responsibility for the family and then the next minute would be dancing on tables; that's who I love. Who is… this person that has a Gulfstream, passports with different names and millions of dollars?'

'I'm the same useless person you know, I just had to do a few things to get us out of that tricky situation a couple of years ago.'

'But I don't know you. The person I know, is a rubbish liar and a non-violent person. If you really have done what you claim, you've been lying to me for the last two years. How can I love you if I can't trust you?'

'I am the same person, but I had to keep my two worlds apart. I did what I had to do as head of the family. Nothing has changed between me, you and the kids. Once we get on that plane, then it'll be as if nothing has changed, just that we have a bit more money and can do what we want. If you love me as I love you, you'll pack our suitcases and tell the kids that we are going on an adventure.'

'I love you, but this is too much; I don't know what to think.'

'It's ok,' I said holding her tightly, my cheek still stinging. 'I'll tell you everything over the coming weeks. I have to go now as there are a few loose ends to tie up. I'll be back tomorrow at 12pm, and then we leave for the airstrip; make sure you and the kids are ready. If you have trusted me ever since we have known each other, trust me now.' Before Amy could say anything, or slap me again, I kissed her on the lips and quickly left.

110. Rising Temperatures

After the discussion I had been dreading with Amy, I was pumped. Next was a meeting I was relishing, Peter having received an email from Jonas three days earlier, this while I was hallucinating.

Peter,

Option A—Be at the Fun House in three days' time.
Option B—Your philandering with multiple mistresses in Tanzania and Dubai will be exposed to your wife, before she, then your kids, and then you are murdered.

The Ghost

I entered the sauna in the Fun House and found Peter with a contemplative look, presumably thinking something along the lines, how the hell did I get into such a predicament. While Peter was mussing the reality of his situation, I sat down next to him. There was a comradely silence for the next minute, until Peter finally looked across and saw me. 'What the…' he stuttered when he recognized my face. 'How the… I thought you were…'

'Dead?' I asked rhetorically. 'I am… I'm a ghost.'

The note Nkhonde left under the rock said he would inform Peter that I was killed. Nkhonde even sent a photo of my unconscious body to Peter, and thus my apparition really must have seemed like a ghost. He slowly moved his pointed finger towards my body. On touching my skin he almost jumped out of his. 'What the fuck is this? Who the hell is playing games with me?' He uttered in shocked confusion as he staggered towards the sauna door. 'What are you doing here?'

'You tell me, Peter, tell me everything.'

'Tell you, what? I don't know anything.'

'Then why are you so shocked to see me? Why would you think… I'm dead?'

'I'd heard rumours you were killed, something about drowning on holiday,' he lied. 'You know, Chinese whispers,' he added with a weak smile. 'It's great to see you're alive,' he put as much enthusiasm as he could into his weak words.

'Yes, it's certainly better to breathing air than sand,' I drove my point home. 'Once again, Peter, what do you want to tell me?'

'It's great that you're alive and from what I hear, it sounds like the court case is going in your favour. Whatever I said before… well, never mind, let bygones be bygones?'

'Let's not worry about spilt milk, eh, Peter,' I coldly spat out.

'Yeah, no hard feelings. You know, I was only following orders. It's company policy to make life as difficult as possible within the confines of the law for anyone who sues us. If you win your case, it sets a potentially very expensive precedent.'

'I was… collateral damage?' Peter could only shrug his shoulders. 'I do understand, Peter, but your excuse of, I was following orders,' I mimicked his whiney voice, 'is what the Nazis claimed at Nuremburg, and it didn't do them many favours. I will ask for one last time, how far is GlobeTel willing to go?'

'Only what is legal, of course.'

'Of course,' I replied sarcastically. 'So, Peter, what brings you to The Fun House?' I changed tact to throw him off balance.

'Fun and games with the whores, what else?' he boorishly laughed.

'Well that's the funny things about rumours, I heard that you were here to meet someone.'

'You're well informed. I was a naughty boy, if you know what I mean, and man-to-man,' he said with a boyish grin, 'someone is holding that over me.'

'Blackmail?'

'Yes.'

'What are you going to do?' I enquired, 'Just between you and me, who do you think is blackmailing you?'

'That's the funny thing, the person claims to be The Ghost. Honestly. I don't know how many people use that nowadays to threaten people.'

'Do you feel threatened, Peter?'

'Of course. But I'm a business man and I'm sure we will come to some sort of agreement once I know what he wants.'

'Negotiate your way out of a mess of your own making?'

'Yes.'

'What do you think he wants?'

'I have no idea. I honestly don't know if it's something personal or he wants to leverage my position at GlobeTel.'

'Maybe a bit of both?'

'No one can have that much leverage over me.' Considering the trouble he was in, I was amazed he'd not yet lost his arrogance.

'Is that so? I imagine if they did you would be shitting bricks knowing how much of a big fucking hole you're in!'

'The Ghost is just a myth. It's probably just the police trying to cover up some internal power struggle.' He didn't sound convinced by this suggestion.

'I once heard, Peter... that the greatest trick the devil ever pulled was to make people believe he didn't exist. What if the devil does exist? What if The Ghost exists?' My voice all the time rising in volume and anger. 'What if The Ghost will punish you with the same retribution that he handed out to others that crossed his path? What if he tracked down every member of your family living in Dubai Heights Flats? What if he knew everything about you and there was nothing he wouldn't do to get even? What then?'

'What did you say about Dubai?' he was fazed. 'What do you know about my family?'

'Just a lucky guess… maybe.'

'Maybe?' Peter mumbled. 'Something is seriously fucked up,' he said to himself but just audible enough for me to hear. 'Nice to talk, but, I'm waiting for—'

'The Ghost. Maybe, his greatest trick was for people to think he doesn't exist?'

'Maybe?'

'I'm also waiting for someone.'

'Why don't you go and meet your friends at the bar?'

'It's not a friend I'm waiting for, but someone who my destiny is intertwined with. I thought it would be good to meet them, here… at one of my businesses.'

'What? What the?' Peter stuttered, not sure if he had heard me correctly. 'What do you mean, one of your businesses?'

'Sometimes, it's the very people who no one imagines anything of who do the things no one can imagine.' I shrugged my shoulders. 'This is just one of my businesses,' I reiterated right into Peter's face.

'But what the… I heard you were a consultant?' he was understandably confused.

'I'm different things to different people, Peter; I have many guises. Someone once described me, as a riddle wrapped in a mystery inside an enigma.'

'Oh.' Of everybody he'd met, I was clearly one of the last people he'd expect to be running the Fun House. 'It seems there's more to you than meets the eye,' he conceded. 'How did you get The Ghost's seal of approval? What do you know of this Ghost? It would be a real favour if you could give me any information; I'm in a bit of a corner.'

'Why the fuck would I HELP YOU?' I shouted, 'you backstabbing, weaselly motherfucker.'

Peter, was taken aback by my sudden change in demur. 'I was only acting on company orders.' All arrogance had left his voice.

'Is that so?' Now was the time to turn up the heat, both figuratively and literally. I made a small signal to the corner of the room where a hidden camera was installed and from which Jonas was observing the conversation; he turned the temperature dial up.

'Peter, indulge me and answer a few questions, but be mindful, that I know more, much more about you than you could ever know about me.' I could see that for the first time Peter was no longer shocked, but scared. 'I'll start with an easy opener, why was I fired?'

'You weren't good at your job.'

'That's what you knew or what you were told?

'What's the difference?' He paused. 'That's what I was told by Ephraim and James,' he clarified.

'And you trusted them?'

'Sure, why not?'

'You didn't think it was worth looking into things properly? You didn't think that they had their own agenda to get me fired?'

'Business is office politics, and you didn't play a good game; you didn't build alliances. I admit though, we hired you too early for the job you were recruited for.'

'It was a business mistake to hire me?'

'Sure, that's life, shit happens. I give you credit for having the balls to take GlobeTel to court.'

'And the firing process?'

'Once a decision is made, it's made. It was just a question of going through the motions of the dismissal.'

'My work meant nothing?'

'Not really. As I said, it was business and GlobeTel wanted you out of the country as soon as possible.'

'One less headache for GlobeTel? You were just a cog in the machine?'

'Exactly.' Peter replied more comfortable with this conversation than the earlier one.

'I believe you. It was easier for you to fire me than to reassign me to another department like you do for your underperforming acolytes.'

'Business is all about office politics. If you want to succeed, you need friends in the right places.'

'And screw anyone else?'

'Sure, you only have one life and you do what you have to.'

'In life, you-do-what-you-have-to,' I repeated excruciatingly slowly. 'I fully understand that sentiment. Is that why you asked Belmont to bribe Immigration officials to deport me? Is that... what you had to do?'

'What... No... I never...'

'No lies, Peter.'

'I had nothing to do with Belmont and Immigration.'

'Is that so?' I sighed. 'Peter, you do remember that the Fun House is my business, the guards are my guards, and that anything I want to do to you,' I paused to let the words sink in, 'is fully at my discretion and whim. I'll ask you one more time, what did you ask Belmont to do?'

'Fuck, fuck, fuck,' he uttered to himself. 'How the hell does he know about Belmont?'

'Last time, Peter, the truth or I'll start to get very personal with you, in much the same way you got personal with me.'

'OK,' he said knowing he had nowhere to turn. 'I was getting pressure from management at head office. They wanted the court case finished quickly—what easier way than getting you deported. Abroad, there is even less chance of a court case taking anything less than five-years; it's very easy to extend the process with a few well spoken words to the right people and paying the correct price.'

'You mean bribe lawyers and the courts?'

'How else do you think this country works?'

'GlobeTel does this often?'

'Not often, but yes, you weren't the first. For most local staff we don't bother unless we think there will be a rush of unfair dismissal cases. But, if we see something that could cause problems down the line, we make sure the process is slowed as much as possible while keeping plausible deniability.'

'How can bribing officers of the court, be plausibly deniable?'

'Who's going to investigate a judge? Besides, we can bribe whoever it is to put the file in the proverbial bottom drawer.'

'How did you manage to convince Gordon to help you?'

'Depending on the value of the case, if we want a claimant's lawyer on our side, we simply either give them a fixed fee for disruption or a percentage of the expected pay-out; Gordon was cheaper than most.'

'So, Gordon slowed things down in the hope I would leave Tanzania?' Peter nodded his head in confirmation. 'And when that didn't work, you tried Immigration?'

'Something along those lines, yes. Gordon represents a number of claimants against GlobeTel—he makes good money from us.'

So, that's how he afforded a brand new Range Rover Sport and three girlfriends, I realised, the evidence of purchasing vehicles and female company gleamed from Watson and Terry's investigations.

111. A ONCE IN A LIFE CASE

Now that we had video confirmation of the complicity between GlobeTel, Gordon and the courts, Jonas set in motion the next phase of my plan. The Blue Label Bar member, Regional Police Commissioner Julius Mbogoye, arrested Gordon Wills and the corrupt officers of the court, this being arranged three days earlier when Jonas had met Julius at the Sheraton, informing him, you are about to get the case of your life.

When Julius had asked for details, Jonas gave him the outline of our dossier, though for obvious reasons, namely we could never fully trust the weasel, he didn't mention GlobeTel by name.

'It's never good to upset the status quo,' Julius had made an idiom filled argument. 'A lot of people like the way it is. Everybody makes money on the merry-go-round; why upset the apple cart?'

'There are three reasons why you will upset the gravy train, apple cart or whatever. 1) If you open this case you will become the biggest personality in Tanzania for a considerable amount of time and which will give you much influence and power. 2) We will put $100,000 into an offshore bank account of your choice, $25,000 down payment and a further $75,000 on release of a police statement, an affidavit and a video transcript, to all media at exactly 4:30pm on Friday. This will show a signed and verbal confession of complicity between a certain business and the judiciary of Tanzania. 3) Lastly, well, let's not go down that road, other than to say we have worked together for some time and it wouldn't be good for you if that knowledge got out.'

'The carrot and the stick, as you Brits like to say.'

112. Blood is Thicker Than Water

As Jonas set in motion the other parts of my plan, back in the sauna I continued grilling Peter—pun intended. 'GlobeTel bribed: my lawyer, court officers and immigration officials, but when none of that worked, you were desperate…' I stopped mid-sentence as I saw Peter looking increasingly uncomfortable; he had no idea what I might reveal next.

'You've got me. What can I say?—'

'You were just following orders?' I interrupted.

'Yes, I was just following orders.'

'And head office was fully aware of what you were doing?'

'Not explicit agreement, but certainly encouraged. Though are always very careful so that they can claim plausible deniability if needed.'

'So, if the shit hits the fan, Peter carries the can?'

'Ah, yeah'

'Guess what, the shit has hit the fan.'

'Enough of the games; what do you want?' He aggressively demanded, attack his best, only form of defence.

'What do I want? I'll come to that later, but for now, tell me more about your meeting with The Ghost.'

'He's blackmailing me.'

'What does he want?'

'I honestly don't know?'

'Let me guess… he has pictures of you with a girl, maybe multiple girls?'

'I told you that earlier.'

'A naked girl snorting… what looks like cocaine off your chest.'

'How do you know—?'

'The same girl, that when you were unconscious, stole your clothes, wallet and car.'

'What the?' his jaw dropping at the realization of my knowledge and probable involvement.

'Which happened on the night we met at La Dolce Vita two years ago.'

'How do you know about that? Why would The Ghost tell you?'

He still had no idea who I really was. 'Peter, don't be naïve. Do you remember threatening me that night? Well, you picked a fight with the wrong person. I told you, when some-one is motivated anything is possible, and you made me very motivated that night.'

'But how?' was all he could muster.

'The night is young, and you still have a lot to learn.'

'Did you get me thrown out of here, naked?'

'Guilty as charged,' I smirked. 'I am the owner after all,' I reminded him.

Peter was numb. 'For these last two years, when I have been watching over my shoulder, it has been due to you?' he uncomprehendingly uttered.

'Yes. We have been playing a game of chess and I've let you take a few of my pawns, but we are coming to the end game and you are in checkmate. You shouldn't have underestimated me or fucked with my family.' Peter stayed in stunned silence. 'So, Peter, no more futile chasing a cheetah… last week, you hired Nkhonde to assassinate me.'

'I guess I did.'

The fight had gone out of him. 'Why did you let things go so far?'

'It has gone too far and I'm sorry for that.'

'I bet you bloody are!'

'I was backed into a corner due to office politics. I'd bet my reputation at several head office meetings that I could handle your unfair dismissal case. No significant unfair dismissal cases had been won against GlobeTel, and the first wasn't going to be on my watch. I had the backing of the corporate Chief Financial Officer who understood the financial implications of multiple unfair dismal cases. If word got to the press about a large number of cases, it would be very bad for our brand; there could be a mutiny from employees and shareholders alike. You know GlobeTel positions itself as the brand of the people. Joost Wielhelms, GlobeTel's Chief Executive Officer, was worried that you were the tip of a very slippery slope.'

'You would use any means possible to stop me, including murder?'

'Why not. If we can bribe the police and immigration, and manipulate the judicial process, there was minimal risk?'

'Did you personally order the hit?'

'No, of course I didn't, directly,' he replied, all resistance now gone. 'After your case was expedited, we hired Nkhonde and paid him through an offshore bank account.'

'How did Nkhonde find me in Savannah Lounge?' this was a loose end which I hadn't so far been able to come up with a satisfactory answer. 'You don't know who tipped me off?' Peter lent back and laughed, this his sole victory in an otherwise utterly squirm-inducing experience for him. 'What's that information worth?' he tried to negotiate.

'Nothing. I'll find out sooner or later.' I nonchalantly answered while balling my fist. I was more than eager to find out who the rat was, but I couldn't let Peter become aware of this fact; I dared not show any weakness.

He gave up the name surprisingly easily. 'It was… Watson—'

'That motherfucker!' I exploded, much to the delight of Peter. 'Why?' I demanded.

'His wife is a cousin of Gordon. When Watson saw the noose tighten around your former lawyer's neck, he reached out. For Watson, blood is thicker than water.'

What can you do? I contemplated as I sat in the sauna profusely sweating. You can't mitigate against every possible scenario or investigate every relationship, after all, there are six degrees of separation between everyone in the world, and in Africa with extended families it must be a lot less.

'Watson, showed a modicum of loyalty. He told Gordon to play it straight with any cases he was arguing; he didn't mention your name. We had no inkling at the time that you were pulling the strings, but you were the only client, or so Gordon claimed, that he was screwing with. We had no choice but to take all precautions and hire Nkhonde—'

'And lucky for me, as you just said, blood is thicker than water; Nkhonde had a half-brother in prison.'

'What?'

'Why do you think Nkhonde let me go? And for that matter, the unfair dismissal case got expedited?'

'I have no idea,' Peter looked like he really didn't have a clue.

'Let's just say, I have power.' I wasn't going to divulge more than I needed at this stage, I still wanted Peter to keep guessing as to how far my span of influence stretched. 'Peter, you will put all you have told me in an affidavit.'

'Like hell I will; I'll be killed.'

'By GlobeTel?'

'Yes, by bloody GlobeTel. They can never let this story come out?'

'Peter, you are between a rock and being truly fucked. Ask yourself this, how could I know everything you would say?'

'I don't, I really don't know,' he started to cry as he shook his head.

'Guess.' I was enjoying this interrogation immensely.

'I have no idea,' Peter mumbled.

'Let me tell you a little story, Peter, but before then look carefully to the corner of the room, you will see a small camera.'

'Oh, fuck.'

'Oh, fuck, indeed.' I waved my arm, the signal for Jonas to stop recording. 'The camera has been turned off. Peter, what do you think links me with The Ghost?'

'You're his bitch?'

'Great one, Peter, you still have some fight left in you,' I laughed. 'Be very careful with your next words. Try again.'

'I have no idea,' Peter said, but this time in a resigned voice.

'The greatest trick the devil ever pulled was for people to think he didn't exist. In the same way, Peter… who would've thought that… I… was… The Ghost?'

'No. It's not possible, it can't be?'

'Time is running out. Let's take a walk to my office and allow me to convince you that I am. On our way, you better decide if you want to be under a GlobeTel rock or the hard place of doing everything in your power to save your family from my wrath.' I had no intention of harming his family, as in a few hours I would be in the Gulf Stream and the world would never hear of The Ghost again, but he couldn't have known that.

'Ok,' he relented. It was open to speculation what Globe-Tel might or might not do once Peter spilled the beans, but in his mind, there must have been no question of the imminent threat I posed.

'This is what will happen,' I informed him. 'You will go to a certain place with two of my trusted lieutenants where you will be met by the Attorney General and two Supreme Court Judges who will take your affidavit.' Two days earlier, I'd put messages in the pigeon holes of these three gentlemen to be at the appropriate place. 'You will then be put under the protective custody of the Regional Police Commissioner, Julius Mbogoye. At exactly 11:15am tomorrow morning, you will give a statement to the assembled press. You will then be put into a witness protection program. You will be called to give evidence against GlobeTel in a fast-tracked whistle-blower case. You will only mention about what we talked about prior to the hidden camera being turned off. I'm sure I don't need to tell you what will happen if you disregard this last instruction; are we clear?'

'Yes,' confirmation, the only reply the stupefied Peter could possibly give.

113. I Luv It When a Plan Comes Together

While I was still stewing over Watson's betrayal and deciding what I should do about him, the day-of-days, the culmination of two-years of unimaginable risks began. Our plan had to run to military precision if we wanted to get out from under the criminal cloud that like rainmakers we had formed.

8:25am UK Time / 11:25am Tanzanian Time (GMT+3)

'Phone troopers, its quarterly results day. For my busy bees who were studying last night, you know that economies in Africa are growing fast and the mobile operators are always profitable, so what are you going to do?'

'Buy, buy, fucking buy,' came the chorus.

'That's right my little bunnies, but who are you not going to buy?'

'Those motherfuckers, GlobeTel?'

'And why aren't you going to buy GlobeTel?'

'Because THEY'RE FUCKED,' the phone troopers roared back.

'And why are they fucked?' Gillian whispered to the almost silent room.

'FAIRY GODMOTHER GILLIAN SAID, THEY'RE FUCKED!' they roared to her delight.

'And why do you listen to me?'

'You are the maker of money,' a voice at the back of the room shouted out.

'Little worker bees, pick up those phones and talk sweet money music to your clients.'

8:35am UK Time / 11:35am Tanzanian Time

The average price of mobile operator shares in the countries that GlobeTel operated in started to rise on the above target quarterly key performance indicators, as indeed they had universally done for the last three quarters. GlobeTel's average share price rose the anticipated 2%.

12:15pm Tanzanian Time / 9:15am UK Time

Danny Nyonda had been promised an exclusive, though his wasn't the only newspaper to be present at the Central Police Station when Peter gave his statement to the assembled national and international press crops. However, Danny's was the only paper that ran the story within five-minutes of the briefing, Jonas having anonymously emailed him the press release and the GlobeTel dossier two-hours earlier, this having been skilfully compiled by Watson, the rat bastard, and Terry.

GlobeTel executive hired hit man to assassinate former employee

A senior executive of GlobeTel was arrested late last night in conjunction with perverting the course of justice through bribing lawyers, arbitrators, officers of the court, High Court judges and immigration officials. The senior executive of the self-proclaimed, mobile operator of the people, GlobeTel, admitted, "When necessary, I would authorise the use of underhand tactics. In one extreme case, I was given the go-ahead to organise the assassination of a rogue former employee."

The revelations from the whistle-blower have shone a very unfavourable light on one of the country's best performing sectors. These shocking revelations, bring international businesses and the very fabric of Tanzanian life into disrepute. If the judicial system is not above being corrupted, this puts a knife straight into the heart of democracy and the Tanzanian constitution. The questions that His Excellency, The President needs to ask, are: How to build capacity of public organisations to stop corruption? What should be done to crooked officials if the very systems in place to stop corruption are riddled with dishonest civil servants? And what should happen to GlobeTel?

9:18 UK Time / 12:18pm Tanzanian Time

Knowing the airwaves would shortly be filled with stories of GlobeTel's corruption, bribery and murder, Gillian rang her bell. The office of DWL1 was totally silent within five-seconds. 'SELL GLOBETEL,' Gillian shouted at the top of her lungs. Traders immediately put on hold any other deals they were pursuing until every single client had sold their GlobeTel portfolio.

'WHEN YOU HAVE NO MORE GLOBETEL TO SELL, KEEP BUYING OTHER MOBILE OPERATOR SHARES,' Gillian ordered.

12:50pm Tanzanian Time / 9:50am UK Time

#GlobeTel #murder plot – If you going to do it, do it properly; revenge will be the will of the people

#GlobeTel #bastards – justice is the right of the people

#GlobeTel #corruption – read the National Enquirer website for the complete story

With similar messages on The Ghost's Facebook account, soon hundreds-of-thousands of Tanzanians and foreigners alike were reading the homepage of the Enquirer website and learning of Peter's revelations.

10:15am UK Time / 1:15pm Tanzanian Time

The selling spree of GlobeTel's shares by DWL1 had little immediate impact on GlobeTel's share price; Gillian had gotten us a good price. But as the news of the scandal started to hit the airwaves, the trickle of shares being sold turned into a stream and then a tsunami, GlobeTel's share price dropping like a rock. Within twenty-five minutes of my Tweets, the share price had dropped 10% and was continuing to fall rapidly.

114. Oh Shit!

12:25pm Luxemburg Time (GMT+1) / 11:25am UK Time / 2:25pm Tanzanian Time

An emergency conference call for all GlobeTel country general managers was called by Chief Executive Officer Joost Wielhelms, when he saw on his monitor the cliff like graph of the share price. He'd already called an emergency meeting of the Board of Directors that afternoon.

'Gentlemen,' there were no female General Managers in any of GlobeTel's operations, 'by now, you may have heard that there are problems in Tanzania.'

'Yes,' came the universal reply.

'GlobeTel is a company with fifteen operations in: Asia, Africa and South America. Whatever one rogue executive has done, doesn't devalue the overall balance sheet worth of the company. Sales will still rise, fixed assets will still be invested in and, our customers have a short memory; with an aggressive price promotion you can reclaim loyalty. I hope this will not have any impact on your operations, but we must implement a short-term strategy of containment. You must immediately put out the press release I emailed. If we act quickly, we can control the situation.'

Five minutes later, Joost was reading the press statement from the foyer of the corporate Head Office.

> GlobeTel has high standards of employee welfare and holds
> in high regard the laws in all the countries we work. We aim
> to treat each other with respect and dignity, and value indi-

vidual and cultural differences. We recognize our exceptional teams and hire the best people. We give individuals the authority to use their capabilities to the fullest to satisfy our most important asset, our customers. Our environment fosters personal growth and continuous learning for all the GlobeTel family.

We also believe in personal responsibility and accountability. Those who do not follow GlobeTel's code of conduct, our ethical standards or the laws of the country, will be immediately dismissed, and where appropriate, dealt with by the relevant local authorities.

Our code of ethics states: that core to our principles of good business are that employees are expected to protect and enhance the assets and reputation of the GlobeTel Group. Our business is based on a tradition of trust and dependability. Honesty and integrity are the cornerstones of our ethical behaviour. Our continued success depends on doing what we promise—promptly, professionally and fairly. Our businesses are evolving rapidly and are challenged by a complex environment. The actions of one rogue employee does not reflect GlobeTel who is here to support our customers, respect the laws of the country and uphold our code of ethics.

He refused to take any questions from the assembled press.

12:45pm UK Time / 3:45pm Tanzanian Time

Joost's press conference had the desired effect, the haemorrhaging of the GlobeTel share price stopped; there was even a slight bounce.

4:40pm Tanzanian Time / 1:40pm UK Time—The Enquirer website

In a fast moving and increasingly shocking story, only a few hours after the global press release by Joost Wielhelms, the CEO of GlobeTel Group, he has personally been implicated in GlobeTel-gate. At 4:30pm local time, Regional Police Commissioner Julius Mbogoye released a statement.

"The Tanzanian Police Force has arrested Gordon Wills, a lawyer acting on behalf of a former GlobeTel employee in an unfair dismissal case and, a number of court officials for being complicit in perverting the course of justice. From a transcript involving the GlobeTel executive at the centre of the outrage, it appears what started out as a case of office politics soon took on a personal angle when the former employee was unwilling to lie down quietly and used his constitutional rights for a fair hearing for compensation. GlobeTel management went to increasing lengths to stop the process, the executive claiming. "It was not that we didn't believe that he had a fair case, but that if he won, Joost Wielhelms was worried other former employees would take us to court and which would damage our brand."

This story has lifted the lid of big business in Tanzania and revealed a very unpleasant stink of cooperates taking advantage of their staff for the indulgence of a few executive managers. Where this leaves the reputation of the Tanzanian justice system and GlobeTel, no one can tell at this early stage. Is it a case of a few rotting fish or is there deep rooted corruption at the very heart of the liberalised Tanzanian economy? The more this story unfolds, and how business is ready to intervene on the seemingly triviality of an unfair dismissal case, the more it looks like there is a very un-transparent relationship between big businesses and a handful of the high and mighty politicians and bureaucrats. With the coming of the oil and gas sector, and what should be the light of a new dawn to reduce poverty across the country, serious questions need to be asked and appropriate balances and checks put in place.

4:50pm Tanzanian Time / 1:50pm UK Time

> #GlobeTel #CEO – is murder in your Code of Ethics?

> #GlobeTel #truth – get found out, put your hands up, don't try to cover up – truth will prevail.

> #GlobeTel #what's next? – What's next? GlobeTel thought they were masters-of-the-universe, and not servants to their customers

With the revelations from the affidavit and video transcript quickly becoming the lead story on all social and traditional media, globally, there was an immediate impact on GlobeTel's share price; it plummeted over the next two hours to 60% of its value from the beginning of the day, while their continental competitors share price jumped 5% across the board, 20% where there was in-country competition.

3:45 UK Time / 6:45pm Tanzanian Time

'Gillian, ring that bell,' I said to one of my best friends. 'The share price is where we want it; let's cut and run.'

'When I ring it, our lives and many others will change forever. GlobeTel will in the short term no longer be a mobile operator powerhouse, at least according to their share price.'

'When I came to you with my proposition, I told you we would make a huge amount of money and that I would use it to make a difference to those that needed it most. What will happen next?' I asked, though already knew, or hoped I knew the answer.

'Now you can buy three times as many GlobeTel shares compared to the beginning of trading, so either, A) the price will bounce from our purchases. B) The expected actions of GlobeTel Board of Directors over the weekend will take effect on Monday and will stabilize the price. C) If the price stays low, then you as a major shareholder can push through institutional change and help push the share price back up. D) A competitor sees an opportunity for a takeover, this will definitely push the price up. E) A combination of the above. As long as the share price doesn't drop through the floor, or GlobeTel declare bankruptcy, which looking at all their financial indicators and in-spite of this disaster, is very unlikely; there really is no downside.'

'Ring that bell, Gillian,' I quietly confirmed, remembering the journey I had been through over the last fifteen years to get to this destination.

Down the end of the phone line, I heard Gillian ring the bell; it was the first time she'd ever done that twice on the same day.

'Ladies and gentlemen,' I heard her address the employees of DTW1. 'The time has come to sell all mobile operator shares and buy GlobeTel. Why? You might be asking, seeing as the other mobile operators' shares are on the up and up and GlobeTel is in a world of shit. Well, my little dears, this is a win-win for us and our major investor. So, my little chickens, get on those phones... AND... WHAT?

'SELL, SELL, SELL THE SHIT, AND BUY, BUY, BUY GLOBETEL'

'Yes,' Gillian whispered.

I quickly calculated, the half billion dollars that we had at the beginning of yesterday's trading ($100 million cash in bank, $100 million from sale of the business and $300 million loan from the cartel) would be worth close to $1.5 billion this time next week, minus the $300 million owed to the cartel; I would soon have $1.2 billion to do as I pleased.

115. EPILOGUE

Gillian removed her hands from behind her back and waved her left hand in front of me, 'You are one jammy bastard… or one jammy dodger?'

'Whatever you might be able to do on the stock market with your phone troopers, or whatever you like to call them, I can read you like a book… the twenty-five East Caribbean Cent coin is in your left hand.'

'You're sure of that?'

'You're easier to read than Jackanory'

'Wanker,' Gillian said opening her left hand to revel the shiny coin.

'Fat man, your guess.' I looked at my co-conspirator and moved the coin from hand-to-hand behind my back, 'What's it going to be? A cocktail with umbrella and a cherry,' I waved my right hand, 'or fresh coconut juice with a dash of lime and a shot of vodka.'

'You cheeky twat! I know you too,' Jonas confidently replied. 'The coin is in your left hand.'

'You're sure? I know you even better! I knew you would initially go for my left hand and that's why I put it in my right.'

'You can't fool me; open your left hand.'

'I'm telling you, Jonas, it's in my right fist.'

'Just open your frigging left hand.'

'I told you, Jonas,' I laughed as I opened my empty left fist. 'You should've trusted me. Be a good boy and toddle off to the bar and get some of those aforementioned coconut, lime and vodka cocktails.'

'Tosser,' Jonas smiled. 'Come on then, Tony,' he looked over at our other conspirator, 'let's go to the bar for these fools.'

'I don't know how you two did it,' this from Gillian as Jonas and Tony walked to the beach bar, 'and I don't want to know all the details, but what are you going to do with all that money?'

'When Jonas and I got into this two years ago, we knew we would have to do some pretty bad stuff, and we did. In agreement with Jonas, 70% will go into a trust account and invested in various charities. We will be overseers of the account but not have any day-to-day responsibilities; we need to keep a low profile. 15% is being split between you, Tony and the gang in Tanzania—Sasha, Chidi and Terry.' Watson's name was conspicuous by its absence from the list. Apart from Jonas, I hadn't yet told anyone about Watson's betrayal, I was still mulling over what, if anything, I should do to the snake. On the one hand, he more than deserved a reprisal for what he'd done, but on the other, he hadn't completely dropped me in it and, I desperately wanted to rebuild trust with Amy, this starting by leaving violence and death in my past. 'The fat man and I will keep 7.5%... or to put it another way, $90 million each.'

'But how, Liam, how?' This time curiosity getting the better of her.

'It's funny how all the highs and lows of life are intrinsically linked. For instance, if I hadn't gone through all those troubles with Steph, I never would have known that Amy was the one for me. If it wasn't for Amy, I wouldn't have had kids and thus less motivation for all I've done. At university I studied marketing and which was key to building The Ghost brand. Working in London and then for my uncle, gave me the understanding of how to run a business. London, and those crazy years in the houseshare, is where I met Jonas and Tony; I had a group of friends I could trust my life with.'

'And I guess it all started when you were a volunteer teacher in Tanzania before university?'

'Exactly, that's what set the whole thing in motion. That's what made me decide to leave Steph, to search my heart for passion whatever the consequences. That's what has kept me going through some on the darker times over the last two years. Of course, Amy and I are much financially better off but the majority will be put back into various African community projects; there's a LOT of money to do immeasurable good with.'

MY LAST REFLECTION # 18

As I look across the St Lucia beach and watch Amy and the kids playing on the deck of the yacht bobbing on the current of the Caribbean Sea, my first purchase once I had liquidated the GlobeTel shares two-weeks earlier, this at a time when the share value had risen back to 95% of the pre-GlobeTel-gate price, I pondered on what I had just revealed to Gillian, how the story of my life and all the little pieces went into making a big puzzle. Maybe, there really is such a thing as destiny, I concluded.

So, there you go. I never said my story ended with a bullet or me drowning. This is not one of those stories written from beyond the grave. I'm happily married and have a loving family. I'm wealthy beyond my wildest dreams and which allows me to make the changes and contribute to society as I feel best; I'm now living the life I wished.

Would I have changed anything along the way? Sure, some of the finer details, a brush stroke here or there, but not the essence of the painting. So, my question to you, dear reader, are you doing it your way? Will you aim for the impossible? Are you living like a freebird with all the opportunities and challenges that might bring or are you afraid to live your dreams? Ask yourself this, if you were neck deep in sand, the tide fast approaching and an assassin sitting five metres away enjoying the taste of your Cuban cigar, could you say: I'm glad I've done it my way?

THE END

If you enjoyed reading *18 Reflections and 3 Statements of Relief*, you might like *Crying for Afronia*, the first volume in the Afronia Series.

For Jacob, moving to Afronia means opportunity and love, but a terrorist attack could signal the end of everything he has worked so hard to achieve.

A handful of politically connected elite families control Afronia, but for many, and especially rural villagers, the future holds nothing but poverty and despair. President Solomon's authoritarian administration has been mired in corruption, cronyism, nepotism since riding roughshod over parliament. He has removed all checks and balances to his power and is neither accountable nor transparent in how he rules.

Jacob comes to Afronia as a business consultant and falls head over heels in love with a work colleague. Thinking he has finally found peace in his life, his new world is suddenly shattered by the Independence Day terrorist attack which kills hundreds and sends the country into turmoil. Seeking the truth behind the attack, Jacob discovers more about the way Afronia works than he ever wanted, and what he learns could lead the country on the road to civil war.

Crying for Afronia **is a story of power, greed, love, betrayal, and the quest to uncover the truth.**

PROLOGUE

ALI LANYA'S LIFE WAS filled with far more fear than hope, fear for the future of Afronia. He'd just graduated first from his economics and social development class at Umoja City University. The previous week he had attended the protest in Presidential Square where the security forces had indiscriminately massacred 172 and wounded many times that number. The protest had been called because of the government's inaction after the Corruption in the Capital scandal and which implicated President Solomon and his cronies in the mass looting of state funds.

Ali had mourned his university friends and was now taking a holiday before starting his new job as the economic advisor to the Umoja City Chamber of Commerce. He was returning to his home village of Chambe near the mountaintop town of Denga, in Southiland, the rugged western region of Afronia. He was primarily going home to see Adela, his sixteen-year-old younger sister who'd fled her abusive husband two-and-a-half years earlier to go and work in Saudi Arabia as a domestic helper. She'd recently been deported in a crackdown by Saudi immigration authorities.

Ali's coach passed the eastern shore of Lake Afronia and which not so long ago had been full to the brim with fish but was now heavily polluted and largely devoid of life. The coach passed lush green hills with rich soils and which cascaded down to the lake, the fertile land capable of producing two harvests a year. Theoretically, this meant that no one in

Afronia should ever go hungry… but many nonetheless did. Seeing this sight pass before his eyes, Ali spoke to his travelling companion. 'Afronia should be one of the most prosperous countries in Africa. We should have a strong agricultural sector to compliment our precious metals, minerals and other natural resources, and yet… we are still some of the world's poorest.'

'Corruption and poverty have dogged us for so long, my friend,' Ali's neighbour replied. 'We're so used to being poor that we now accept it as normal. President Solomon is a cruel tyrant who has little interest in developing, let alone running the country,' he glumly concluded.

'I hear you, brother,' Ali agreed. 'Mining profits drain into offshore accounts. There is no rule of law and the army and police do as they please. In every measure of human development: safety, food security, access to water, healthcare, education etcetera, we scrape along at the bottom of the proverbial barrel,' he said for the hundredth time. 'We have all the resources one could wish for, but they have only brought us misery. We die of hunger, disease and lost hope while the regime and their foreign sponsors line their pockets.' The two travellers stayed in comradely silence, each considering the suffering of their fellow countrymen and women.

As the bus crossed the regional boundary between Wahilistan and Southiland, it was stopped at a military checkpoint. The passengers nervously got off the coach as four policemen searched fruitlessly for contraband. Once the search had concluded, all but one passenger got back on the coach.

It was five minutes to eleven on the morning of the 7th of July 2014 when Ali asked his neighbour, 'Where's the girl who was sitting across the aisle? I hope she didn't get on the wrong bus.'

Ali's neighbour raised his eyebrows, 'Who knows, brother? The soldiers do what they like, to whom they like and when they like. My best guess, they will probably rape the girl and put her on the next bus, that's if she's not too traumatised and accepts what happened to her without complaint.'

Talking about the brutalisation of an innocent girl in such a matter-of-fact way is so deeply shaming, Ali thought of his neighbour's depressing answer. 'What do you mean?' He asked, even though he was not sure he wanted to hear the answer.

'If she complains, they will kill her to shut her up. The army do whatever they please to us Southis; we never fight back. We're so timid and accepting, and should be ashamed for not living up to our warrior heritage.'

Ali considered what his new friend had said while remembering what he'd witnessed at the Presidential Square massacre. 'How can it be that we just cower?' he beseeched. 'Why don't we hold those responsible to account?'

'I don't have answers, brother, just tears,' his neighbour shrugged his shoulders in dejected resignation.

The coach continued gaining altitude as it passed through the foothills of the Southi Mountains towards Nyala, the regional capital. Approaching the village of Bhumi, the passengers noticed a large number of soldiers wearing the red berets of the Counter Terrorism Unit, Afronia's paramilitary special forces. The passengers also saw a number of unmarked government cars which they correctly assumed belonged to the dreaded Afronian Internal Security Services—Afronia's secret police. Silence fell over the bus as it passed through the village, the passengers not wanting any reason, whatsoever, for the military or secret police to stop and enter.

Exiting the village, the coach was diverted and the reason for the heavy military presence suddenly became clear. Ali could see the burned, twisted and smouldering remains of an Armoured Personnel Carrier, its wheels in the air and a large hole in the road. He guessed, *An IED (Improvised Explosive*

Device) was probably planted and subsequently detonated. Most likely, the ambush would have been carried out by the Southi Republican Army, this being the terrorist faction of the Southi Democratic Unionists political party.

The Southi Republican Army had carried out their first attack four years earlier against an army barracks in Nyala, this after Life President, Altimus Solomon had refused to countenance an independence referendum. The violence on both sides had been escalating since that first terrorist assault and the subsequent iron-fisted response. In recent months, the president had favoured using Russian-made military drones and which the Southis had christened Death Eagles.

The silence in the coach grew grimmer still as the bus was called to a halt by the side-of-the-road shortly after leaving Bhumi. Ali and his fellow passengers feared there would be a Counter Terrorism Unit response, and fervently prayed, *That it wouldn't be this coach or our village attacked in the reprisal.* As if to confirm the tension, a movement in the sky caught Ali's attention. Shading his eyes from the sun and squinting, he saw a Death Eagle circling ominously.

The coach continued on to Nyala without incident where, upon arrival, Ali changed to a minibus for the last part of his journey home. The minibus drove through the Southiland valleys and over the mountain passes and soon Ali was only thirty minutes away from the final stop, Denga. From there he would walk the last hour to Chambe.

There were two villages left to pass through and in both Ali had many friends from school days. In the first village, Bandros, Ali recognised his friend Abdul and who after leaving school at the age of fourteen had started to work with his father in the small village garage. Ali reminisced about the games they'd played in days gone by, *Hide and seek in the mountains, swimming in the frigid rivers and stealing apples for impromptu picnics.*

Abdul had taken over the running of the garage since his father's vanishing two years earlier. Friends and family assumed the disappearance had been at the hands of the secret police. They believed, correctly, that Abdul's father would have been tortured and executed. It was well-known that he was involved with Cell 156, a group of outlawed Afronian political activists. It was most likely that he had been reported to the secret police by an informer.

Ali was waving at Abdul when suddenly, and very violently, the minibus was thrown like a toy into a mud and thatch house and instantly knocking Ali out.

Minutes later, Ali awoke to see his neighbouring passenger dead, a metal pole sticking out through the centre of his chest. He looked around the upturned minibus and saw two other passengers who also appeared deceased, their necks twisted at an unnatural angle. Ali heard moans from the front of the bus and saw the driver trying to pull his bloodied and broken body through the shattered windscreen, screaming in pain as he did so.

Dazed, confused, but with the help of nearby villagers, Ali managed to crawl out of the vehicle. In the sunlight he saw three more blood-soaked people, each with a look of total bewilderment, *But at least they are breathing,* Ali considered. *Probably villagers going about their daily routines*, he decided, not recognising any as passengers. He then checked his injuries, and which, remarkably, comprised only minor cuts and bruises.

Staring at the scene of utter devastation, Ali instinctively knew, *It must have been an explosion for the minibus to be so completely destroyed. But was it a Southi Republican Army IED that went off by mistake or something else?* Ali looked around to try and acquire some reasoning as to what had just happened. Turning 180 degrees he saw a huge plume of smoke billowing from where Abdul had been standing, waving and smiling just a few short minutes earlier. Stumbling towards the smoke pouring from his friend's garage, Ali grasped his head in his hands and tried to make sense of the scene in front of him, but to no avail. Looking to the sky for answers from God, he saw the glint of sun on metal and suddenly it all made sense. *A rocket fired from the Death Eagle!* It was the same one he'd seen a few hours earlier. *The attack was in retaliation for the ambush in Bhumi and yet another example of President Solomon's tyrannical response.* Seeing three Counter Terrorism Unit jeeps closely followed by a truck of smiling red berets come roaring up the road and screeching into the village, Ali knew his logic for the rocket attack was correct.

From where Abdul's garage had once stood, Ali saw a bedraggled man come staggering out of the smoke and scattered bricks. The figure was carrying a small baby in his right arm, the left hanging listlessly by his side having been shredded in the explosion. Advancing towards the Counter Terrorism Unit soldiers, the blood drenched figure chanted, 'Tomorrow we will be free, tomorrow we will be free.' Ali recognised the pitiful figure, it was Abdul.

'Stop,' a soldier warned, but Abdul couldn't hear as both eardrums had been perforated in the explosion. Having failed to obey their orders, the soldiers mercilessly opened fired and slaughtered Abdul and his baby son. The killers casually sauntered up to the dead bodies and fired a burst of rounds into Abdul's head, his once handsome face now unrecognisable. The soldiers had been ordered to disfigure enemies of the state by their Commanding Officer, Colonel Hamza Leso, and were only too willing to carry out their orders as indeed they had been doing for the previous six months as they went from Southi village to Southi village murdering anyone in their way.

ABOUT THE AUTHOR

CHRIS STATHAM is a business consultant by day and novelist by night. The son of a British Army officer, he volunteered in rural Tanzania and subsequently fell in love with the effervescence and immediacy of Africa, his home for the last twelve years. He has lived and worked in Ethiopia, Germany, Jordan, Ireland, Malawi, Saudi Arabia, Tanzania and the UK. *18 Reflections and 3 Statements of Relief* is Chris' fifth novel… he refuses to say what's inspired by fact and which parts are fiction.